FRANCES

Walk on
The Dark
Side

Copyright © 2013 Frances Macarthur
All rights reserved

ISBN: 1494437457
ISBN-13: 9781494437459

ALSO BY THE AUTHOR

The Pulpit is Vacant
Death of a Chameleon
A Christmas Corpse
Courting Murder

ACKNOWLEDGEMENTS

My beloved husband, Ivor, died suddenly on holiday in October 2013.

This book was ready to be published before we went away and he was going to help me with the next one.

I dedicate this book to him…he told everyone we met about my books…and also to Heather and Arthur Paikos who supported me so wonderfully on holiday before I came home.

June 15th 1977

The contractions which had wracked her body for some time seemed now to be slicing her body in two. The nurse mopped her brow with the wet cloth and told her to push hard. She did this, moaning with the different pain which met this effort.

"Stop pushing. Take deep breaths, the way you were taught in your classes. Good."

"More gas and air. Please!"

Another contraction engulfed her and her body arched, her feet pushing against the rail at the foot of the bed. The pain ebbed and she relaxed against the soaked pillow.

"Now, push again. Good girl, I can see the head. Push!"

The cry of the new-born baby was heard in the next room where the young husband was waiting with his mother-in-law. They waited expectantly for someone to come in to tell them the news but nobody came.

"Marjorie. What is it? What's happened?"

"I'll go in. Don't worry. I can still hear the baby crying."

Marjorie left the waiting room and stood outside the delivery room, listening. She heard the nurse telling her daughter-in-law to push. It was unusual to have to push to remove the placenta. What was happening? She was about to go and knock when she heard the excited words of the nurse, "Well done. You have another beautiful baby boy."

The older woman slipped away, smiling. Her son-in-law looked up anxiously as she came in.

"Marjorie. What is it?"

"You have twin sons, my dear."

"Twins! Two sons! No one told us she was expecting twins."

"It sometimes happens that one baby is behind the other and the second heartbeat isn't spotted. Do you have two names? I never asked you before."

"We had a boy's name and a girl's name but not two of each sex, Neil and Lesley."

"What do you think now for another boy? Maybe Leslie as it's a boy's name too

"That's an idea. We thought of and discarded so many possible names."

"What about your father's name…gosh, here I am planning names. We can't talk about this without Lorna being present!"

"Don't worry, she'll not be left out if I know my wife!"

"Yes, my daughter knows her own mind."

They grinned like two conspirators.

"So you're a grandmother, or gran or maybe nanna. What do you want to be called?"

"I'd prefer Grandma What about your own mother?"

"She wants Gran and my father wants Papa."

"We haven't discussed what my husband wants. I'll suggest Grandpa and then there'll be no confusion."

They sat for a while. She explained to the new father that new babies had to be washed and wrapped up warmly before visitors could be called. He relaxed.

The sound of babies crying was audible as the door to the delivery room opened and the nurse came in to tell them that they could go through.

June 15th 2009

CHAPTER I

He had been feeling bad for some time now but today was even worse. The crawling sensation in his stomach made him think of the spider he had seen once in his room. He had caught it and pulled its legs off, watching the dismembered body twitch then finally lie still. He wanted to do this to another creature, the one which he hated so much. He grinned at the thought, showing his rotten teeth.

Clutching his stomach, he moved forward, guided by the pale light from the twilit sky. He peered out of the trees.

In the distance sat the car. He didn't know it was a car but he knew what it contained: the hated one and another. He had perfect vision in his imperfect body and he could see the dark curly hair.

When he was a child, he had been taken to the zoo and had seen the gorilla. He sometimes felt like the gorilla and he did so now. He lifted his long arms and grabbing a branch, swung himself along, then upwards to a thick branch where he rested.

He had no concept of time and was not to know that he remained there, crouched and silent, for almost an hour. Beneath him, the car door opened and in the light from inside, he saw her. His teeth drew back in a snarl, a silent pulling back of his teeth, and he swiftly slithered down the tree and with the gait of the gorilla, his long arms trailing his hands almost on the ground, he made for some bushes.

The hated one passed him, a shadow in the darkening night and silently he emerged from the bushes and followed her. Her woman smell was strong. He began to feel aroused. He wondered where the small animal was. It was usually with her. It puzzled him and upset him too as he loved to see it.

He had almost caught up with her. His movement in the bushes made them rustle and she turned round.

With primitive instinct, he acted. He put his long arms round her and pulled her through the bush. She struggled and he put his huge hands round her throat, pressing hard under her chin. She lay face down and motionless in the grass and he felt a warmth build up in his groin then came a wonderful surge as release came and he felt a stickiness. This was new and he moaned a little.

He knelt down, lifted the top half of her body and put his mouth to her neck, sucking once.

He saw a light in the distance and he tasted fear for the first time. Swiftly, he bent down and bit hard. The taste of the blood almost chased his fear but not quite. Leaving the hated one and picking up his spoils, he went back to the safety of his branch. The lights passed him, briefly bathing him in their glow. He swung down and along and back to his lair.

CHAPTER 2

Thursday night Weightwatchers' class in Newton Mearns' church hall was very busy. Pat McLean had meant to come early as this was a busy time for her with all the S1 reports to write up before parents' evening, always a busy one in the middle of June. She got in line at the end of the queue of hopeful people waiting to be weighed. There were one or two men this evening, quite a rare event. One, immediately in front of her, looked quite handsome. He had thick brown hair, neatly cut at the back and when he had turned round, obviously looking for someone, she had caught a glimpse of vivid blue eyes. He was tall too and she could not see why he had to come to weightwatchers. He turned round again as the hall door opened and a smile lit up his already attractive face. He spoke to the person who had just joined the queue behind Pat.

"Thank goodness you're here, Fiona. I thought you'd left me to go through this by myself!"

Although she was in a hurry, Pat turned to the woman and told her to join her friend. She stepped back to let the woman in. She was shorter than the man and a bit on the plump side. Her hair was short, fair and neatly cut. Soft brown eyes had smiled their thanks when she had taken up Pat's offer to change places in the queue.

"He should have the brown eyes and she should have the blue," thought Pat who always noticed things like that.

The queue moved forward slowly. She picked up some of her favourite goodies from the stacked table and moved forward to hand over her prepaid card, pay for her food and get her index card with her weight details on it. She had lost about six pounds so far, another eight to go before she would be satisfied.

The man was on the scales and she saw him laughing at the woman who was noting his weight. He took the hand-outs she offered him and stood aside as his friend took her turn. She did not appear happy with what the scales said and made a face at him as they walked off together.

Pat was next and was delighted to be told that she had lost another two pounds. She had purchased last time a little pedometer which measured how many steps she had taken every day last week and she mentioned this to the woman who said that that was probably why she had lost more weight.

"Keep up the walking, Pat. It all helps."

She ran out through the arcade to where she had parked her car. It was raining, again. She had hoped that the weather would have picked up in June, as it had done last year but not so far. It was easier to walk when the weather was at least dry.

The couple she had been watching were standing by the car next to hers. It was a silver grey Audi, quite a new one she noticed, a 12 registration.

"Ok for you, Charles. You're slim enough as it is and you've lost weight since your first visit but I've put on a pound and it's me who's overweight. You're like my dad who always said there was nothing to fear from the dentist but he had great teeth and never needed any fillings! I'll never get slim enough for the bikinis I've bought. I'll probably just wear my old swimsuits."

"Well we both ate a lot at our special meal last night. You'll be slimmer next week."

"So, I'm now fat *and* forty!"

She sounded really glum and Pat sympathised with her. That was the reason she was dieting too, to get into a bikini in July.

"Fiona, don't get obsessed with weight. You look great to me and I want to see you in your bikinis, slimmer or not."

A smile spread over the woman's face.

"Charles Davenport. You're an A1 flatterer. Now get in your car and get off home. Pippa will be wondering if you've got lost and your sister will be wanting to get off home."

The man laughed, tipped up her face and kissed her gently on the lips. Then he noticed Pat who by this time was inserting the key into the car door. He had thought she was small in the queue but realised now that she must be only just over five feet. Like Fiona, she was fair haired but it was almost white he saw now, one of those women whose hair aged prematurely and wisely did nothing to change it. It suited her, reaching to her shoulders then curling softly. "Thanks for letting Fiona skip the queue," he said. "I needed moral support tonight."

Pat laughed, said it was no bother and slid in behind the wheel of her Passat. She wished, as she often did, that her husband did not always want a large car as getting it out of parking spaces like this one was always tricky. Still, it was about six years old and maybe as he was driving less than her now that he had retired, he would agree to something smaller next time.

As she drove away, the couple still had not moved and she wondered what the relationship was between them. Pat was a people-watcher, much to her husband Greg's amusement and she reckoned that the couple were not married, at least not to each other and maybe not at all as although they seemed to be planning a holiday together, they obviously did not live together.

It took her about ten minutes to get home to Waterfoot and she felt her shoulders relaxing for the first time that day. Greg, bless him, would have the dinner ready as he always had. He had retired four years ago and had promised to make all the meals and do the housework so that she would benefit from his giving up work early as much as he did. They had both been teachers at the same secondary school in Bridgeton and he had been offered early retirement when the school had closed, being over fifty. Pat, at forty-four had gone to another school, a more academic one, nearer home but then she did not want to retire early as she loved her job, demanding though it was.

She parked the car, being careful to leave enough room for her neighbour who had a disabled space next to her, to manoeuvre her car in. Next door's cat came to meet her as it often did but did not roll over as usual, the ground being too wet for that. She tickled it under its chin and scratched it behind the ears, receiving a purr of thanks.

Pat would have loved a dog but she and Greg went on faraway holidays every summer and she would have hated to abandon a dog in kennels so that would have to wait till she retired and the long-haul holidays stopped.

The rain had almost ceased so she did not get wet going up their short path. The door was unlocked and Greg was in the kitchen.

"Well, how did you get on, love? Lose any more weight?"

"Yes, another two pounds. She said it was the walking that was doing it."

"Well, it's too late for that tonight. Dinner's ready and after you've done the school work which doubtless you have to do, there are some good programmes on TV."

Pat took off her jacket and hung it up behind the door of the kitchen cupboard, thinking as she did so that she really ought to have a trawl through the coats and jackets hanging up there. She could hardly get the cupboard door shut and there must be things they did not wear anymore which could go to the church weekly Nearly New sale.

"I'm going to walk every second day, if possible," she said as she sat down at the dining room table, sniffing the air appreciatively as Greg brought her a plate of smoked haddock with mashed potatoes and sweetcorn. This was followed by a yoghurt as both were trying not to eat so much, now that summer holidays were within thinking distance.

She spent an hour in their small study, assessing some essays done by her third year class who were, on the whole, bright youngsters and writing up some reports and then she joined Greg in the living room to watch, "New Tricks". She was not much of a TV fan but loved this programme with its catchy introductory tune and well-known cast.

As they lay in bed together, her husband, who was a bit of a worrier, cautioned her about going regularly on the same walk.

"Someone might be watching you and decide to mug you. That's a quiet walk round the Keel Estate. Do you always take your mobile phone?"

"I promise to always take it, worrywort," she muttered sleepily. "And why would anyone want to mug me when you take all my hard-earned cash?"

He gave her a gentle dig in the ribs and told her that he had to worry for both of them as she never gave these things a thought. She kissed the top of his nose which was just reachable above the duvet and turned over, smiling happily.

Life was good.

CHAPTER 3

"Penny! Do you have a copy of those stolen goods from last week's robbery at the newsagents in Pollokshaws? I can't find my copy and I'm off to look at the things recovered from a suitcase abandoned in Pollok Park."

"Frank, do you never file anything? What d'you think your filing cabinet's for?" Penny Price asked him, exasperatedly. She was very methodical and loved keeping her filing cabinet in the room she shared with Frank Selby and Sergeant Salma Din, neat and tidy and up to date. It had been an innovation on DS Macdonald's part to have them all issued with their own filing cabinet and Penny had seen a small red one which she was going to buy for her bedroom in the flat she shared with a friend, Alec. She had only recently moved in and was still getting a lot of pleasure in buying things for the flat. She could not wait to have files marked 'electricity', 'gas' and 'council tax'. Salma often laughed at her friend's methodical ways but then she still lived at home with her mother and sisters and brother in the West End and had no responsibilities. Her family had moved soon after their last murder case and she was revelling in having a large bedroom all to herself. She did not want to have responsibilities. She had no intention of marrying yet and would not be allowed to move out to her own flat. Her younger sister, Shazia, who was a primary teacher, had showed signs of wanting her freedom last year and her mother had been so upset that Shazia had stopped talking about it. Her brother Shahid was the lucky one. He had escaped to London to work for British Airways and had refused to come back home even when their father had died. This was almost unheard of in Muslim families, as the oldest brother was expected to take charge of the family in these circumstances. Although Salma loved her older brother dearly, she often felt resentment at him for landing her in the role of head of the family, after her Mum.

Frank, untidy at home where his mother did everything for him as her youngest son and therefore her baby, was no better at work, his computerised notes being the only tidy thing about him. He loved using the computer but Penny often had to decipher his written notes and put them into some semblance of order for him.

Penny now handed Frank her copy of the stolen goods and suggested that he photocopy it in case he had lost his in the seas of chaos which were his cabinet drawers. Grinning, he went off to do what she suggested.

Salma took this chance to ask Penny about Frank's relationship with the girl he had been going out with since Penny's flat-warming party.

"What was her name again, Penny? Was it Sandra?"

"No, it was Susan, Sue she prefers to be called, Sue Wilson. Yes, I think he's still going out with her. That'll be about five weeks now."

"Has he had many girlfriends since you've known him?"

"Yes but they don't ever last long. Always turns out that something's wrong with them. He never seems to think it could be something wrong with him."

The girls laughed and DS Macdonald coming into the room at that moment asked what the hilarity was about. Frank had passed her in the doorway on his way out.

"Just gossiping about Frank's love life, ma'am" said Penny. The DS had unbent a lot since her arrival a year ago but was strict on being given her title. Penny had heard a rumour of a broken relationship in her last station but she would never have pried about this and had not even told Frank as he was convinced that there was going to be a relationship between Fiona Macdonald and their boss Charles Davenport, even going so far as to nickname them Bonnie Prince Charlie and Flora Macdonald and whistling Scottish tunes whenever possible.

"Don't tell me there's a mad woman around who fancies our Frank," laughed the DS.

"Yes ma'am, there is and she's quite clever too. In her last year at Strathclyde Uni, doing pure maths."

"I just hope she's white, Catholic and doesn't drive," said Salma, jokingly.

"Actually, I met her at Sunday school years ago and she still goes to the same church as I do, so she's a Protestant, and a practising one at that," Penny told the astonished pair. "She *is* white but she drives."

"Maybe Frank doesn't know her religion," said the DS then, remembering what she had come in for, told Salma that she wanted her to go to the local secondary school, Bradford High, and see Mrs Martin the headteacher, about a pupil who had been found in possession of cannabis.

"On my way, ma'am," said Salma, going to the hat stand and getting her hat. She fastened her jacket and smoothed her jet black hair before putting the hat on.

"Any work for me, ma'am?" asked Penny, hopefully. She did not like being what she called 'quiet' at work and was delighted when DS Macdonald asked her to check out the local shopping centre. There had been a report of illegal immigrants selling goods there.

Having sent all her staff about their business, Fiona walked up the corridor to the DCI's room. The door was shut and she could hear voices, one raised and one softer. She had seen Grant Knox, the chief superintendent in their corridor, earlier on. He had simply ignored her in spite of her smiling at him and saying, "Good morning, Sir" but this was not unusual and she had remained unfazed by it. He was obviously in the DCI's room and a visit from him was never good news. He was irascible and a bit of a control freak. He was also bad at handling the press and always blamed someone else when newspaper reports showed the police in a bad light. Fiona was pleased that she never had to deal with him and knew that the DCI preferred to talk to Solomon Fairchild, the assistant chief superintendent. She went back to her own room and stayed there until she heard the brisk footsteps going down the corridor.

The DCI's door was now open as it usually was but she knocked on it before entering. Davenport was sitting with his head in his hands but looked up as she entered. He looked beyond her as if checking that his boss had gone out of earshot.

"That man will send me to an early grave, Fiona."

"No chance, Charles, only the good die young."

"Thanks."

He grinned. They did not usually call each other by their Christian name but there was no one else in sight.

"Come in and shut the door."

She did as she was bid and, shutting the door, went and sat down in one of the chairs across the desk from Charles.

"What did he want, or is it private?"

"No, not private. He wants all departments to produce a department manual, a potted history of all personnel, jobs applied for, discipline procedures carried out etc. Also he wants a summarised account of all big cases, backdated to when I took up my post here. Well, I assume he means big cases and not every single theft or cat stuck up a tree!"

"Is that *all* he wants? Sure he doesn't want the women's bra sizes and the men's inside leg measurements?" Fiona was outraged, thinking of the time this would take up.

"No, that's not all. All handbooks in the department have to be catalogued and I've to inspect all filing cabinets regularly."

"Is he giving us any time to solve cases?"

Sarcasm dripped from Fiona's tongue, like honey from a knife.

"That's all this job is becoming, paperwork and more paperwork," said Charles.

Fiona, realising that Charles was as despondent as she was, tried to cheer him up.

"If it has to be done, I suggest you put Penny onto the filing cabinet part. Ask her to sort them out. I think she likes doing things like that, then you can inspect them once they're ready. Discipline procedures are all logged already but in a separate book. I don't like the idea of putting, for example, Selby's reprimands about uniform etc onto what is in effect his cv."

"That's how I felt too. How do you feel about, in effect, writing a book about every big case?"

"It's something that could make an interesting read but we're police people not novelists!"

"I suppose at least we're quite quiet right now so we'd better make a start. I pity those in other departments who've been here longer and so will have more cases to write up. We've got the Elizabeth French case last summer, the Cathy Cameron case last summer also, the Ewing twins' murders at Christmas and the recent murder at the tennis court. What say we take two each or do you think we could involve any of the others in the team?"

"Well, we could involve Salma and Penny. They're good writers but I'd feel bad about leaving Selby out and there's no way we could involve him in anything literary like that."

"I agree, Fiona. If Penny is doing the filing cabinets, that's enough for her to be going on with.

Could I ask Frank to catalogue the handbooks and hand outs if we said it was just alphabetical or chronological?"

"How about by date first and then alphabetical once that is done?"

"Good idea. Then we could ask Salma to do one murder case."

Relieved at having parcelled out the work, Charles sat back and relaxed his shoulders then leaned forward and switched on his coffee machine. Fiona got up and took two mugs out of a cupboard, along with sweeteners. Neither of them took milk in coffee any more. She came back to the desk, just in time to see Charles pull his left ear lobe and knew that something was worrying him.

"What is it, Charles?"

"What do you mean?"

"Well, you're pulling your ear so something's troubling you."

"Am I that obvious?" he grimaced. "I was wondering if it would be OK to delegate like that or if I'm supposed to do all these things myself."

"Don't be ridiculous and anyway, you'll have to check everything once it's done so in a sense you're still responsible."

Penny returned first, to report that there was no one selling anything illegally at the shopping centre. She was delighted when told about her new task and, being Penny, asked if she could start right away. Told that she could, she went off to remove her hat and jacket and roll up her sleeves and make a start on Frank's filing cabinet. She had not told her boss that her own cabinet was ready for inspection right now as that would have sounded boastful, something Penny could never be accused of.

The next to arrive was Frank, armed with his list of found goods. He had written down a description of everything found and just needed now to sit down at his desk and check off that list with the list of stolen goods. He had had a quick glance at this list and knew that what had been found were indeed the things stolen from the newsagent's in Shawbridge Street. Realising that he was going to be busy for some time, Davenport decided not to tell Frank of his next job. Time enough for that when he was idling around.

Salma came in about twenty minutes later, having had a tough interview with the mother of a fourth year boy found to be in possession of cannabis. The mother had sworn that her son must have had the stuff planted on him and, on hearing that the boy had taken that line too, Salma had spoken to Mrs Martin who had informed her that the boy was a bad piece of work and there was no way he could be forced to do anything he did not want to do. Salma had interviewed some of his cronies who did not know what his chosen line of defence was and not one of them had mentioned the boy being an innocent victim. They were more inclined to praise him for being the leader in this drug scene so eventually the boy had admitted his guilt rather than lose face with his pals. Mrs Martin had thanked Salma for her handling of the incident and had suspended the boy for six weeks, recommending that his mother found him another school.

Davenport asked her to make a narrative of their last murder case, feeling that as that one would be fresh in her mind, it would be the easiest to do. She seemed quite pleased with this task and did not question his reason for asking her to do it but he explained anyway, telling her that all the team were being given something to do to help their boss obey Mr Knox's instructions.

"I've asked Penny to tidy up all our filing cabinets. That is probably the longest task."

"Well her own will be in pristine condition, Sir and I think mine is quite acceptable. Frank's... well..."

"It's OK Sergeant, we know what Selby's will be like," laughed DS Macdonald. "I think the top two drawers of mine will be in order but can't say the same for the bottom two as pressure of work stopped me finishing my sort-out recently."

Davenport looked a bit sheepish when she said that and admitted to not having tidied out his two cabinets for a while.

"I guess women are better at that sort of thing than men," he said.

Fiona Macdonald gave him a mock glare.

"Sexist comment that, Sir. Will we log him, sergeant?"

"Well...maybe we should let him off this time, ma'am."

Salma left, laughing, and DS Macdonald went off to her own room to get started on what had been her first case with DCI Davenport, and the DCI, feeling happier about what he saw as this unnecessary, extra work being foisted on them, went into his room and got out his reports on the death of the deputy head at Bradford High. It would be a two-part 'story' as the head of PE had also been murdered.

Silence reigned till lunchtime.

CHAPTER 4

True to her word, Pat decided to take a walk on Friday evening. She waited an hour after her evening meal, then laced up her walking shoes and, putting her mobile phone into her jacket pocket, she kissed Greg and set off. The worst bit was the walk uphill to the main road from their wee cul de sac but once she had reached this and crossed over to enter the Keel Estate, she began to enjoy herself. Originally there had been a derelict house at the entrance to the estate but a property developer had built two large houses, one at each end of the road through to the quiet narrow road which led from Waterfoot to Newton Mearns. These two houses had stood empty for some time but were now inhabited. The first one she passed obviously belonged to a family as there were two tricycles in the garden, one red and one yellow and washing hung on the line, a little girl's dresses and a smaller pair of trousers which could belong to a younger brother or sister.

Being an imaginative person, as she walked past, Pat saw in her mind's eye a table set for four with mum, dad, son and daughter. The son was in a high chair and was banging his spoon happily as he waited for his meal, the little girl feeling grown up as she was sitting in a chair similar to her mum and dad's chairs, for the first time. She was sitting quietly beside her dad and smiling up at him. Mum was in the kitchen plating their meals.

Pat mentally shook herself. What she was imagining was a fairy tale setting and the reality might be very different. In the distance, she could see a woman with the rough collie dog. They were both walking slowly as neither was in the first flush of youth. She had met the woman many times. The dog was friendly and loved being patted. As she came up behind them, she pitied the poor thing as its coat was very thick and must be making him very hot in this warmer weather. In the winter it had been matted and dirty although the woman had been quick to point out that she brushed him every day and that it was the rain and mud which he acquired through rooting through the long grass and bushes which did the damage. Pat had, earlier in her life, had a Shetland collie, a smaller version of this large dog and she remembered how long it had taken her to brush Rob's coat. She had a soft spot for this breed and planned to persuade Greg to buy this kind of dog rather than his favourite, the golden retriever, when she too was retired.

She drew nearer. The woman turned and smiled and the dog pushed its nose into her hand.

"Hello, Mrs Fraser and how are you and Cooper tonight?"

She was not sure how the dog's name was spelt and she asked now.

"It's C.O.O.P.E.R. Funnily enough we got him in Fife, as a rescue dog but he isn't named after the town of Coupar, in Fife," Mrs Fraser replied. "It looks as if this evening's weather will be changeable. I wonder if we'll get a decent summer this year."

"Well I read somewhere that we've to have a BBQ summer this time," said Pat, laughing,

"but I think I've heard that story before," she added.

They spoke for a little while longer then Pat said cheerio and walked briskly away. It was indeed a lovely evening, not too warm for walking yet not cold either and the street lights would not come on for about another hour. Some clouds suggested that it might rain later. She turned the corner and looked as she always did at the building housing Keel Products. They had been given permission to set up in the estate if they promised to keep the building low so that it could not be seen from the road or spoil the view. They needed peace and quiet for their expensive turn-tables as fine tuning was essential.

There was only one light on in one of the ground floor rooms. The rest was in darkness. The factory closed at 5.30 so this was probably the caretaker's room. Once again Pat imagined the man.

He would be sitting reading his paper with his feet on the table and a mug of tea in his hand.

The last part of the walk had been quite hilly and she slowed her steps, feeling the backs of her legs aching. She hoped that this would stop once her body had got used to the exertion. Maybe after a few weeks of walking, her calves would strengthen. She noticed some flowers by the roadside and slowed to examine them. After the long winter, it was so good to see some colour appearing. She took out her mobile phone and took a picture of the little yellow flowers. Greg would be able to tell her what they were. His father had taken him on many walks when he was young and had told him the names of flowers and trees.

Walking on, she looked at the picture she had taken and zoomed in to get some detail of the largest flower. What was that? She magnified the picture as far as she could. It looked like a fingertip with a red nail. Surely not. She must be seeing things. Really, her imagination ran away with her! She walked on but curiosity got the better of her and she turned back, trying to find the exact spot where she had taken the picture. There it was!

The largest yellow flower was at the back of the display and there was something red next to it. Pat knelt down and peered more closely, wishing that she had worn her glasses. Then she recoiled sharply because it *was* a finger. She gingerly parted the grass and saw that the finger was attached to a hand. Feeling a bit sick, she moved further in towards the bushes which separated the part with the flowers from the field. An arm was sticking through the bushes. This was horrible but she had to do it. She put her two hands into the bush and parted it. The arm led her to a body which was lying on its stomach. It was the body of a woman. She could tell by the clothes and the hairstyle, probably a young woman, as the trousers were what a young person would wear, cropped trousers and the jacket was a short denim one. Pat took in all this detail and she knew she was paying attention to the unimportant because she was scared to look closer. She just could not touch the woman to feel for a pulse. The flies, buzzing round the body, told her that it was a dead body. She stood up and looked round. Mrs Fraser had reached the bend in the road and was turning back. She never came this far as she said the hilly part was too much for both her and the dog.

"Mrs Fraser! Mrs Fraser!" Pat called loudly and the woman turned. Pat got herself back on the road and ran down the hill. The woman looked alarmed.

"What is it, Mrs McLean? What's happened?"

"Oh, Mrs Fraser, there's a woman lying in the grass half in and half out of the bushes. I'm sure she's dead. I'm too scared to feel for a pulse. I'm going to phone the police. Will you wait with me, please?"

"I was a nurse. I'll come and have a look."

The woman was brisk and Pat could imagine her taking charge of a ward.

They went back together to the spot which would now be forever etched on Pat's memory. Pat held Cooper while Mrs Fraser parted the bushes.

"Don't turn her over. I'm sure the police would want her left as she is," she warned the woman.

It took only a minute for Mrs Fraser to find out that the woman was indeed dead. She looked pale as she re-joined Pat.

"Yes, definitely dead and has been for some time I think. Her arm's rigid. I think rigor mortis has set in."

Pat took out her mobile phone and dialled the emergency number. It sounded surreal to be asking for police and then telling them that she had found a body. She gave her mobile number and her address and told them where she was. She told them that another woman was with her and had confirmed that the body was a dead one. They asked for her address too and Pat asked Mrs Fraser what her address was and relayed that to the police constable. She hung up.

"We've to wait here until the police come," she said.

"Could I use your phone to let my husband know why I'll not be back when he's expecting me?" asked Mrs Fraser.

"Of course."

The woman asked Pat to get the number for her as she was not used to mobile phones. Pat waited till someone answered then handed the phone over.

"Hello, George. It's me. No I'm fine but we've found a dead body...me and a woman who was walking here. We've to wait till the police come. See you later."

She handed the phone back to Pat. Pat explained how she had come to find the finger, then the arm, then the body. They exchanged first names and Pat told her where she stayed. They were in adjacent streets. Pat told her about her own dog, anything to keep away from the subject of the body.

It was not long before they heard the sound of a car coming up from the main road in the direction Pat had been walking. The police car stopped and two constables, a man and a woman got out and approached them.

"Mrs Maclean?"

Pat introduced herself and Mrs Fraser.

"I'm PC Selby and this is PC Price," the man said. "Can you show us where this body is, please?"

Pat and Mrs Fraser - Elaine - led the police to the spot. They squatted down on the other side of the bushes and then stood up again, the young man reaching for his phone.

"Sir, Selby here. It *is* a dead body, that of a young woman, I think. She's lying on her stomach. We haven't touched her...yes...OK...will do."

The policeman straightened and stood up.

"You can both go home. We'll see to things now. Penny, will you contact Martin Jamieson and Ben Goodwin."

The man asked for Pat's address, noted it, then took Elaine Fraser's address too. Pat had given this already on the phone but did not like to say so.

"There will be someone round to see you both but probably not till tomorrow or Sunday."

"I go to church, Constable," said Pat. "Could you make it after 1pm if it's Sunday?"

"What about you, Mrs Fraser?

Elaine Fraser said she would make sure she was in at that time and she and Pat left the scene. Both had recovered from the immediate shock and were now curious about who the woman was and how she had come to be lying dead in a field.

Pat walked with Elaine until they reached her house and then went off home to tell her husband about her eventful walk.

"I told you it wasn't safe to walk up there alone," was his reply.

CHAPTER 5

Penny Price and Frank Selby stood by the corpse for about half an hour before the police surgeon, Martin Jamieson arrived, looking even more immaculate than ever in a dinner suit complete with silk, black cummerbund and black velvet bow tie. Penny, who had known him now for some years, risked a wolf whistle and Martin grinned.

"Yes, I know, a bit over the top for clambering into fields but I had just dressed to go out for a special dinner at the Lodge."

Martin's speech was as perfect as his sartorial elegance. He spoke like someone who had learned English as a foreign language and never abbreviated words, as now when he had said, "I had" and not "I'd". Frank felt very inferior when Martin was around. He had confided this to Penny last month.

"I always think I'm making grammar mistakes…"

"…grammatical mistakes," Penny corrected him.

"See what I mean. I was never very good at English at school and I'm sure he notices."

"Martin's not like that, Frank," she had told him but faced with Martin in his dress suit, Frank stuttered.

"Hello Martin. G...good of you to get here so quickly. I'll show you the body."

Frank went off the road and Martin followed him, carrying his case of tricks. Penny remained where she was. She had spotted a jogger coming in their direction and wanted to make sure he or she did not stop and nose into what was happening as the fewer people who knew the better, until the press was told officially. As it was, the man was listening to music on his iPod and merely smiled as he ran past. Penny parted the bushes and joined her colleagues.

Martin had turned the body over and they could see that it was that of a youngish woman, maybe in her late thirties.

"Notice anything, Frank?" Martin was saying.

Frank knelt down and looked closely at the body. He stiffened and turned pale.

"God, someone's chopped off a finger!"

"Yes, her ring finger."

Penny looked at the hand that had obviously not been the one that had led to the discovery. It had been red nail tipped and whole, according to their eye witness. She looked at where the ring finger should have been. There was a bloody stump and this had attracted the flies. Penny felt sick and excused herself, going back through the bushes and returning to the road.

When Martin and Frank joined her, she had just seen a van coming up the road towards them. It came to a halt and she saw that it was the van to take the body to the lab for closer inspection. Martin took off his latex gloves which looked so incongruous with his evening attire.

"Bert, Frank will show you where the body is but do not take it away until SOC have marked where it is lying."

"Here they come now, Martin," said Penny and a minute later a silver Mercedes pulled up and Ben Goodwin joined them. His passenger got out and started talking to the van driver.

"Wow! Some car, Ben!" Frank exclaimed.

"It's my baby. I don't use it for work but I was out tonight when I got your call. Just had time to pick Gerry up."

Frank was walking round the beautiful car, admiring it.

"Well, what have you got for me tonight young Penny?" Ben asked.

"A young woman missing a finger, Ben," said Penny.

"Right lead me to her. I'll mark the site then erect my tent and you can take her off with you, Martin."

Penny and Frank were no longer needed, so saying goodbye to Martin and Ben, they walked to where their car was parked. Martin followed them. Frank got into the driver's seat and wound down the window.

"Tell your boss we have a woman aged about 30-35. She has been dead for a couple of days I would think. Ring finger chopped off. Not a clean cut, an amateurish job I would say. Tell him I will be in touch as soon as possible."

"Thanks, Martin," said Penny as she got in beside Frank.

They drove to where the road came out onto Glasgow Road and, seeing the house positioned there, Penny decided to phone their boss to see if he wanted them to make any enquiries that night.

"What do you think, Sir? Is it too late now. It's…" she peered at her watch, "….almost nine o'clock."

She listened.

"OK, Sir."

"He says we've to get off home and we've to come up first thing in the morning and interview the folk at any nearby houses. We passed another large house on the way in at the other end of this road, didn't we?"

"Have we to go into the station first, Pen?"

"No, so drop me off at home and pick me up there at 7.30am. Better get here before anyone goes to work."

Frank groaned. He was managing to get into work on time these days but he would have to get up about 6.30 if he was be in time for Penny.

"Don't moan. You can have an early night. You'll be home by 10 at the latest."

"I was going to meet my pals at the pub tonight."

"Sue by any chance?"

"No, not Sue by any chance."

"Are you still seeing her Frank?"

"Yes."

Sensing that she was not going to get any information from her colleague, Penny wisely decided to keep quiet. He would tell her in his own time. He stopped outside the block of new flats, one of which she shared with an old friend, Alec and she got out.

"See you tomorrow, pal," Frank called after her as she put her key in the lock of the main door.

"Another day; another murder. Life was anything but dull," he thought as he drove off.

Penny found the flat empty when she went in. There was a note from Alec on the hall table telling her that he was spending the night with his friend. They always left each other notes if they were going to be out all night so that the other could double lock the door. Penny occasionally stayed with her Mum and Jack. Her relationship with Gordon, her vet boyfriend, had not reached the staying together stage, in fact he had only ever kissed her as so often their dates had to be cancelled either because of her work or his. There was a message from him when she dialled 1571, asking if she would go out with him this Sunday. It was his birthday and he had forgotten this when they made their arrangement to meet on Saturday. She rang him now and said she would be delighted to see him.

"Is that instead of tomorrow night?"

"We could still see each other tomorrow night as well if you like, Penny."

"Yes, I'd like that, as long as the new murder doesn't get in the way, Gordon."

She explained what had happened that night, mentioning only a dead woman. Davenport would have her guts for garters if she divulged details at this stage. Gordon understood and did not ask questions, just said he would pick her up around 7 pm on Saturday, if he heard nothing to the contrary.

Deciding to have the early night she had recommended to Frank, she hung up her uniform, sponged it where it had got muddy that night and laid out a clean white shirt and clean tights. Finally she brushed her black shoes till they shone.

Sleep did not come immediately. It seldom did when she wanted it to. She lay and thought of the woman who had been murdered and who had had a finger chopped off, then thought about more pleasant things, about where Gordon could be taking her on Saturday and Sunday and if their relationship would develop.

Finally she slept.

CHAPTER 6

It was a minor miracle that Frank arrived on time to collect Penny. He tooted his horn once and she appeared almost right away, looking as fresh as she always did. Frank said very little on their drive to Waterfoot. He was not a morning person and neither was Penny. Salma had often teased them both about this. She was at her best then and ready to chat.

The journey took only about fifteen minutes as most of the traffic was going in the opposite direction, into Glasgow. They passed Eastwood Toll and went on up Eastwoodmains Road, one of Penny's favourite roads with all its trees fully green now. There was a bit of a hold up at Sheddens' roundabout as a silly driver had blocked the entrance to the Eaglesham road. Frank scowled at him and the man waved an apologetic hand.

"Probably have given me the v sign if I hadn't been in a police car," grumped Frank.

However, they were soon on their way and reached Floors Road just after 7.15. They drove carefully round the sharp z bend and up the quiet country road till they came to the entrance to the estate. There was a very large, very new house right at the entrance. Frank pulled in off the road and together they went to the front door. It took a few minutes before the door was opened by a man in a navy and red plaid dressing gown. He was very tall and completely bald and by the expression on his face, none too pleased at this early visit.

"Yes? Who are you? Do you know the time? It's only just 7.15."

Could he not see who they were, thought Penny grumpily.

"Sorry Sir," said Frank feeling, and looking, sympathetic. "I'm PC Selby and this is PC Price. I'm afraid that a body was found in the fields near you last night and we hoped you might be able to help us find out who the person is."

The man's expression changed. He looked curious.

"Please come in. I'll call my wife."

He showed them into a lounge which was obviously newly decorated. The walls were what Frank thought was called magnolia and the suite was in white with pale green cushions which matched the curtains which were full length. There was no other furniture in the room except for a standard lamp and the carpet was deep pile and creamy coloured.

"Obviously no dogs or children," thought Frank. He sat down gingerly on the edge of the settee and Penny sat down on one of the matching chairs. She was looking at the one magnificent painting above the fireplace, the scene of a battle somewhere. The colours were muted, the figures precise and detailed.

The woman who came into the room with her husband was in her dressing gown too, well, a silky equivalent. Frank knew it had a special name but could not remember what it was. She was not tall but had what is called a 'presence'. Her dark, greying hair was immaculate, pulled straight back from her face and caught up into a roll at the nape of her neck with just one curly tendril escaping artfully. Her face was devoid of make-up but still beautiful. As the man joined her, they made a handsome couple.

"I've told my wife why you're here, constable," he said now, coming forward to stand by the fireplace while his wife took the other chair. Frank got up and offered him the settee.

"No, constable, I prefer to stand, thank you."

Frank remained standing too.

"Were you at home last night, Sir?"

"Yes."

"I see that this room overlooks the road through the estate. Did you hear or see anything unusual?"

"Yes it does but we sit, when we're alone, in a smaller lounge which faces Floors Road and we were there last night until we went up to bed at about..."

"About 10.30, dear," his wife volunteered.

"Now Mr..."

"Cook."

"Mr Cook. What about the night before that, Thursday night?"

"Thursday? Oh yes we were in Bearsden visiting my son, Neil and his family. We got back at about ten o'clock."

"Did you notice anything strange or see anybody about?"

"No."

"What about you, Mrs Cook?"

"No, nothing, constable. It was quite dark and I saw no one. We went straight to bed as we'd had supper at my son's."

Penny had been quiet for longer than usual and she spoke now.

"What about Wednesday night?"

"We were at a concert in Glasgow, a Wagner concert. We got home later, at about eleven. Had a cup of tea then went to bed. It was wet that night I remember. I saw nothing. Did you dear?" she asked her husband. Penny thought that the 'dear' which she kept using was rather forced.

Mr Cook thought for a minute as if he might be remembering something.

"Sorry, no."

Preparing to leave, Frank shut his notebook and walked to the door with Penny, stopping only to give the man the station phone number in case anything came to their minds.

"Was the person murdered, constable? Was it a man or a woman?" Mr Cook asked.

"We don't know yet, Sir, if the person was murdered. A young woman, that's all we know at the moment."

Back in the car, they drove along the estate road, passing the murder scene, then the factory and were almost at Glasgow Road before they came to any other houses. One large one was almost a replica of the one they had just visited. This time Penny took the lead when a young man came to the door, drying his thick, dark hair on a large, bright yellow towel and wearing only navy sleepshorts.

"Sorry to disturb you so early, Sir. A body was found last night near the factory. Were you at home last night?"

"With two young daughters, we're always at home," the man said ruefully.

"So you were at home on Thursday and Wednesday nights too then?"

"Yes. What do you want to know?"

At this point he was joined by a young woman in an advanced state of pregnancy. Her fair hair was tousled.

"Who is it?"

She saw the two police constables.

"What's wrong?"

"There's been a body found near here, Mrs...?"

"Mrs Fensom. Was the person murdered?"

"We haven't got any details yet but it was a youngish woman. Can you remember seeing anything out of place on any of the three nights, either of you?" asked Penny. "That's Wednesday, Thursday and Friday," she explained again for the sake of the woman.

A little girl, still in red and white striped pyjamas and aged about three ran up behind her mother, followed by her elder sister, dressed for school in a navy skirt and white blouse and aged about five.

"Anne pet, take Karen back into the kitchen please."

The elder girl tugged her sister's arm and then went back into the room they had come from.

"There are hardly ever any cars on this road after the factory empties at about 5.30," the man said and his wife nodded.

"We tend to sit in the family room most evenings as that's where the TV is... and that room looks out onto the fields," he added. "Sorry we can't help you."

Penny gave them the number to call if they remembered anything and they turned their steps to the semi-detached house across the road.

A teenage boy answered their ring. He was smart in school uniform, even had the tie tied neatly which was unusual these days, Frank thought.

"Could we speak to your mum or dad, son?" he asked

"Dad doesn't live here anymore but I'll get Mum for you," he replied politely and went off into the recesses of the house.

The woman who appeared, looked harassed and shouted back, "Craig, get yourself up now, do you hear me!"

"Sorry...constable."

She looked worried when she saw the uniformed man and woman at her door.

"Is anything wrong? I hope Craig's not in trouble again."

"Craig is?" asked Penny.

"He's my younger son. He's been getting into trouble recently, skipping school, things like that. He misses his Dad. Edward left us about six months ago."

"Well it's nothing for you to worry about, Mrs Harris." Penny had read the name on the door plate. "A young woman was found dead last night up the road quite near the factory and we wondered if you'd seen or heard anything the last three nights."

The woman thought.

"Well on Wednesday, I was at Parents' Evening at the school, for Kenny. They were both with me as I had no one to leave Craig with and the school like the child being discussed to be present. Got home about 9.30 I think. I saw no one then and after I packed the two of them off to do the last of their homework, I was in the kitchen getting a meal ready for the next day and the kitchen's at the back of the house."

"And on Thursday night?" Penny prompted her.

"I was in with Craig. He wanted to go out but he'd been grounded. We watched TV together. I heard nothing, no cars going up the road and we see headlights usually on the wall the TV's on. It's not often a car goes past later in the evening."

"What about Kenny?"

The woman shouted into the house for Kenny and he came to the door holding a slice of brown toast and marmalade.

"Son, when you came home on Thursday night, did you hear or see anything unusual?" Frank asked.

The boy thought for a minute.

"No, Sir. I came off the bus and no one else got off."

"When was that?"

"About 9 o'clock. I'd been to my friend in Eaglesham to do chemistry homework together."

"What about last night, Mrs Harris?"

"Craig and I were in again. He was in his bedroom most of the evening, listening to his iPod, I imagine."

"And I was at the BB, Sir and again I came off the bus alone at about 9.40."

"Well," said Frank, "if you do remember anything odd or unusual, please call the station."

He handed over the phone number once again and they thanked the woman and her son. As they walked away, Mrs Harris called after them:

"Mrs and Mrs Smith next door are elderly and very deaf. You'll have to knock loudly. They don't usually hear the bell."

Grimacing, Frank thanked her and he and Penny walked to the next house. They knocked loudly and waited but nothing happened. Frank knocked again even more loudly and they heard footsteps coming slowly down the hall. The door opened and a wizened face peered round the chain-locked door. Frank was reminded of a walnut with white hair.

"Who is it? What do you want?"

"It's the police, Mrs Smith. We need to ask you a few questions."

"Put your card through the letterbox, sonny."

The door was shut.

Feeling a bit silly, Frank dropped his warrant card through the letter box and after a few minutes the door was opened fully and a little old lady stood there, dressed in a wrap round blue overall and with her snowy-white hair in a hairnet. Once again Frank told what had happened but it was obvious that she would have heard nothing as she said they had sat with the TV on every night.

"Loudly, because my husband is very deaf," she shouted.

"You heard nothing in the road?" said Frank loudly.

"What's that about a toad?"

"The road," bellowed Frank. "Did you hear anything in the road?"

"No nothing."

That they had probably heard nothing was confirmed when her husband joined them as he could hear even less well and Frank had to shout everything at him.

"Let us know if you remember anything unusual or odd!" Frank shouted.

"God, what about God?" shouted the old man back. "Are you one of those Jehovah people?"

"He's the police you silly old coot!" shouted his wife.

She smiled at Frank.

"He's stone deaf you know."

Frank felt as if he'd done two rounds with Mike Tyson as he and Penny walked back to the car. Penny had taken a fit of the giggles. It was now about 8.20 and time they got back to the station. They had nothing to report. This was a good place to commit a murder, an isolated road with only four houses anywhere near.

They arrived back in time for a cup of tea in the staff canteen. Salma was there and she told them that there was a meeting scheduled for nine o'clock.

"Comb your hair, Frank," Penny told him.

He was thinning on top but that did not stop one lanky bit of hair from falling over his forehead and she did not want him to be reprimanded as he sometimes was for his untidy appearance. Grinning, he did as he was told.

CHAPTER 7

"Right, team," said Charles Davenport.

He was standing in front of them in the Incident Room. They were all seated. Fiona Macdonald had come in last and was seated nearest to the door. She was wearing a light grey skirt and pink blouse, having left her suit jacket hanging up in her room. Penny had thought as she came in that her boss had lost some weight and it suited her. Penny smiled at her and Fiona smiled back, thinking as she often did what an attractive young woman PC Price was.

Next to Penny was Sergeant Salma Din, looking immaculate as always, her black hair shining and up in a neat pigtail pinned on top of her head. At the end of the row, Frank Selby sat, trying not to grin at his boss's opening welcome. He often mimicked the, "Right team" and pulled his left earlobe as Davenport did when worried or concentrating. He thought about humming, 'The Skye Boat Song' but decided not to as there was serious business in hand today.

"We've got another murder case on our hands. A young woman was found in Waterfoot, in a field beside the back road leading from Floors Road to Glasgow Road. All I know so far, courtesy of Martin Jamieson who spoke to Penny and Frank last night, is that she was probably murdered about two days ago and has had her ring finger chopped off in an amateurish way. She was probably in her thirties. Penny, you and Frank have interviewed the people in nearby houses. Any information for us?"

"We saw the man and woman who live in the big house at the entrance to the Keel Estate on Floors Road, Sir," said Frank. He looked down at his notebook.

"A Mr and Mrs Cook. They were in last night but we asked about the previous two nights and they were out the night before, at their son's in Bearsden and the night before that they were at a concert in The Concert Hall."

"They hadn't seen all the activity last night, Sir," said Penny eagerly. "They sit in a lounge that overlooks Floors Road, not the road connecting the estate to Glasgow Road. We told them that a young woman had been found dead, nothing else, Sir."

"OK, and at the other houses?" asked Davenport.

"There's another similar large house at the other end of that road, Sir," said Frank. "A family lives there, a Mr Fensom and his wife and two daughters, aged..." Frank had to look at his notebook again... "five and three."

"There were in all three nights, Sir," said Penny. "But they didn't hear anything. They were further away from the scene than the Cooks. They said there were seldom any cars on that road after the factory closed at 5.30."

"There's a semi- detached house across from them, Sir," continued Frank. "One family, consists of a mother and two teenage sons. Harris, their surname is and the other belongs to an elderly couple called Smith."

"The elderly couple say that they go to bed early, around 10pm and can't remember hearing any cars the last three nights but then they're both a bit deaf, Sir," Penny put in her two pence worth, grinning at Frank as she said this.

Frank added, "And the Harris family were out on one of the nights as it was Parents' Evening at the boys' school. That was two nights ago and mother and younger son were in the next night and last night. The older boy was out both nights till between 9 and 9.40. He saw no one when he came home either night but he got off the bus in Glasgow Road and his house is right at the entrance to the estate and really quite far from the crime scene, Sir."

"Thank you both," said Davenport. "Our biggest problem will be getting the identity of the murdered woman. Maybe SOC will come up with something helpful. Meanwhile, Salma you check records, see if any young women have been reported missing recently on the South Side."

"Yes, Sir."

Salma got up and went off upstairs to the room where records were kept.

"Penny, you and Frank get up to Waterfoot and take a statement from the women who found the body."

"We told them we'd probably be coming up to see them, Sir. One of them goes to church so she asked if we could come after 1pm. Is that OK?"

"That's fine. Nothing else we can do till we hear from Martin and Ben. Luckily we can rely on them both to be as quick as possible."

He smiled and the others knew that he was thinking of the last head of SOC, Vince Parker who had been rather slow in reporting back, being more concerned with interviews for promotion than with his day to day work. Martin Jamieson had worked with the South Side police for longer than Davenport and Fiona Macdonald and they had always found him speedy in his reporting. He was a workaholic and liked to get work done as soon as possible. Davenport thought that his wife Kath must be a saint to put up with his irregular and often long hours. His own wife had given up the struggle and they had divorced, amicably, Davenport getting custody of Pippa their daughter as his wife had wanted to move down South to work and Pippa wanted to stay at her school. She had had to move recently after all when Davenport had been sent to this large station, Shawbank, in Govanhill but by this time she was settled with her dad and her mother seemed satisfied with seeing her at holiday times.

All that happened that day was a phone call from Mr Cook to say that when they arrived home on Wednesday night, he had seen tail lights disappearing in the direction of Glasgow Road. He had thought it might have been a courting couple, as the road, with no street lighting, would be perfect for an assignation.

"Perhaps we disturbed them," he said now.

"What time would that have been, Sir?" Davenport had asked him.

"About 10 - 10.15. Our son has young daughters and they went to bed at 9pm and we left Bearsden about twenty minutes after that. It takes us about three quarters of an hour to get across the city."

Davenport thanked him, telling him that they would probably be seen again once the police had more to go on.

Salma came to his room with the information that no women had been reported missing in the last few days.

"The last person was someone from Pollokshields on the 15th of May and she turned up a few days later, Sir. Been staying with her new boyfriend and didn't think to let her parents know."

"Tell the others, Salma. I'll tell DS Macdonald. There's nothing to do now so get on with your other work. Try to get it up to date to leave yourselves free for this case."

Salma left the room and Davenport went into the DS's room to inform her. Frank would have been interested to hear him say that he hoped that this case would be resolved quickly as they had a holiday coming up in mid- July.

"Only about four weeks to go, Charles. A tight time scale for us."

She smiled at him and he thought again how her smile transformed her often serious face.

"We can do it," he said, hoping that his optimism would not prove unfounded.

CHAPTER 8

Penny had enjoyed her Saturday evening with Gordon. He had picked her up from the flat at 7pm as promised and they had gone for a Macdonalds' meal on the way into town. Penny loved Macdonalds' thin chips and enthused over the toffee dessert. She laughed all through the meal as Gordon told her about some of his animal patients.

"This wee black and white spaniel was brought in yesterday, Penny. He'd fallen down about seven feet onto rocks and broken a leg. He was lucky not to have been killed, wee chap. He was so good but I had to keep him in overnight to do an operation today and what a difference without his owner. He was vicious. Lorna and I were both terrified!"

"What did you do?"

"Well I managed to stick a needle in and knock him unconscious. Got his leg pinned but then when he came round he was vicious again. Lorna managed to slide some food into the cage he was in."

"Has he gone home now?"

"Yes. When his owner came he transformed into a cuddly, friendly, tail-wagging wee dog again."

"Have you had any unusual animals in?" Penny wanted to know.

"I think the oddest was a python."

"Ugh. I'm terrified of snakes."

"They're not slimy, Penny. They're quite dry to touch and this was a baby one luckily."

They had finished their desserts and Gordon asked Penny if she still wanted to go to the pictures.

"I'd rather just chat if that's OK with you."

"Do you want to come to my flat or do you want me to come to yours or do you want to go to a pub somewhere? asked Gordon.

Penny felt herself blush. She wondered what he meant by inviting her to his flat. She had never had a serious boyfriend, usually going out with church pals and she was quite inexperienced in the physical side of dating.

Gordon had noticed the reddened cheeks and was quick to reassure her.

"It's not like, 'Come up and see my etchings, Penny'. I'll not rush you into anything you don't want to do. Just come up for a chat, a few drinks, a coffee then I'll run you home in time for your beauty sleep."

"Oh, think I need help with my looks then?" she teased him, warming even more to this young man.

Laughing and holding hands, they left the restaurant, found his car in the large car park and drove to his flat in Kingspark. The flats were quite newly built and there was a car park at the back for residents. Gordon took her in the back way, showing her his little patio on the way. It was dark but she could make out some tubs of plants, a table and four chairs.

His flat was one of two on the ground floor and the hall was carpeted in a dark beige colour. The light was on in the hall.

"Want a quick tour?" Gordon asked as he shut the front door.

"Yes please."

He showed her his own bedroom with ensuite shower and toilet, the guest bedroom near to the communal bathroom, the tiny kitchen and finally they went into the lounge with its sliding doors opening onto the patio.

"Give me your jacket. Have a seat and I'll get us a drink. What do you want? I have the usual things."

"Do you have martini and some lemonade? I'm not much of a drinker."

"I do have martini - the dry one. Would you rather have coffee?"

"No, I'd like a drink. It'll be a nice change. I'm usually the driver when I go out in a car."

While Gordon was in his kitchen getting their drinks, Penny looked round his lounge. The carpet, like the hall one was beige, the settee was black leather and there was a round table with four chairs. A TV and music centre was in one corner flanked by a teak bookcase holding books, videos and DVDs. She went over to have a look. The books were what she termed, 'man books'. Jack Higgins predominated and there were some Wilbur Smith and the whole series of Quentin Jardine.

"What do you like to read, Penny?" Gordon asked coming in with a tray holding two drinks and a bowl of crisps.

"Oh I read anything. Nothing highbrow I'm afraid. I'm not one for the classics. Afraid school put me off Dickens and Shakespeare, though I like to see his plays."

"Who's your favourite?"

"I suppose Georgette Heyer, though believe it or not I like crime fiction."

"Have you read any of his?" Gordon picked up one of Quentin Jardine's books.

"No. Are they any good?"

She laughed.

"Silly question when you have so many!"

"They're all based in Edinburgh and there are lots of relationship bits as well as crime. Borrow the first one if you like."

The talk went on to films and plays and Penny was delighted to find out that Gordon did not like classical music either, neither did he like ballet and he said he never visited museums and art galleries. She began to think that she must have found her soul mate.

"Stop it, Penny," she told herself. "You don't want to get serious at your age."

They both talked about their colleagues, Gordon laughing at Frank's pairing off of the DCI and DS. Penny told him about Frank Selby's racist comments to Salma Din when she first arrived, talking about the smell of curry in the station, making a play on her surname with his mention of the terrible 'din' in the room and how Salma had got her own back by calling a girl, Frank's 'selby/sell by' date. He told Penny about his assistant, Lorna and how she loved animals but had nearly fainted when someone brought in the python, even though it was only young and quite small.

"She had to hold it while I sedated it," he laughed. "She thought that she deserved a medal for that."

"She did!" retorted Penny. "I'd have left you to deal with it by yourself. The only time I've even looked at a snake was in the first Harry Potter film where Harry set the snake free and it said, 'Thanksss,' as it slid past him."

This led them on to a discussion about Harry Potter which they both enjoyed and they agreed to go and see the latest film the following weekend if work permitted. This in turn led to Penny talking about the last few murder cases she had worked on and she told him how much she liked working with her two bosses.

It was after twelve o'clock when Penny looked at her watch and asked Gordon if he would mind driving her home. She had noticed that he had only drunk diet coke and respected him for that.

They drove home, still chatting. Gordon was taking her to a new restaurant in Merrylee Road for his birthday the following night.

"The restaurant is called 'Merrylee Road'," he told her. "Some friends went recently and they recommended it. Is that OK?"

Just as Penny was saying that it was fine, they were drawing up at the flats in Kilmarnock Road. Gordon kept the engine running while he made arrangements to pick her up, in a taxi this time so that he could have wine with his meal. He leaned over and kissed her gently on the cheek. She turned her face towards him and he kissed her again on the lips. For the first time, she liked the feeling and kissed him back. His tongue explored her lips and parted them and she felt a warmth spreading over her, a pleasant warmth.

He pulled back and in the light from the street lamp she could see that he was looking at her fondly.

" 'Night, Penny. Sleep well. See you tomorrow."

She stood and watched him drive off, waving till he was out of sight.

CHAPTER 9

Pat McLean and her husband Greg passed Sunday in their usual way. Pat went down to church in Pollokshaws where she was an elder. She had continued to go to the church she had been baptised in as she had lots of friends there and had been married in it, Greg being an agnostic and having no affiliation to any church. She always picked her Mum's elderly friend up in Coustonholm Road. Betty was waiting for her as she always was and gave her a kiss as she seated herself. She was always so smartly dressed, as now in a peacock blue suit with white shoes, that Pat felt untidy in her grey trousers and pink polo shirt.

"Hello, second Mum," Pat greeted her. Her own Mum had died five years ago and this lovely little lady who was as thin as a sparrow, had been like a mother to her ever since.

They were almost late for church this Sunday as a multi-storey building in Shawbridge Street was being demolished later that day and the road was blocked so they had to turn round and go by way of Lidl Stores. The church was humming with excitement as the church building was being refurbished and this was the last Sunday of the service being held in the large hall. There was no tea and coffee being served after the service this Sunday as the smaller hall was packed with the new chairs for the church and after dropping Betty off earlier than usual, Pat went for one of her church friends and they went to the nearby golf club for lunch as usual. It was just after three o'clock when she arrived home.

"Did you make an arrangement with the police to interview you today at 1pm?" were her husband's first words to her.

"Oh, no! I completely forgot. What did they say?"

"They were OK. They said they would come back later this afternoon, about 4pm."

Greg had spent all morning with his Observer as usual. He had made himself his normal late breakfast cum lunch and was ready for a walk.

"Do you think we'll be allowed to walk our usual way, past the Keel factory?" he asked Pat as she came into the lounge, prior to going upstairs to change into her casual trousers and flat shoes.

"I really don't know, Greg," she replied. "Do you want to go that way and see or do you want to take the car to the Hill of Birches, park it and walk from there instead?"

"Let's just try our usual way. You can point out where the body lay," he added in a dramatic voice, then laughed when he saw her face.

"If you don't want to revisit the crime scene, Sherlock, we can always go the other way."

"No. I'm quite curious myself to see the place again."

She ran upstairs and came back down, wearing navy jogging bottoms and a tee-shirt.

They walked briskly up the street, crossed over the main road and entered the estate. It was not till they reached the factory environs that they could see evidence of police activity. Yellow tape sealed off half of the width of the road and led into the field through the hedge, making a curve then coming back out further down the road. A lonely policeman guarded the spot and Pat felt sorry for him as there was nowhere for him to sit. As they drew nearer, she recognised the constable from the night before and smiled at him.

"I'm so sorry, constable, about forgetting your visit. We're not being nosy. This is where we always walk on Sunday afternoon."

Frank Selby smiled back at her. He had been standing for a few hours, having relieved Bob at 1.30 pm and he would be here for another hour before Penny came back to take over from him till Bob came back again. SOC had done most of their work last night but Ben Goodwin had returned during Penny's shift to have a clearer look round in daylight rather than dusk. The body had been removed to the mortuary for Martin to run tests on but Davenport did not want the public tramping over the scene today so the constables had been assigned duties until it got dark.

"Have you found out anything about the dead woman or can't you tell me?" Pat asked him.

"I couldn't tell you if we had but we haven't," Frank answered. "Once we have a photograph, we'll be going round the houses in the area to see if anyone recognises her. See you later, Mrs McLean."

Pat and Greg skirted the yellow tape and continued with their walk, Pat wanting to ask if the constable knew how the victim had died but not wanting to seem ghoulishly curious. As they passed the large house, Greg commented on the fact that both large houses had not long been sold and that now the two families had landed themselves at a murder scene.

"Especially this one," he said. "It's so near where the murder took place."

They had both taken an interest in the new houses, Greg commenting on how lovely it would be to live in one, especially this one so far from other houses but Pat preferring the one nearer them because it was close to a bus stop.

They continued on down Floors Road, passing their favourite house with the little river, bridge and miniature, wooden water wheel. One car passed them going towards Newton Mearns and they passed a girl with a black and white collie dog. Pat smiled at her as they had passed each other many times, then, realising that she would be turning into the estate, she stopped her to tell her about the murder.

"Maybe I shouldn't go that way," the girl said. "Do you think I should just retrace my steps?"

"Glen will be disappointed not to be let off the lead," said Pat, having seen the collie excitedly sniffing in the undergrowth on other days. "But I'd keep him on the lead until you get past the policeman. He might smell where the body lay and dive in there."

Thanking her for the advice, the girl went off into the estate, with her dog firmly on the lead.

Another car passed them, this time a police car.

"Probably relief for the guy who was there," commented Greg. "Don't fancy their job. Very boring work."

The hardest part of their walk was the part on the main road as it was uphill so they said little, conserving their energy for the climb. It was a busy road and they were passed by many cars, mostly going far too fast, and by one bus, going to Eaglesham. This was their least favourite part of the walk as it was the least healthy with all the engine fumes but there was no other way to go unless they took the car and that seemed to defeat the point of a walk. Pat felt the muscles at the back of her legs tighten and knew that her pace had slowed. Greg slowed too so that they could walk side by side even though the pavement was quite narrow. He kicked at the pebbles which cars had displaced from driveways.

They turned into Barlae Avenue and Greg remembered to post a letter, then they continued, downwards now, to the bottom of the road.

"I wonder if the dead woman lived round here, Greg," said Pat.

"I can't think where else she would be going unless she was going the other way, got off a bus and walked through going to Floors Road. No… that would be silly as the only houses on that road are down by the main road and she could just have stayed on the bus for one more stop and got off almost at her house," her husband replied. "Did she look familiar at all?"

"You know I told you I hardly looked at the body. It was face down anyway. She had short dark hair and youngish clothes though it could have been an older person wearing young clothes. Most people wear denims these days."

They had reached their own house by this time and Greg went up the path first as he had the key. Next door's cat was in their garden again, probably trying to get away from his own house as there were two young children who gave him little peace.

Pat followed Greg in and shut and locked the door, wondering as she did so if the dead woman would indeed prove to have lived near them.

"I wonder if the murder will be in tomorrow's Herald," she said. "Buy that as well as your Guardian, just in case, Greg," she told her husband.

Later that afternoon they had their visit from the police. Greg went into the kitchen while Pat told exactly how she had found the body. She showed Penny the photograph on her mobile phone and was thanked for her prompt reporting of the event.

CHAPTER 10

There was nothing in Monday's Herald. Greg and Pat were not to know that that was because Davenport had not yet informed his chief constable, Grant Knox, hoping to have at least found out who the woman was before he reported to his quick-tempered and impatient boss.

Martin was, as usual, first to get in touch and as he often did, he rang in with the information so that Davenport would get it before the written report landed on his desk.

"Martin here, Charles. The woman was 5 foot 3 inches, 128 lbs in weight - 9 stones 2 - I know you like it in the old form. She was in her late thirties, I would say. Her hair was dyed black, probably treated about three weeks ago by herself more than likely as it did not look as if it had been professionally done. She was manually strangled, from behind, probably once she was down on the ground on her knees which were grass-stained and a bit muddy"

"Size of hands? Could you tell from the marks on her neck?"

"Large."

"Anything else, Martin? Had she been sexually assaulted?"

"No she had not but I found semen on her denim trousers so the murderer must have ejaculated over her, most likely after she was dead as it was on the back of the trousers and we found her lying on her front. She had been sexually active recently but it was not rape or even penetrative sex."

"What about the missing finger?"

"I have spoken to Ben and the finger was not found in the field so we must assume that the murderer took it with him. The finger had not been chopped off but bitten off. There was skin under the finger nails of her right hand so she must have gouged him. It was facial skin, from the jaw, minute traces of dark bristle."

"So it was definitely a man. Time scale?"

"The call to me was recorded at 7.48 on June 17th. She had been dead about 48 hours, so that takes it to somewhere on the evening of Wednesday 15th between 6pm and 10 pm I would say, if I were pushed to narrow the time."

"Anything else of interest?"

"She had some recent love bites on her shoulders. There might have been some on her neck which is a more common place to find them but the injuries to the neck will have hidden them."

"When you say recent, do you think they were done by the murderer?"

"That is the odd thing. One was definitely done after death but the rest were before. Sorry I cannot tell you any more than that."

"So the murderer might have seen these bites and copied them after killing her?"

"Yes or done it before and after killing her but I would suggest that she had a liaison with someone before she met the murderer. It is impossible to give you a more definite time I am afraid."

Davenport thanked his lucky stars for Martin who was not afraid to make statements like this.

"Thanks Martin. I'll expect the written report later today and thanks again for being so quick. Oh..."

"Yes?"

"Will you attach a photograph this time as we need something to show around, preferably something not too gruesome."

"It has been done already, Charles. I took a photograph of her face. I am afraid she looks a bit 'doctored' as she obviously died in agony."

Martin rang off. Davenport noticed, as he had before, that Martin spoke like a grammar book. He had mentioned on another case that he had been sent to elocution lessons as a boy.

He decided to make himself a coffee before giving the information to his team and was glad of that decision because the phone call from Ben Goodwin came through while he was drinking.

"Charles. Ben here. That information you want on the recent murder….sign of a struggle in the field and the hedge showed signs of someone having been pushed through it."

"Penny told me that the woman who found the body only parted the hedge and looked through but the other woman who had been a nurse went through to feel for a pulse."

"That wouldn't have damaged the hedge in the way it was damaged. No, there was definitely a struggle. Someone with big feet I would say, going by the marks on the grass."

"Martin said there was no sign of the finger."

"No, no sign. We searched to the borders of the field and along the verge on the road side of the hedge and nothing, so unless it turns up, we have to assume that the murderer took it with him. We did find a key on a ring beside the body. It could have fallen from her pocket. I'll send it over for you."

"Thanks, Ben… Martin said that the murder probably took place on Wednesday evening."

"Well it rained on Wednesday evening if you remember. Started at about 7pm. I was going to go bowling and changed my mind. Now the ground under the body was wet so she must have been killed after 7."

"Great. That narrows the time to about 7 to 10pm. That's a help."

Davenport thanked Ben for his speedy verbal report. He would wait till the written reports arrived then ask for an interview with Grant Knox who need not know that he had been given the information earlier. He drained the now lukewarm coffee, rinsed his mug and went down the corridor, calling out to Fiona as he passed her room, "DS Macdonald, Incident Room please."

Her door opened and she hurried after him, pausing only to shut both his door and hers.

By this time Davenport was at the door to the room where the sergeant and constables worked. He looked in. Penny was at a filing cabinet, busy with her new filing project, Frank was almost buried under a pile of catalogues. He had just been told what his part in the new duties was and Salma was at her desk, writing away, busily. The only other constable who sometimes augmented the Davenport 'team', Bob, was on duty at the front desk.

"Stop what you're doing, folks. I need you in the Incident Room now."

When they were all seated, he told them what he had just heard from the police surgeon and the head of SOC.

"The woman was quite small, 5' 3 inches..."

"Same as me," Penny could not resist commenting.

Davenport smiled at her. It was hard to rebuke Penny.

"She was of medium weight, aged around 35 to 40, dark-haired. She had struggled with her attacker, probably scarred him or her. I would think it was a man as Martin found minute traces of facial bristle, dark bristle under her right finger nails. She was not sexually assaulted but he had ejaculated over her dead body, onto her back. She was probably killed between 7 and 10pm on Wednesday night. She was strangled from behind. She had probably had some heavy petting prior to the attack but had not had sexual intercourse and was not raped.

We have to show her face to the people who live round about. Not to the public yet. Hopefully we won't have to do that. Martin has tried to make the face more...palatable, wrong word but you all know what I mean. She had struggled with her attacker. There were some love bites, one given after death but some before, on her shoulders."

"So she might have had a meeting with a boyfriend just before she was killed, Sir," Frank said.

"Yes. One other thing, her ring finger was bitten off, not chopped or sawn off as we thought at first. No sign of the finger."

"Yeuch!" said Penny, shuddering.

"What now, Sir?" asked the DS.

"Well, no point in rushing off till we get the photograph. Martin has sent his report over so it should be here shortly. I suggest that we all busy ourselves with the work in hand, try to clear our desks as we'll have to leave the filing and the sorting and the writing till this case is over."

"Will you see the chief constable, Sir?" Fiona asked.

"Not yet. I'll wait till we have the photograph and the written reports."

They all filed out. Going back up the corridor to his room, Charles spoke to Fiona out of earshot of the others who were some steps behind.

"Wish I could put off seeing Knox till we find out who the murdered woman is, but he'd be furious if he wasn't told as soon as possible."

Fiona agreed with him.

"Well, better see if I can finish off the narrative of Robert Gentle's murder," she said. "I'll leave William Paterson's till after this case is finished."

"I'd just started the David Gibson case. I hadn't reached the other teacher's murder. What was her name again?"

"Irene something," said Fiona.

"That's it. Irene Campbell."

"Our first two cases together had two murders, so had the third..." Fiona commented.

"...and the last one had three," Davenport added.

"Let's just hope there's only one this time eh?" Fiona said wryly.

She opened her door.

"Let me know when you're off upstairs to see the big chief."

Smiling at her, Davenport promised to do just that. He had just finished tidying up what he had done of his narrative when Bob arrived with the reports from Ben Goodwin and Martin Jamieson.

"Both arrived one on top of the other, Sir," said Bob.

Davenport had a quick glance over both missives, combed his thick brown hair, put on his suit jacket and going off down the corridor, glanced in at Fiona who had left her door open.

"Off to beard the Knox lion. I feel like a Christian martyr."

"I'll be thinking of you," was her reply.

CHAPTER 11

Davenport, in the lift on the way to the top floor, felt irreverently that he was being whisked upwards to God which was how he often described his superior to himself. Fancifully he thought that Grant Knox should have a large open book in front of him, a book containing all his failures. He had read a poem once by Studdart Kennedy, nicknamed Woodbine Willy, the war poet, in which God was believed to say only one word when faced by someone newly dead.

"Well?"

This was what Knox would probably say to him in a minute.

The lift came to a halt and he stopped grinning. It would not do to be caught looking happy when he did not even have a name for his latest corpse. The lift doors opened and Solomon Fairchild, the assistant chief constable was waiting to go down.

"Good morning, Charles," he said with a smile. "Anything interesting happening downstairs at the chalk face?"

Charles was holding the lift door open but Fairchild was obviously not in a hurry so he let it close and they heard the lift purring its way downwards.

"There's been another murder on the Southside, Sir."

"That must be about your tenth murder since you arrived here!"

Charles counted them off silently on his fingers.

"Spot on, Sir. Ten it is."

"The South Side's becoming like Midsomer. Murders must be attracted to you like they are to John Nettles."

"Or Angela Lansbury, in 'Murder She Wrote'," laughed Charles.

"Who is it this time?"

"Afraid I don't have a name yet, Sir."

"Oh dear. Well good luck."

Charles could tell by the look on his superior's face that he knew that the interview approaching was going to be a fraught one. They grimaced at each other and Fairchild pressed the down button for the lift. Charles straightened his shoulders and walked towards the office of Grant Knox. His secretary looked at him disapprovingly. Perhaps working for a man with little humour had made her treat life seriously. She had been much friendlier working under her last chief constable.

"Yes, DCI Davenport?"

"Can I see Mr Knox, please?"

Charles felt like a small schoolboy asking to see his headteacher. He almost corrected it to, "May I see Mr Knox, please", as he knew his old English teacher would have told him to say.

"You don't have an appointment, do you?"

She inspected her diary, knowing he thought, full well, that his name was not written in it.

"Sorry, no I don't. I didn't know in advance that a murder would take place but a murder has taken place, on Wednesday."

"Wednesday! This is Monday."

Tempted to say that he was well aware of the date and determined not to be browbeaten by the secretary as well as by the chief constable, Charles attempted humour.

"Gosh is it Monday already?"

Her face went red and she shut her diary with a snap, picking up the intercom phone.

"Sir, DCI Davenport here to see you."

She listened.

"No Sir, no appointment but there has been another murder...on Wednesday, Sir."

Charles could hear the reply as his boss's raised voice spoke back.

"Wednesday? Send him right away."

Wilma Sharp, by nature as well as by name, Charles thought, smiled sweetly at him.

"Please go in, DCI Davenport."

Solomon Fairchild would have ordered coffee for both of them before asking him to take a seat but Charles knew not to expect anything sociable like this from Knox. He was not disappointed.

"Davenport. Another murder? On Wednesday! Why wasn't I informed at the time?"

"It was late on Friday, Sir, before the body was found. You would have left the station by the time I knew. I didn't think you would want to be disturbed at home during the weekend and I had hoped that by today I would have a name for the victim…"

"…and have you got a name?"

"No Sir. We've only just got a photograph from the police surgeon, not a nice picture to show around unfortunately."

"Why not?"

"The woman was strangled, Sir."

"So the police surgeon, Jamieson isn't it, has made his report?"

"Yes, Sir, so has the head of SOC. I have them both here."

Charles laid a folder on the desk. Knox picked it up, opened it and extracted the two sheets of paper. He sat back in his chair and started to read. Charles shuffled his feet, hoping to be told to sit down and when he was not invited to sit, he decided to risk a reprimand and sat down anyway. Knox was engrossed in what he was reading and did not seem to notice. After about ten minutes, during which Charles studied his finger nails, he looked up.

"Not sexually assaulted I see, but there had been some petting maybe before the murder took place. Nasty things love bites!"

"Murder is nastier," Charles was tempted to say but he remained quiet.

"And the murderer seems to have ejaculated over the dead body. A man who craves sex but has no girlfriend and couldn't force the woman to have sex with him, couldn't rape her. Wonder why not?"

He might be a difficult boss to work with but he had a point, something to bear in mind, Charles thought.

"Not likely to be smaller than her, Sir. She was only five feet three inches but maybe he was frail or she struggled so violently that he just killed her quickly."

"Mm. Yes that's possible, I suppose. Or maybe he heard a car coming and just pushed her through the hedge and strangled her quickly. Has anyone been interviewed?"

Charles was glad that at least he could say they had started the investigation.

"We've interviewed the people in all the nearby houses, Sir."

Knox looked down at the SOC's report.

"I see it took place in a field adjacent to a minor road running through an estate in Waterfoot. How many houses were there on that road?"

"Four, Sir."

"Did anyone hear or see anything at all?"

"One man saw a car's lights disappearing as he arrived home with his wife on the night of the murder but that's all, Sir."

"At what time was that, Davenport?"

"About ten o'clock, Sir, 10 to 10.15 the man thought."

"It could well have been the murderer then if Jamieson put the time at between 6 and 10 and head of SOC, Goodwin isn't it, said we could narrow it by an hour because of the rain, to between 7 and 10."

Davenport had to hand it to him, he certainly absorbed details quickly and accurately.

"That's correct, Sir, all supposing the murderer wasn't one of the inhabitants of the houses."

"Tell me about these inhabitants."

For the next half hour, Charles went through the contents of his second folder then Knox asked him if he thought that giving the news to the press would be a good idea. Not like the man to ask for advice from an inferior, thought Charles. Maybe it had dawned on him that his dealings with the press had not always been successful.

"I don't think we should release information to the papers for a day or two, Sir. The picture of the murdered woman, as I said, isn't a very nice one, is it?"

Knox agreed.

"Right then, Davenport. I'll give you a couple of days to see what you and your folk can do. Report back here on..."

He rifled through his large desk diary.

"... Thursday at 4pm."

"Yes Sir."

Charles rose to his feet. The interview had gone better than he had hoped.

"Ask Miss Sharp to come in here on your way out."

Charles picked up his two folders.

"No. Leave those with me!" barked Knox.

On his way our through the office, he told the secretary that she was wanted in the inner sanctum and was pleased to see her fairly scuttle to the connecting door. His heart was lighter as he waited for the lift. Three full days he had been given. Surely they would find the woman's identity in that time.

The lift arrived empty and it made its way without stopping, to the ground floor.

"Right folks, Incident Room please," he called out, as he passed the main room and the room of his DS. Going into his own room, he removed his jacket and picked up the master copy of the picture of the dead woman. He took a copy of his

A-Z street map from the desk drawer then made his way back down the corridor. His colleagues came in just after him and sat down.

"Penny, get some copies of this made, ten please."

He handed her the photograph and she rose and went off to the room which housed the photocopier, returning with the copies and handing them to her boss who was studying a map.

"There are four houses, the ones you've already been to and there will be more, probably, on Floors Road. Salma, you and Penny, divide these houses among you and show the inhabitants the picture. No point in telling them not to mention this to anyone. The ones you've already seen have probably already told some folk and we know from experience that the public will tell other folk even if we ask them not to. Don't give them any details, of course, other than what they'll gather from the photo."

"Is Mr Knox telling the press, Sir?" asked Fiona.

"Not yet. I think I've got till late Thursday afternoon, maybe Friday morning. It's a nasty photograph to publicise. He could see that."

"What about me, Sir?" asked Frank.

"I want you to do the houses at the other end, the two streets across the main road from the entrance to the estate. One of them was the street Mary McGregor lived in."

They were sombre, remembering the murder of the teenager a few weeks ago.

"Right folks, off you go. Get on with your routine work. Better to visit houses early in the morning, so go tomorrow. Salma, you and Penny meet up with Frank after you've done your own houses and help him out. The woman must have been heading for either the houses you are going to Frank, or in the other direction, towards the houses in Floors Road, unless she was making for a bus stop."

"Could she have been visiting someone, Sir?" asked Penny.

"Perhaps, Penny. Perhaps a lover or boyfriend, the latter more likely if we take the love bites into consideration and the fact that she had not had penetrative sex recently. If she was visiting someone, they could be in one of the houses you'll be visiting, I imagine, as she's unlikely to have walked further. I hope so anyway."

They went off to get on with their work.

"I'll drive us all up there tomorrow," said Frank. "No point in taking two cars."

"No, better take two in case one of us has to come back before the others," argued Salma.

Davenport walked up the corridor with his DS, suggesting that they go out for lunch as there was nothing much they could do until the others reported back.

"I need a stiff drink after my interview with God," he said.

CHAPTER 12

Frances Harris was worried, a common experience for her since her husband Edward had walked out on her or rather since she'd driven him to his latest girlfriend's house and told him to stay there and never come back. The face that looked back at her in the bathroom mirror these days was lined and she had black smudges under her eyes from lack of sleep. There were days when she longed for Edward even though he had tried to control her all the time but especially so now that Craig was proving to be a source of constant anxiety to her.

Edward had strayed a number of times during their seventeen year marriage and she had accepted his apologies and his assurances that it would never happen again but this had been the last straw, a fling he said but a fling which she had discovered had been going on for nearly a year and had started almost immediately after she had found out about another girl. So much for his apologies which never had sounded sincere, almost as if he should be allowed stray on occasion. To make matters worse, this last woman was older than herself, not his usual age as he had always chosen women about ten years younger than her. His favourite game when he was a child, she had shouted at him, must have been 'Doctors and Nurses', as he inevitably had affairs with the nurses at the hospital where he was a gynaecologist.

"You're supposed to treat women's private parts, not sample them!" was the last thing she had shouted at him before bringing down a suitcase which she had packed for him earlier. His look of utter surprise had been almost comical.

She had driven him away from their house in Newton Mearns because she had every intention of keeping their bigger car and was giving him no chance to drive off in it. She had almost immediately sold it and bought a small one.

Maybe they had made a mistake in not explaining things more clearly to the two boys, thinking Craig, especially, too young to understand adult problems. She had simply told them that their father had left to live with another woman and that they could see him whenever they wanted to but not in the house they would be moving to with their mother.

Kenny had taken it very well, saying that most of his friends' parents lived separately. He saw his father every week and had even, much to Frances's displeasure, met the 'other woman' and claimed that she was "OK" but Craig had gone very quiet and subdued at first. This was easier to cope with than his second phase, the one he was in now, his rebellious phase. He had, from the start, refused to meet Edward at all which had hurt his father as the two had always been very close. Frances did not know what to do about that. She supposed that deep down she was quite pleased that one of her sons was not prepared to forgive and forget.

Edward had been a lieutenant in the local church's BB company and both boys had attended. Kenny still went and was taking his Duke of Edinburgh Award course this year but Craig had come home one Friday night to say that he was not going back. At church on the following Sunday, the captain, a bearded young man who was extremely enthusiastic about his company, came up to Frances and explained that he had had to tell Craig not to come back as he had become totally disruptive and non-cooperative. This had been going on for some time and was beginning to affect some of the younger boys who had begun to copy his exploits. Expelled from the Boys' Brigade! If it had not been worrying, it would have been laughable. She had asked Kenny who, reluctant at first to tell tales on his young brother, had eventually admitted that Craig had been rude to all the leaders and had deliberately made mistakes in group activities such as marching.

Next came the school reports. Naturally, Craig did not volunteer the times when he had had detention, the times when he had been given punishment exercises and not handed them in. The first intimation Frances had had that his school behaviour had deteriorated was the letter informing her that her son had been suspended from school for three days and asking her to make an appointment to see his Guidance teacher. She had immediately rung the school and asked what he had done. The list of demeanours was frightening. He had played truant a number of times, been caught smoking in the boys' toilet, been rude to teachers and recently had started bullying some of the younger boys. She made an arrangement to see his Guidance teacher and went up the next day. At that time she did not have a job though she was looking for one.

The young man who met her and took her to his room, was very sympathetic and also very puzzled.

"Craig was always such a lovely young guy, Mrs Harris. I'm also his chemistry teacher and he worked so hard and was one of my best pupils. He seems to have completely lost interest in the subject and reports from other teachers show the same thing."

Frances had explained about her husband leaving and how Craig did not even want to see him. She told him about the BB and about how Craig's sunny nature at home had been replaced by a surly, uncommunicative one.

"I know youngsters can go through rebellious phases in their teens but Kenny didn't and I suppose I expected the same from Craig," said his mother.

"Yes, I teach Kenny too, a charming young man."

Frances had promised to speak to Craig, to try to find out what had altered him but she was afraid it was his father leaving and she could do nothing about that.

The next day was Saturday. Kenny had gone out to play football for the BB and Frances had cornered her younger son.

"Craig, love. Can you tell me what's bothering you? What's made you change from such a lovely, affectionate son into a grumpy bear?"

She tried to keep a light tone, not wanting to alienate him.

"Nothing's bothering me."

"But son, you've been put out of the BB and now you've been suspended from school. Your school work is suffering. You won't get to be a doctor at this rate."

"I don't want to be a doctor anymore!"

"Why not? You've always wanted that ever since you were wee."

"Dad's a doctor, isn't he? That's why!"

She could get nothing more from him though he had promised to stay out of trouble. He had kept his word until they had moved house to the small semi-detached house in Waterfoot, then things had got bad again. Another suspension was given. Frances went back up to the school and spoke this time to a depute head who warned her that if Craig got many more three-day suspensions, he would end up being expelled.

"And he doesn't want that on his school record, Mrs Harris."

This time, a talk with Craig elicited eventually, after much persuasion on her part, that his friends had lost interest in him. They were all hard workers and also all lived in Mearns whereas he was now in Waterfoot. He had got in with another crowd, boys and girls who saw school as a place to be endured and who chose to cause trouble to enliven their boredom. Luckily Frances had seen the frightened wee boy underneath the sullen young man. The day before the police had turned up at her door, she had gone to the school nearest to their new home and enrolled Craig there. He had agreed to make a fresh start and had also agreed to go down a year in order to catch up on what he had missed.

"I still don't want to be a doctor, Mum. Dad deserted us and he makes a fool of himself with the nurses."

"How do you know all this, love?"

"One of my old pals told me. His dad works in the Victoria too and he said Dad's a laughing stock there. They say he's really pompous but flirts with all the young nurses."

Frances had tried to convince him that his dad still loved him and that it was her that he had left, not them really, though they were affected by the move too. He had told her that he had blamed her at first. He had heard her telling Edward that she was sending him away, taking him to his other woman and he had been angry with her for not forgiving him. By the time he had realised that she was not at fault and that he was wrong to try to punish her with his bad behaviour, things had gone too far to stop and he had dug his heels in and tried to live up to his bad reputation.

Frances had told Kenny and asked him to help his young brother whenever he could and he had agreed, though now of course they would be at different schools. Kenny was a prefect and model pupil and son but Craig did not seem to resent his brother though the two were not close and never had been. Kenny wanted to go into the army but wanted to get a degree first. He was a handsome young man with a group of close friends, no girlfriends as yet, unlike Craig who had always made friends easily with girls in spite of being rugged in looks rather than handsome.

Now that she had sorted out Craig's problems, she hoped, Frances wondered if the fact that his father was a womaniser had turned her elder son away from the female sex but when she spoke to Kenny about it he had just laughed, his usual cheery laugh and told her not to be silly.

"No time for girls yet, Mum. I've got too much to do with school, exams, BB, the Duke of Edinburgh Award, football. I'll get to girls at Uni."

Craig had set off to school that day, wearing his new uniform and promising to be a star pupil.

"Some things are impossible," she had laughed and rumpled his curly hair. He had grinned back.

When she saw the policewoman at the door, this time she was not afraid.

CHAPTER 13

"Will we work together or do separate houses, Sarge?"

As they got out of the police car at the beginning of Floors Road, they had counted more than nine houses, all detached and Penny knew that it would be quicker if they split up but she guessed that Salma might prefer to work together as she sometimes met with rudeness because she was Asian.

"We'll go separately, to start with, Penny. I'll take the second house. You do the first one."

Salma knew she had to bite the bullet and do interviews by herself. She was competent at her work which was why she had been promoted to sergeant and knew that if she wanted to rise further in the police force, she had to have confidence and be able to deal with any racism that she met in the course of her job.

She walked briskly up the path to the first house and rang the bell which she heard chiming in the hallway. As she waited, she looked back at the garden which was well tended, a riot of early summer colour, yellows and reds predominating. She turned back to the door. It was panelled in shaded glass and she could see the shape of a woman coming through the hall.

The door opened and a tall, elderly woman stood there, looking anxious through pale, faded eyes when she saw the police uniform. Salma was used to this reaction and hastened to reassure her.

"Please don't worry. This is a routine investigation, nothing personal, Mrs...?"

There had been no nameplate on the door.

"Winters. Miss."

Salma could have kicked herself. She had made an elementary mistake and not looked at the woman's ring finger. She saw now that it was empty of rings.

"Sorry, Miss Winters. There's been a murder locally and I wondered if you recognised this person."

She handed over the photograph. The woman took it, putting on the glasses which hung from a cord round her neck and inspecting it thoroughly.

"No. Sorry. I've never seen her before."

She sounded almost disappointed.

"Where was she murdered?"

The news would soon be in the papers so Salma saw no harm in telling her that it had been in the Keel Estate which was the truth but a bit vague. She thanked the woman, took back the photograph and walked back down the short path, meeting Penny at the gate.

"Any luck, Penny?"

"No. The woman has two small children who came to the door with her. She looked harassed. Family called Ferguson. She hadn't seen the woman in the photograph. She didn't even ask any questions ! What about yours?"

"Same. Hadn't seen her either but wanted to know where it had happened. I saw no harm in telling her and luckily she didn't ask anything else."

As they were early, they caught everyone in except at one house where there were letters and circulars lying behind the door. As it was the last house, they had gone to it together and Penny frowned when she saw this proof that the occupants were probably on holiday.

"They should have used Keepsafe from the Post office, silly people. They're just advertising that the house is empty."

"Better take a note of their name and address so that we can come back if we're not lucky getting someone to recognise our body," said Salma, and Penny wrote down in her notebook the name, Henderson, and the house number.

They walked back to the car and with Salma driving, went up to where the street met the road through the estate.

At the large house, Mrs Cook answered the door. Penny had remembered her as elegant, so was surprised to realise that she was quite small, about the same height as herself and smaller than Salma. She was one of those women who would look glamorous in a pillow case, as her Mum would say, thought Penny. She was wearing denim trousers and a cashmere sweater in palest lemon. Her hair was not combed up today but curled gently on her shoulders, a soft grey which on her looked anything but ageing.

"Mrs Cook. Sorry to bother you again," said Salma. "Would you please have a look at this photo and see if you recognise the woman in it?"

She handed over the photo and Mrs Cook took it and grimaced. She handed it back.

"Is this the dead woman? No, I don't recognise her. Sorry."

She shouted into the house and her husband came to join her at the door. The balding, tall and quite well built man looked a lot older than his wife. He was smartly dressed in a dark suit. Obviously, he still worked.

Salma handed him the photograph but he did not know the woman in it either.

"Does anyone else live in the house, Mrs Cook?" asked Penny.

"Yes my other son, Robert lives at home. His marriage broke up some time ago. There were no children. He and his wife got half the value of their house each and he's still looking for something suitable. Will I get him for you, Constable?"

Penny thanked her and Mrs Cook vanished inside.

"I take it that this is the young woman whose body was found," said Mr Cook.

"Yes, Sir," said Salma.

The young man who accompanied his mother back to the door, looked to be in his early thirties. He resembled his mother, though he was much taller and had a full head of dark hair shot through with silver which made him look very distinguished. He was dressed smartly but more casually than his father, in grey trousers and a white shirt, open at the collar.

Shown the photograph, he denied ever having seen the woman.

"When did you come home on Wednesday evening, Mr Cook?" Salma asked him.

"Robert, please. Mr Cook makes me feel elderly," he laughed. "I didn't come home on Wednesday at all. I stayed overnight with a friend in Lawrence Street, off Byres Road. We'd drunk rather a lot and I didn't think I should drive home."

"Unusual on a weekday, Sir," said Penny, noticing the look of disapproval on Mrs Cook's face.

"Afraid I've just got the taste of freedom recently, Constable. I was still capable of doing my job the next day though."

"What do you do, Sir?" asked Salma.

"I'm an estate agent in Shawlands. Is this relevant?"

"In a murder enquiry everything is relevant, Sir," said Salma.

"Are we being suspected then?" said Mr Cook, bristling.

"No Sir but we do like to ..."

"Well, I'm a lawyer, based in town, in Bath Street and my wife has never worked. Is that all?"

Salma could sense Penny tensing at her side. She decided to end the conversation before her young colleague said something she might regret.

"Yes, thank you, Sir. Please let us know if you can think of anything that might help us."

Salma stepped back from the door and tugged Penny's sleeve. The three Cooks stepped back too and Mr Cook closed the door.

"What a rude man!" said Penny indignantly.

"As a lawyer you'd think he'd know we were only doing our job."

They got back into the car. By the time they were driving past the factory, workers were arriving and cars were behind them and also coming towards them from the Glasgow Road end. Salma pulled in to let a large van pass them on the narrow road then she drove on and stopped outside the other large, detached house.

"I meant to ask you, Penny. How did the meal out with Gordon go?"

"I wasn't much taken with the restaurant. They served tiny meals though you could choose a number of dishes. I prefer a large plateful of something I like. We had so much to chat about that it was after 11 before we realised that we were last to leave. We sat and did more chatting outside my flat."

"Did you not invite him up for ...coffee?"

"No, not for...coffee, Sergeant Din."

Penny had gone a bit pink so Salma stopped teasing her and they got out of the car again.

The door opened before they could knock and the young man nearly bowled them over.

"Oh, sorry. I'm a bit late. Trying to catch the 8.30 down at Clarkston."

"Can you spare a minute, Sir or do you want us to come back tonight?" Salma asked.

"No. It's OK. I run my own IT business in Cumbernauld. Find it easier to get there by public transport so I leave my car in Clarkston car park. Suppose it's OK for the boss to be late occasionally."

He went back inside and invited the two women into the hallway. Like the other house, it was recently painted but had some dirty marks on the walls.

"Now, what was it you wanted?"

"Would you have a look at the woman in this photograph, Sir and see if you recognise her?"

The young man put on the hall light. He frowned.

"I don't know who she is but I've seen her, I'm sure of it. I take it that this is the woman whose body was found on Friday?"

"Yes, Sir."

He shouted.

"Grace! Grace !"

"What is it?" called a woman's voice, sounding a bit irritated, Penny thought.

"The police are here. Want a word with you."

The young woman, still in her dressing gown, came out of a room at the back of the house. She was followed by her two daughters, one in shorts and a tee shirt and one in school uniform.

"Sorry to bother you again, Mrs Fensom," said Salma.

"Grace. Have you seen this woman before? I have but I can't think where," said the man.

Grace peered at the picture. She took glasses out of her pocket, put them on and looked again.

"Yes, I think I've seen her, probably walking past here. Does she have a dog?"

"We don't know, I'm afraid," said Penny.

"Mummy, mummy, can I see the photo?" said the older girl.

"No, darling. It's not a nice picture for you to see. Is that all? I'm already late getting dressed and the school bus will be here soon. No help from their father as usual."

Salma thanked them both. Mr Fensom came out with them and went to his garage.

"Must be doing really well in his business to be able to buy a house like this," commented Penny.

"Yes and I don't think his wife works," added Salma. "She looks as if she might be pregnant."

"She is. I noticed that the last time. Quite far on too, I think."

"It sounded as if they've been having a domestic," said Salma.

They walked across the road to the semi-detached houses. Salma offered to take the two deaf people Frank had told her about and left Penny to talk to the Harris family.

Mrs Harris looked much more cheerful this time. She invited Penny in to a family room where one boy was watching TV.

"This is Craig, my youngest. His school is nearby so he can leave later. Kenny, my eldest has already gone. What can I do for you?"

Penny proferred the photograph once again, asking if the woman had ever seen the girl it showed. Mrs Harris looked at it and made a face.

"Can I see it, Mum?"

Mrs Harris looked as if she was about to say no but changed her mind.

"Right, Craig but it isn't pleasant."

Craig looked. He did not seem unduly disturbed by the image he saw. Instead he looked excited.

"Mum. I've seen her and you must have too. She walks past the house quite often with her dog. It's a black and white collie, called Amigo. I've spoken to her and patted him."

Frances Harris looked again.

"Are you sure, Craig? I remember the woman you mean but I would have said she was younger than the one in the photo and her hair was curlier, more like this lady's."

She gestured at Penny as she spoke.

"Mrs Harris. The woman had been lying outside for a few nights, some of that time in the rain so her hair would be dishevelled."

"You're right, Constable."

Mrs Harris had yet another look at the photograph.

"I think you're right, Craig. With curlier hair and a rosy complexion this could be that girl who walks her dog."

"Do you know her name by any chance or where she lives?" Penny asked hopefully.

Their faces fell.

"Sorry, I don't know either," said Mrs Harris.

"Me neither," said Craig. "I only know the dog's name. I think she turned in from the right so maybe she came from Barlae or Riverside. I hope the dog wasn't with her when she was attacked. It could be running around anywhere."

"Craig, it's time you went for your bus. It'll be along in a minute."

Craig looked at his watch, grabbed his bag from the settee and loped off. Penny thanked Mrs Harris and left too. There was no sign of Salma so she leant on the garden wall and put her face up to the sun. The Harris garden badly needed weeding and the bushes cut back.

It was another five minutes or so before her sergeant joined her, looking a bit…shell-shocked… was the word which came to Penny's mind.

"How did you get on, Salma?"

"Get on? That's a mad house, Penny. Each one told me the other one was deaf and they're both deaf! I asked if they had seen the woman in the picture and they seemed to think she had been in a film. They told me they never went to the pictures any more. I said she had been killed and the old man asked me to repeat what I'd said and I said, "She's dead" and he said, "Said? What did she say?" Then the old woman said, "She didn't say 'said', she said 'red' you silly old coot. Was she wearing red in the film, pet?"

Penny started to giggle then realised that her friend was looking frustrated.

"So you got nowhere with them. Do you want me to have a try?"

"Yes please, Penny. Your voice is maybe clearer than mine."

Penny walked up the path, rang the bell then knocked on the door. She went in, returning a few minutes later with an apple and a smile.

"When I asked if they had even seen this woman before, they said someone else had just been in and no, they had never seen the woman before and was she famous. I just said no then the old woman picked this apple from a bowl on the table and gave it to me for my lunch. I guess it doesn't matter that they think she's a film star. They haven't seen her."

Penny told Salma that next door, two of the family had seen the woman before, walking a collie dog.

Salma looked at the apple then she too grinned.

"Well, at least one family had seen her and we know she must be local if she walked her dog here regularly. Maybe Frank's had some luck. I think we should find him and help him."

"Yes, that's what the boss wanted us to do. Frank's got two whole streets to cover and by now folk will be leaving for work," Penny agreed.

They went back to their car.

CHAPTER 14

Frank had been successful in finding everyone in so far but unsuccessful in that none of them remembered having seen the woman in the photograph. He had covered the top part, both sides, of Barlae Avenue, when Penny and Salma caught up with him.

"No house to go back to so far," he informed them. "Everyone's been in but I think that's going to change. Listen."

They listened and could hear some car engines revving up. A couple of minutes later cars began to pass them. Salma told Frank about the collie dog and about the fact that they were quite sure that the woman had lived near here somewhere.

"Do you want us to make a start with Riverside Road, Frank?" asked Penny, anxious to get going.

"Yes please. I'll carry on with this street."

Penny and Salma took opposite sides of their road. There were detached houses at the start, the low numbers. In these detached houses there was still somebody in but only one remembered the woman and then only because Penny mentioned the collie dog.

"I've seen her with that wee dog but the picture isn't a good one of her. She always gave me a cheery smile when she passed if I was in the garden," the woman said.

Asked if she knew where the woman lived, she pointed down the hill vaguely.

"She came from that direction," she offered. "Sorry not to be more helpful."

Penny had crossed the road to tell Salma that they were probably in the right street.

The houses became terraced on one side about half way down the road and Salma met with less success, some doors remaining closed, until she was at the second terrace. Penny was at a large house opposite. A woman came to the door with a lively toddler at her heels.

"The woman with the dog? It's a lovely dog, so obedient and yet friendly too."

"Dog!" said the little boy, pointing down the road.

She did not know the woman's name but thought that she lived by herself as she had never seen the animal with anyone else. Penny thanked her. She walked down the path. Salma was crossing towards her.

"I've just spoken to a man who walks dogs for about half the neighbourhood. The man next door told me about him. Said if anyone knew the woman who owned the collie dog, it would be him and he was right. Mr Galbraith took Amigo out for Mrs Findlay if she couldn't do it herself for any reason. He recognised her from the photograph."

"So we have a name now," Penny sounded triumphant.

"Yes, Moira Findlay and an address. Number 79."

They walked down to number 79 and rang the bell. Immediately there was a cacophony of barking and through the opaque glass door, they could see the shape of a dog. The door remained unanswered and the animal began to whine.

"I'm going to go back up to Mr Galbraith to see if he has her key. That poor dog won't have been fed since...Wednesday, maybe even Tuesday," said Penny. "What number was he, Salma?"

Salma looked in her notebook.

"Number 61," she said. "I'll give Frank a ring on his mobile and tell him to get over here."

Penny came back with Mr Galbraith and they walked up the path of Number 79 and he opened the door. The black and white collie greeted him ecstatically, then ran back inside and returned with a empty, red, plastic bowl which he dropped at the man's feet.

"Can I feed him, constable? I know where the food is kept," said the neighbour.

"Do you have any dog food in your own house, Sir?" asked Salma.

"Yes I have. Would you rather I took him home with me?"

"Yes, Sir, if you don't mind. We don't want to disturb anything in the house."

"Poor lassie. It's obvious from the photo that she's dead. Well, you know where I live if you want me. I'll look after Amigo meanwhile."

A red lead was hanging by the door and he took it, clipped it on to the dog's collar and walked off up the road.

Frank reached them at this point. Salma took out her mobile again and called the station, asking to be put through to either DS Macdonald or DCI Davenport.

"Ma'am, it's Sergeant Din here. We've found the address and name of the dead girl. A neighbour had a key... no Ma'am, nobody has gone inside but I let him take the woman's dog home with him to look after and feed. Her name is Moira Findlay."

She ended the call and put her mobile back in her pocket.

"One of us is to stay here. The other two have to go back to the station. For some reason they want me to come back." She sounded puzzled.

"I'll stay," volunteered Frank. "You two get back."

Back at the station, DS Macdonald had informed Davenport about the successful outcome of the house to house visits.

"The name of the dead woman is Moira Findlay and she lived at number 79 Riverside Road. A neighbour's taken the dog to look after."

"I hope no one's gone inside," said Davenport, sternly for him. "If they've let that neighbour trample about inside, I'll have their guts for garters."

"No it's OK. Salma said no one went inside so I imagine the dog came out willingly."

"It'd be hungry, poor brute, left alone since Wednesday evening. Now will you go or will I go?"

"That, coming from you, Charles, means that you want me to go," Fiona Macdonald laughed. "OK I'm off. Just the usual search for address book, diary, correspondence?"

"Take that key that was found. See if it's the house key. I should have given it to Salma but they got in anyway. Did you give Salma the news?"

"How could I over the phone?" Fiona was sombre now. "I told her we wanted her to come back. I take it that's why you want to stay?"

"Yes."

Salma and Penny got back to the station at around 10.15. The call to the station for Salma had come just before she had rung in with the news of their success. Her mother had collapsed and died while out shopping in Great Western Road.

Penny and Salma were chatting excitedly as they came up the station steps and Davenport heard their laughter as they came along the corridor. He gave them time to remove their hats and jackets and he boiled his kettle for tea, before going down to their room and asking his sergeant to come to his room.

"Me too?" asked Penny.

"No, Penny. I need to speak with Salma alone."

Seeing her boss's serious expression, Salma wondered if she had done something wrong. Maybe she should not have let the neighbour take the dog away. He would not want to tell her off in front of Penny. He was good like that.

"Sit down, Salma."

She sat.

"I'm afraid that there's no easy way to tell you this..."

"What is it, Sir?" She was scared now. Her heart had started to beat too fast and she felt a bit dizzy.

"It's your mum, Salma. I'm afraid she collapsed in the supermarket ..."

"Where is she? Have they taken her to hospital? I'll need to get there, I..."

She had risen to her feet in panic.

"Salma sit down. You can't do anything. She died instantly."

"Died? No she can't have died. She wasn't ill."

"There'll be a post mortem. There always is with a sudden death. It was your sister who rang us. She was contacted at her school. Have this tea then I'll get Penny to run you home."

In a daze, Salma sipped the hot sweet tea.

"Does my brother know yet?"

"I'm sorry, your sister didn't say."

She got up, placing the cup very carefully on the table as if scared it might break. She walked down the corridor to the room she shared with Penny and Frank. Penny, seeing the expression on her face, ran towards her friend.

"Salma, what is it? What's wrong?"

"It's my Mum. She's dead."

The word seemed to release something inside her and she started to cry, great wracking sobs. Penny caught her in both arms and hugged her tightly. Gradually the sobs subsided.

"You've to take me home, Penny."

"Of course I will. Get your jacket."

Penny had been to Salma's house a number of times since she had moved to the West End so she needed no directions from her friend and just let her sit quietly on the journey across the city. They pulled up outside the flat. Penny switched off the engine, got out and came round to the passenger side. Salma seemed reluctant to get out of the car and Penny realised that, as the eldest of the family still at home, she knew that when she went inside, she would have to be the strong one. This was reinforced when Shazia almost erupted out of the close and tried to drag her sister out of the car.

"Salma, what have we to do? Have you any idea?"

Salma seemed to mentally give herself a shake. She got out of the car, hugged Shazia and said that the first thing they had to do was get in touch with their elder brother Shahid.

"Do Farah and Rafiq know yet?"

"No. I thought Rafiq was best left at school," Shazia said. "I'll phone Farah now that you're home."

"Right, after we get Shahid, if we can, we'll need to phone Uncle Fariz. As Dad's brother, he'll take charge till Shahid comes. We'll need to get the ...body buried before midnight."

She seemed to remember Penny and turned to her colleague.

"Thanks, Penny. There's nothing you can do to help. The family will rally round."

"I'll pray for you all, Salma. It's the same God after all."

Salma gave her a sweet smile. She seemed to have regained her composure and turned to the close mouth ready to go inside and take charge until older help arrived. Shazia clung to her, weeping quietly.

Penny went to the car. Inside, she said a quick prayer that the family would get the strength they needed at this sad time, then she switched on the ignition and drove back to work.

DS Macdonald was standing in the corridor with the DCI when Penny came up to them and Penny heard her say, "I used 1571 and there were three calls. One said the caller withheld their number, another said that she hoped Moira was OK and the third was from a woman saying that a hospital appointment hadn't been kept."

Davenport smiled at Penny.

"Did you get Salma safely home?"

"Yes, Sir. Her sister Shazia was there and they're going to contact their elder brother."

"Come into my room both of you and have some tea. Where's Frank?"

"I sent him to the canteen," Fiona replied.

They talked about deaths in their own families while they drank. Davenport suggested that Penny should go to the funeral, being the closest to Salma and Penny agreed.

CHAPTER 15

It was nearly six o'clock. Grace Fensom looked at her watch for the umpteenth time. She had turned the oven down, hoping to save her casserole from getting dried out. Standing at the window, she surveyed her new garden. It was totally uncultivated as yet. They had only moved in about six months ago. She had been so happy. Brian had done very well in his IT business and they had put in a successful bid for this brand new detached house. Recently however, things had started to go wrong. Brian loved his children but being stretched to the limit to buy this house had left him little extra money and he missed his nights out with his friends and his brother. His brother. Grace thought of Dick, single, wealthy, handsome, envied by Brian. He encouraged Brian to socialise and, she suspected, told him that it was the wife's job to look after the children. She had never liked the man. Right from the start she realised that he had thought of her as a rival for his brother's affections. She had tried to be nice to him, inviting him for meals, asking him to be godfather to Anne. He lavished Anne with expensive presents but ignored her young sister, Karen who luckily was not yet old enough to notice.

Why had Dick never married, she wondered often. Was it that he poured all his love out on his brother? Their parents had died when they were in their late teens and there were no other siblings. Dick had left school almost immediately, Brian had told her, got a job and paid for Brian to go to university. She could understand why he loved his brother so much but she wished he would pay more attention to her and the two wee ones.

Take tonight, for example. She had made the meal, expecting him at around 5 o'clock. He had not rung her to say that he would be late. This happened often, far too often. The girls got fractious and she ended up giving them their meal which should have been a family affair. If he was much later, she would have to bath them and put them to bed and they would cry because their beloved daddy was not there to tell them one of his exciting stories. She found bathing them very tiring now that she was nearly seven months pregnant.

She was in the middle of the bath routine, her hair plastered to her face with the steam, when she heard his key in the lock.

"Daddy! Daddy!" screamed Anne, standing up in the bath. Karen, knocked by her sister's elbow, started to yell. Water slopped everywhere. Grace sat back on her heels and waited. The steps pounded up the stairs.

"Hello, my precious girls. Daddy's home."

He hugged them, wet as they were. Karen's wails stopped as if by magic.

"You finish off here, Brian. I'll go down and try to salvage your dinner."

Grace thumped off downstairs, hearing giggles of pleasure follow her down. It was not fair. She spent all day catering for them and then he came home and she might as well be invisible. She caught sight of herself in the hall mirror, old trousers, faded blouse, soggy hair. Her breath caught in a sob. A wave of nausea wept over her and she sat down suddenly on the bottom step of the stairs.

By the time he came downstairs, she had worked herself up to a temper.

"Well, wonderful daddy, what kept you tonight? Don't tell me, your precious brother persuaded you to stop off for a drink. Am I right?"

She was right. Brian had let himself be coaxed along to the pub nearest to his work. His brother had a large workforce. He had bought up the painting and decorating business he had joined after school and expanded it a number of times till he was not needed for any of the manual work any more. He contrived to be at his brother's IT factory most days at closing time and nearly always managed to persuade Brian to join him for a drink or two.

"The little woman won't begrudge you some relaxation will she?" he would say and Brian, knowing that Grace would be fuming at home, would be too embarrassed to let his brother think he was reluctant to go home late.

He looked at the virago standing in front of him in their kitchen with all its mod cons and shining steel. Where had the gorgeous, happy woman he had married gone to?

"Surely a man can relax with a drink or two?"

Guilt made him irritable.

"And when do I get to relax, Brian?"

"You haven't tried working for years now. Your whole life's one big holiday!"

This conversation had taken place often of late and it was getting them nowhere.

"I'll take you out at the weekend, Grace. I promise."

"Oh yes? And who will look after the girls? Not your precious brother that's for sure. He's never so much as offered has he? He only thinks we have one daughter so even if he did baby-sit which he won't, he'd probably forget to put Karen to bed."

"Don't talk nonsense!"

"Well what has he ever bought wee Karen? Tell me that."

Brian was silent.

"Well. Who'll look after them? You tell me."

"Maybe Mrs Harris would come in. Her two boys are old enough to be left alone aren't they?"

"The girls hardly know her. Forget it."

Suddenly Grace felt very tired, tired of the arguing, tired of never going out anywhere on her own. She felt as if a fog of weariness was enveloping her and she said quietly:

"I'm having Saturday to myself, Brian. I don't care what you say to your brother. Golf is not on this Saturday and that's final."

Grace turned to the door of the kitchen and before Brian could think of a response, she had gone. It was only just before eight o'clock but he was sure that she had gone upstairs to bed. They hardly ever had sex any more. She would be asleep long before he went up and the atmosphere would be as strained next morning as it had been this morning when that policewoman had come to the door.

He finished his dried-out meal and went along to the lounge to watch TV so he did not hear his wife crying in their bedroom. Now he was left with trying to explain to Dick about their cancelled golf game. His brother would make him feel inadequate, tell him he should not let Grace dictate to him. He was between a rock and a hard place once again.

CHAPTER 16

Salma had been unsure about going to a Christian cremation and Penny was now in the same predicament about what to do about Salma's mum's funeral. She had rung her friend the next day and Salma had been quite relieved about the fact that there would have to be an autopsy as her mum's death had been sudden and unexpected.

"Muslims are usually buried as soon as possible, Penny but I want Shahid to be there and we were told that he was coming in from Dubai this afternoon so the earliest he could be here is tonight."

"So do you have a date for the funeral then?" asked Penny.

"Provisionally it's tomorrow afternoon. I'll be going to wash the body with Shazia, Farah and my Aunt Zenib then it'll be taken to the mosque. That's of course if the autopsy is OK."

"Can I come to the funeral, Salma? The DCI says I can come. I mean I'd like to be there but are women allowed at the mosque? Sorry to be so ignorant. We never did have that talk about our religions did we?"

"Of course you can come. The prayers will be said outside the mosque, in the courtyard. There's no bowing or prostrating or anything. Then after that, mum's body will be taken to the local cemetery. Muslims have a special section set aside for them but the women aren't allowed to go to that part. Shazia, Farah and I will go home to prepare food for guests who'll come back afterwards."

"Can I help with that? I'm not much of a cook as you know but I am willing."

"Thanks Penny but all the female relations will be enough and more for our small kitchen. Please do come back though and help eat the food.."

Salma laughed and Penny thought how brave her friend was being. She herself had been too young to remember when her own dad had died but she doubted if she could have been so controlled if it had been her mum who had died so suddenly.

At work, she said this to Frank, who still had both of his parents and did not know how he would react, and DS Macdonald who said gravely that the worst time would be later on.

"Salma has a lot to do right now, Penny so she hasn't had much time to think. It'll hit her later and hit her hard so we'll just have to look out for her in the weeks to come. I coped very well when my own mother died. I even did the eulogy at church but about six weeks later when my friend's dog died, I was distraught and couldn't stop crying."

Davenport had joined them by this time. He asked after Salma and commented that his problem with family deaths was that he wanted to grin at the wrong moments.

"It's nerves of course but it's so embarrassing. I had to tell my aunt that my dad, her brother, had died and I found myself grinning when I told her I had news for her. Of course she assumed it was good news!"

Penny asked if she could have time off the next afternoon for the funeral and Davenport said of course she could; he had already said that she should go. She told them all what Salma had told her about the procedure and Davenport realised that she was nervous about going but wanted to be there for her colleague.

"Perhaps DS Macdonald would go with you. Will you?" He turned to his second in command. Fiona said she would be happy to go with Penny if they could both be spared at this busy time.

"Well Frank and I will make a start on the people in Moira Findlay's address book. You can both help with that in the morning but there's nothing else we can do except find out who knew her well and hopefully find someone who might have wished her dead. I'll get Bob to help in the afternoon and someone can come from another department to man the front desk."

He and Fiona had scrutinised the diary and address book. Unfortunately, Moira Findlay had been the kind of person who put initials in her diary rather than names. Dr R was easy, obviously her doctor and Davenport had rung to make an appointment to see Dr Ross whose name along with the practice address had been in the address book.

In Wednesday's space in her diary, there had simply been an S and he didn't know whether S had been met during the day or, more crucially, in the evening. At the moment they did not even know if the dead woman worked, was divorced, separated, had a husband at sea, was childless. They had found S written in the diary quite often but not every week. There was a V next to 10.15 on the Thursday. There was also an A which kept appearing. Fiona had looked through the rather full address book and found four people who had A as their first initial but there were also three entries whose surname began with A. There were no first names beginning with S but lots of surnames. S and Mac, as Fiona knew from her own, were always the fullest pages in a Scot's address book.

"Fiona. You're a woman..."

"Thanks, kind Sir."

They had been alone in his room and he smiled gently at her and blew her a kiss across his desk. "A very desirable woman but that's for another time. As for just now, would *you* write down the initial of a person's first name or surname in your diary?"

"Possibly first name but I usually write the full name. Mind you I haven't had any secret affairs... yet."

"Don't you dare! Am I down as C in your diary then?"

"You are actually, just in case my diary got lost and one of the constables opened it."

"You're a wise woman. On that topic, should we tell the others about our joint holiday? I know you said no when I last mentioned it but would it not be better to tell them and treat it casually as just friends going away together with my daughter, rather than have them find out and read more into it?"

"I'm not sure, Charles. We're such a small unit here and they'd be watching us closely if we told them."

"Maybe you're right. Women have a better understanding of these things."

They went back to a discussion of the names. There was an Elenor Anderson, a Laura Agnew and Mrs & Mrs E. Allan. Then there was an Alison Jones, an Alan Knight, a Mr & Mrs A. Smith and an A. Livingstone.

"Surely Elenor Anderson would be E. You wouldn't call her Anderson so why use her surname initial?" said Fiona. "The same with Laura Agnew."

"I agree but I think we'd better check them all eventually. We'll leave those two till last."

They turned to the Ss but there being no first names down as S except for a Mr & Mrs S Watson, they had only one name to add to their priority list which now read:

Alison Jones
Alan Knight
Mrs A Smith
Mr A Smith
Mrs S Watson
Mr S Watson.

There was no name beginning with V.

This list had addresses and some had phone numbers, all but Alan Knight and the Watsons but Charles found both of these in the telephone book which Fiona had also brought from the house.

Fiona and Penny decided to take Fiona's car rather than a police car. Charles asked Penny to talk to Frank who wanted to know how Salma was coping, before she left.

Charles and Fiona went into his room.

"Right, I'll see the doctor tomorrow morning if I can get past his receptionist. Some of them are like dragons guarding their caves! You, Frank and Bob divide up the other six names. Phone first and make an appointment to see them as soon as possible. I'll put Penny on to phoning some of the people in Moira Findlay's phone book. That should keep her mind off the funeral. Hope you don't mind going along too. Penny was understandably nervous about going."

"So will I be but two will be better than one. Charles, to change the subject, did you know it's Jean's birthday next week? She'll be seventy."

"How on earth did you find that out?"

"She let it slip when we were getting supper at our last bridge evening. I asked her what she was planning and she said nothing as she and her husband lost touch with most of their friends during his last illness and she has no relatives up here, most of her cousins being in the South of England."

"Let me guess. You want us to plan something for her."

"Yes. I thought we could maybe try to arrange our bridge night on that night. It's easy to plead a heavy work load on our usual night."

"That's fine by me. Have you mentioned it to John?"

"Not yet. I thought I'd run it past you first."

"What night is it?"

"It's a Saturday, a week on Saturday. Do you think John would give his social life a miss for once?"

"I'm sure he would. He's very fond of Jean. What do you think we should do?"

"It's your turn to host the bridge that week so I'll bring her up as usual but instead of coming to you, I'll take her to a restaurant and you and John can be there before us. How about that?"

"What restaurant?"

"I thought maybe that Italian one by the railway station at Giffnock."

"Andiamo I think it's called."

"Yes there. I'll book it once I've sounded out John. I'll ring him tonight and let you know tomorrow. Would you like me to buy her something from you?"

"You're an angel."

"Well it's a step up from 'woman' which you called me earlier."

He laughed and getting up, leaned over the desk and kissed her on the nose.

CHAPTER 17

It was a week after the murder. Davenport was in the waiting room at the medical centre in Clarkston. The receptionist had turned out to be very friendly and helpful and had asked if he had time to wait till 11.30 when Dr Ross finished his appointments. Glad that he was male as all the magazines were old copies of Golf and not much else - did female patients steal the women's ones he wondered - Davenport picked up May's copy of the golf magazine and rifled through it. The waiting room was quite full. A woman opposite him was plucking nervously at a paper handkerchief and staring into space. She was unaware that pieces were falling to the floor. Perhaps she was here to get test results, he thought. Next to her, a young woman sat with a fractious baby on her lap. She had tried walking up and down but to no avail and was seated now with the wee one over her shoulder. Her other child was playing in the play area and making loud banging sounds which were obviously annoying the elderly man near him as he was shifting about in his seat and making tutting sounds. The only other person in the waiting room was a scruffy-looking young man who was speaking into his mobile in spite of the signs reminding people to switch their mobiles off.

"Mr Swan to room 3," came the disembodied voice on the intercom.

No one moved.

The receptionist leaned over the counter and said loudly to the young man, "Mr Swan, the doctor is waiting for you."

The man rose, still chatting into his phone. He walked a couple of steps then stopped and continued talking. The receptionist said loudly, "Mr Swan. Please don't keep the doctor waiting. He's a very busy man."

Totally ignoring her, the man continued to speak.

"Mr Swan, if you don't go immediately, I'll tell the doctor you haven't turned up!"

At that, the man put away his phone and sauntered off up the corridor.

Davenport sent the receptionist a sympathetic look and she smiled back, weakly.

Perhaps because of this holdup, it was a little after 11.30 before Dr Ross was free to talk to him.

A man in his late forties stood at the open door at the end of the corridor.

"Come in, Inspector."

Davenport seated himself where the patients sat and the doctor took his own seat across the desk.

"How can I help you?"

"You have a patient, Moira Findlay."

"Yes. I have."

"I'm sorry to tell you that she's been murdered."

"Murdered! Where?"

"In Keel Estate, last Wednesday, though the body wasn't discovered till two days later. I know there's patient confidentiality but can you tell me anything that might help me find her killer?"

"As she's dead there's no need for secrecy but there's not much I can tell you."

He tapped at his computer.

"Moira Findlay. Mrs. Age 35. She was on blood pressure pills…"

"She was young for that surely?"

"Well no. You'd be surprised at how many young people are on them. She got divorced about a year ago. Can't help you with why I'm afraid. She was reluctant to even tell me about it but she realised that it was a factor in her depression. She was on antidepressants for a while but stopped a few weeks ago. I remember thinking that she seemed much happier when she came to see me that time."

"I don't suppose she mentioned another man in her life?"

"No, Inspector, she didn't. Some patients treat the doctor like a priest and confide everything in him but Moira was a very private person. In fact I was surprised when she admitted to being depressed."

"Was her husband a patient of yours too, doctor?"

"He was but he's left my practice now. He came once some years ago with a bad back and he asked me to send him for sperm tests. I did and they came back saying that he was fine.

I got the impression that the childlessness was one bone of contention between them. When she was depressed, she did tell me he had been very keen to have kids and she wasn't."

Davenport rose.

"Thanks, doctor. You've been very helpful."

It only took Davenport quarter of an hour to get back to the station. Fiona and Penny had left for the funeral and Frank and Bob were not yet back. He logged on to his computer and started working on his narrative of the murders at the local secondary school. He had written up David Gibson's murder and was now on that of Irene Campbell, the PE teacher. So engrossed was he that time passed quickly and it was a gentle cough which alerted him to the fact that Fiona was back.

"That's us back, Sir. Do you want to hear about it or are you very busy?"

"No, I'm not too busy. Have you both had lunch?"

"No, we skipped it as the funeral started so early in the afternoon but we did eat something at Salma's."

"Well, I'm starving so why don't I take you and Penny to our local and you can talk while I eat, then Penny can get on with some phoning for me and by that time maybe the men will be back from their interviews."

When they were comfortably settled, with drinks for the women and food for Davenport, Fiona told him about her one interview that morning as he had gone by the time she came back from it.

"I saw Mr and Mrs Smith. They turned out to be friends of Moira's parents, quite an elderly couple. They saw her about once every six weeks and the last time they saw her they thought she was much happier than she had been recently. She'd gone through a divorce. Irreconcilable differences, they said was the cause. He was a nice fellow, they said, and Moira was quite cut up about it."

"Depressed?"

"They never said."

"The doctor had her on antidepressants for a time but she was off them now."

"So she was happier for some reason, Sir," chipped in Penny, never quiet for long.

"Maybe Penny or maybe just got over the divorce."

Davenport had finished his lunch so he sat back and prepared to listen to what had happened at the funeral.

"We got quite a shock when we got to the mosque, Sir," said Penny. "The coffin was open and we were expected to walk past and look at Mrs Din. She was covered in a white sheet and had a white hijab on her head."

"The men took turns in saying prayers but for most of the time it was silent prayer. One woman started wailing but the men seemed annoyed and quietened her down quickly," said Fiona.

"How was Salma?" asked Davenport.

"I would say dignified, like her two sisters. Her elder brother was there. He said one of the prayers. The younger brother was there too but he was kept in the background," said Fiona.

"Rafiq is ten. There's quite a gap between Farah and Rafiq. Salma told me that her mum lost two babies," Penny informed them.

"When everyone had filed past the coffin, it was taken to the cemetery by the men and all us women went back to Salma's house. The older women were already there getting food ready. We ate a little, had a quick chat to Salma and came away," Fiona summed up, looking at her watch.

"Yes, you're right. We'd better get back to work," said her boss.

When they entered the station, Bob was sending the supply policewoman back to her own department.

"Frank's just gone to your room, Sir. We finished the interviews."

Two had agreed to come home for lunch and two were retired and they had seen them earlier.

Davenport and what he liked to call his 'team', congregated in the Incident Room. Fiona told Frank quickly how the funeral had gone and about her visit to Mr and Mrs Smith, then it was Frank's turn.

"Mr and Mrs Watson are very elderly. Moira was at school with their daughter who emigrated to Canada with her husband and children some years ago. They said she visited them regularly and had become almost like a daughter to them. They were very upset, Sir when I told them what had happened. They knew she had gone through a divorce and weren't aware of any other man in her life."

"Right, what about Alison Jones?" asked Davenport.

"She saw Moira often. Another school chum. They went out every month, either to the theatre or to the cinema and had lunch every Saturday at one of their houses."

"Did Moira confide in her?"

"Well last time they met, Moira told her she had met someone but wouldn't give details yet as the relationship was very new. His name's Sandy Macpherson and she called him Mac. Alison got the impression that the man was married but she's not sure about that, Sir."

"And Alan Knight?" said Davenport looking at the list he had written on the flipchart.

"He's a friend of her husband's. He hadn't seen her since the break-up."

"Do you think he was telling the truth, Frank?" asked Fiona.

"Yes, ma'am. His wife was at home and it seemed that they'd been a foursome. He and his wife seemed very fond of each other. Not long married and David Findlay and Moira had been best man and matron of honour."

"Thanks, Frank. Well is seems that Moira wasn't meeting any of the As and S Watson is too elderly. That right?"

"Yes, Sir."

"So S is probably Sandy Macpherson. It seems unlikely that Moira would be seeing two men at one time whose names began with S."

"Why not put M in her diary then, Sir, if she called him Mac?" asked Penny.

"True."

"I think she might put his first name's initial, knowing that no one would read her diary," said

Fiona. "It's the kind of thing a woman might take pleasure in, knowing it was secret."

"So how are we going to find this Mac, Sir?" asked Fiona.

"Well perhaps the newspapers can help us there. Mr Knox is sure to want to talk to the press and I can ask him to form a request for this man to come forward with the promise of anonymity. If he's innocent he might get in touch."

Davenport did not sound too hopeful. He had been sitting on a desk and now stood up. The others did the same.

"All we have is the mention of a car driving off in the direction of the Glasgow Road on Wednesday night. It might be important. It might not."

"Sir, Mrs McLean mentioned seeing a light on in the factory on Friday night," said Frank who had been looking up his notes. "She thought it would be a caretaker. He might have been on duty on Wednesday night and left in his car."

"Maybe someone else took over from him every night, Sir," said Fiona. "It might be worth a visit to the factory."

"Good idea. I'll do that on my way home as I'm quite near there. Now folks… Penny, back to the telephone and Frank get your interviews typed up before you forget what they said and you can't read your writing."

His grin took the sting out of the words so Frank grinned back. He pulled on his left earlobe as he said, "Yes, Sir" and was relieved to see that Penny had a smile on her face at this imitation of Davenport's little habit. He knew that she would be feeling sad for Salma and had hoped to cheer her up.

"Sore ear, constable?" asked Fiona and Penny had to turn her giggle into a cough.

"No, ma'am, just an itch."

Penny and Frank walked off quickly and Fiona and Charles went more sedately to their own rooms. As she opened her door, Fiona asked when Salma would be back at work.

"She'll be back next Monday, I hope," he replied. "I'm glad that she has her older brother with her. I wonder if he'll stay at home now."

CHAPTER 18

He had been feeling really happy for some time now but this morning when he woke the old bad feeling was back. He tried to go back to sleep but this did not work so he got up and went to his table. He had found that picking up the finger, taking it from the drawer in the table, had made him feel especially well over the last few days. He twirled it in his own fingers. Little bits of dead skin fell on the table top and he brushed them off impatiently, with his free hand. This hand was awkward and not all the pieces went onto the floor. He let out a roar of rage.

At the zoo he had seen lions in their cages. He felt like those lions when he roared. He paced up and down as he had seen them pace. Maybe his keeper would come up and feed him soon. He would have liked a large piece of raw meat that he could have torn with his teeth, the way he had seen the lions do but he had no way of expressing his wishes and had to make do with soft meals which he often threw on the floor.

He lay down on the floor and sniffed the pieces of dead skin. They smelled good. From where he lay, he could see the thing which had fallen from the finger some days ago. It sat under his table, winking at him. The other, duller one remained on the finger. He turned over and lay on his back. This made him feel happy. Maybe he would not get into his bed tonight. He got back up and went to the packing cases under his window. One was upturned and one the right way up. The second one which was larger, contained straw which covered a rowing machine. He did not know what it was but treated it like another lion, patting it and putting it to bed in the case every night. One of his keepers had tried to get him to sit on the lion but he had refused. Now he delved under the straw and pulled the machine from the case but this time he was not interested in the lion but in the straw which he pulled out in handfuls and scattered on the floor.

He lay down in this straw and grinned. He was happy for a few minutes, then the feeling of unease rose in him like a thick, black cloud obliterating all other feelings. He got up, growling, and, pacing to the only window, peered out. It was sunny and he blinked and turned to look into his room. He did not like the light of the sun and only put on the light in his room briefly. If anybody else put it on, he immediately put it off, often scratching the hand that had switched it on. He had not allowed any of his keepers to cut his nails recently though they had often tried. He had bitten the last person. They had stopped trying.

He only ever had four visitors. Three he tolerated; one he loved. He would paw her and try to lick her face. He had a dim memory of a fifth creature, the hated one. He had thought that she was gone but this morning he knew differently and he whimpered now. He turned from the window and going to the table, he pawed the finger till it fell on the floor. Down on all fours on the floor, he patted it till it rolled under his bed. Instinct told him to hide it and he knew one of his visitors would be coming in soon to clean up.

Curling up, he put both paws up to his face. The smell was still there and comforted him a little. Soon he slept.

CHAPTER 19

Shahid Din had, at school, been very active on the anti-racist committee. He had been all for integration between Muslim and Christian pupils and had tried to emphasise his Scottishness. In fact the only time he had shown his Muslim side had been when he had acted the star lead in Bugsy Malone and had been given a hot dog to eat on stage. He had laughed but informed the drama teacher than he didn't even want to hold the pork-filled roll, never mind eat it. Naturally, the teacher had been apologetic and had given him a cigar instead. All his best friends had been non- Muslim at school and Shazia and Salma and maybe Farah knew that his life down in London had included alcohol and women.

Salma and Shazia had gone to Glasgow Airport to meet him the night before the funeral, leaving Rafiq with their aunt and uncle and had at first not recognised him in the black, bushy beard. They had driven into the pick-up area, having sat in a side road until he had rung them on his mobile to tell them that he had picked up his luggage and they were now anxiously scanning the people waiting. Shahid had opened the back door of the car and got in and they had turned and stared at him for so long that he had had to remind them that they only had fifteen minutes before they would be charged a fee.

Salma put the car into gear and drove off quickly, leaving Shazia to do the talking.

"Shahid! What's with the beard?"

In the driving mirror Salma saw her brother look a bit sheepish.

"Remember I went over to Pakistan a few months ago?"

"Yes," his two sisters chorused.

"Well I met someone there."

"Someone? Who?"

"Her name's Bushra. I want to marry her."

"So? That doesn't explain the beard," said Shazia.

"Well, I decided that if I wanted to marry a Muslim girl, I had better become a good Muslim."

"So what happened to Amanda?"

"It wasn't working. I was away too often. She got fed up being on her own at weekends when I was away."

"And does being a good Muslim mean no more alcohol?" teased Salma and was surprised to hear her beer-drinking brother say that he had drunk nothing alcoholic since meeting Bushra.

"And the wedding?" asked Salma.

"Next year. Colin's agreed to be my best man. It'll be held in Pakistan. Bushra is only fourteen."

"Fourteen!" exclaimed Shazia. "She'll still be at school."

"She can go to school here."

"Where's here? Glasgow or London?"

Salma hoped it would be here as she wanted her brother to take charge of the family and she knew that Shazia felt the same.

"I'm coming back here after the wedding. We'll stay in the family home and I'll take charge of the family."

Although this was what she had wanted to hear, Salma did not like the tone of his voice when he had said that he would take charge of the family. Shahid could be very dogmatic when he chose to be and she hoped that he would not decide to try to interfere in his older sisters' lives. Still, now was not the time to discuss anything heavy. Things were serious enough with their mother's death and funeral to cope with. On the rest of the drive home, they discussed practical matters and the journey passed quite quickly.

Aunt Zenib and Uncle Fariz were delighted to see their favourite nephew and doubly delighted with his appearance. They had loved him when he was turning out to be the bad boy of the family and they were overjoyed to seen his reformation. For a while they listened to him talking about his future bride and they talked about his wedding in Pakistan, then talk turned to his mother's death. They told him that the autopsy had shown that she had taken a massive heart attack and that death had been instantaneous. Shahid, who in spite of his independent streak, was quite soft at heart, cried a little at the thought that his beloved mother would now never see his chosen bride nor his future children.

Salma made some tea and persuaded Rafiq to go to bed. Although he was upset, he was also quite excited at the prospect of being off school, dressing up and going to the mosque tomorrow, although he was a bit sullen about the fact that he would not be allowed at the cemetery with the other men. Salma had a bright idea and told him that one man was needed to look after the women when all the men had gone off and he seemed content with that.

With Rafiq safely in bed, the adults talked into the small hours. Their aunt and uncle left at about 1am, promising to be back early the next day though the funeral was not till the afternoon. Shahid showed his sisters some photographs of his future bride, a shy-looking girl, and the couple who were to be his new in-laws and in turn, Shazia talked about her teaching job in Govanhill where the class was predominantly Muslim. Salma told him of her new position, also in Govanhill, and told him about her experience at a cremation recently. Farah had only recently started at Santander so had little to say. Shazia made them more tea and eventually they yawned off to bed at around 2.30am.

Salma took a long time getting off to sleep. There was so much to think about and she was determined to talk to her sisters about this change in their brother, seeking allies in her determination not to be straight-jacketed into a marriage by Shahid, now that he had reverted to being what he called a 'good' Muslim. Their mother had been easy to side track when she mentioned marriage and as long as they did not try to leave home, she had been happy.

At about five o'clock, as the sun was rising, Salma fell into a deep sleep.

CHAPTER 20

Davenport was just about to leave for Waterfoot on Thursday morning when his phone rang. It was Bob at the desk to tell him that a Mrs McLean was on the line.

"She says it's about the murder, Sir."

"Put her on, Bob."

Pat McLean had remembered more about the light she had seen on the ground floor of the factory on Friday evening. It had seemed to be permanently on as she walked past, but she commented that a light had gone on in another room very briefly, upstairs. Probably the caretaker doing his rounds but said that she thought that he ought to know and apologised for not remembering sooner.

"Surely it was light at that time of night, Mrs McLean?"

"Not very light, Inspector. It was a very nice night to begin with but I think it rained later."

He thanked her and rang off.

He arrived at the Keel Products factory just before 4.45. He parked his car in the half empty car park and went to the reception desk where he asked if he could speak to the manager.

"I'm sorry, Sir. He's away overseas right now," said the pretty, young receptionist, looking lively and interested. Davenport thought how nice it was to be met by someone like her instead of the bored young things he often came across.

"Who's next in line?" he enquired.

"Well if it's a sales' matter, it'll be Mr Mackay and if it's an advertising matter it would be Mrs Caldwell and if...."

"...It's a murder matter," said Davenport, cutting across her list.

The girl looked startled.

"Murder?" she said. "I don't know who to put you on to, Sir. The depute manager's out at our other factory."

"Do you have a personnel manager?"

She looked relieved and, picking up the phone with one beautifully manicured hand, she pressed some buttons.

"Jackie? Lisa here. Would you come down to reception please. There's a man here a - she looked inquiringly at Davenport who said,' DCI Davenport' - a DCI Davenport. Yes a police DCI, Jackie, what other kind is there? He wants to see you about a murder."

She put the phone back on its stand.

"Jackie will be right with you, Sir. Please take a seat till she comes down."

Davenport sat down on one of the blue, straight-backed chairs across the hallway. He was not there for long before a slim, blonde whirlwind flew through the swing doors. She must have been poured into her dress that morning, thought Davenport. No room to hide even a feather. Her breasts thrust themselves against the jersey material of the dress and he doubted if she was even wearing a thong.

"DCI Davenpost?" she asked him though there was no one else there.

"Davenport," he replied, trying to keep a straight face.

"Sorry. How can I help you? Lisa said that there'd been a murder. Not in the factory surely?"

"No, not in the factory but nearby, in a field just off the road out there."

He pointed through the large, glass window of the hallway. She followed his gaze like someone transfixed, as if she would be able to see the body if she looked carefully enough.

"All I want to know is… do you have a watchman who remains on the premises at night?"

"Yes, there is. I hired him only recently as Bert our last watchman retired at Christmas. His name's Eddie Rankin. He comes in about - she looked at her watch - about now and stays till 1am when he's replaced by Bill Townsend."

Almost on cue, a buzzer sounded and Lisa let in a rugged man who looked about fifty.

"Good evening, Lisa my lovely and Jackie too. My luck's in tonight."

Lisa grinned back but Jackie looked a bit peeved as if she thought that this kind of banter was OK for the girl on reception but not for someone of her rank.

"Eddie. This man, DCI Davenpo...rt is here to see you."

The man held out his hand. Davenport shook it.

"Eddie Rankin. I was Sergeant Rankin in another life. Retired last August. What can I do for you?"

"Is there anywhere we can speak privately?" asked Davenport, aware of two pairs of curious female eyes upon them.

Rankin led him across the hallway to a door at one side of the only window. It led to what must be his living, and sleeping quarters. There was a desk and chair, an armchair and a single bed, a one-ring cooker, kettle and small sink.

"Welcome to home," said the watchman.

He sat on the edge of the desk and Davenport took the chair.

"There's been a murder, Mr Rankin. The body of a woman was found in the fields by the side of the road through the estate."

"I knew that something had happened because I saw police standing in the road on Sunday when I came on duty. When did it happen?"

"The body was found by a woman having a walk, early on Friday evening but the murder took place on the evening of the previous Wednesday. Someone saw a car leaving here on Wednesday evening and I wondered if it might be you."

"At what time?"

"Between 10 and 11pm."

"No not me and not the man I replaced, as he left when I arrived at about 1am. We take weeks about with the shifts. I'm on early shift this week."

"Where can I contact the other man, Bill..."

"...Townsend. Can't help you I'm afraid. I just know he lives locally and comes on his bike. Lisa will be able to tell you. She has all the staff details. So has Madam Jackie."

Thanking the man for his time, Davenport let himself out of the room and went back across the foyer to the reception area.

"Will you give me the address of Bill Townsend please?"

Lisa, concentrating on filing her nails, had not seen him at first and jumped guiltily, catching at the open bottle of red nail varnish to prevent it spilling. She got up and, going to a filing cabinet behind her, extracted a file. She came back to the desk.

"William Townsend. 180 Bonnyton Drive, Eaglesham."

Davenport thanked her.

"Do any staff ever stay on to do overtime, Lisa?"

"I don't know."

She looked embarrassed.

"I get off right away every night at 5.30 so I wouldn't know."

"Who would know?"

He knew the answer just as he asked the question.

"Jackie," they said together.

Jackie was visibly annoyed at being called down to reception again.

"Sorry, Jackie...Miss...?"

"Ms Hobbs."

"Sorry, Ms Hobbs but Lisa couldn't answer my question. Do any of the staff ever do overtime?"

"Very seldom."

"Do you keep any sort of record for salaries?"

"No because when I said they sometimes did overtime, it isn't really overtime but flexitime. If they stay late they're either repaying time they've used up or stocking up time."

"So at any one time, no one knows who is staying late in the building?"

"They have electronic passes so no one needs to know."

This was like chasing a butterfly, difficult and unproductive.

"Can you tell me, Ms Hobbs, who works on the ground floor facing the road."

She thought for a few minutes.

"Two of the windows are toilets. One window is Mr Grant's office and the other is a storeroom."

"Thank you. I would like to see Mr Grant if possible."

"Lisa, ring through to Mr Grant please. Ask him to come to reception. The police want to talk to him."

Something in her tone of voice told him that she did not like this Mr Grant and had enjoyed relaying the bit about police. He soon found out why.

Through swing doors erupted a small, middle-aged man in a white coat.

"This had better be important, Miss Hobbs. I'm in the middle of an important experiment with a turn-table."

"Ms Hobbs, Mr Grant. How often do I have to tell you, it's Ms?" Jackie said angrily.

She gestured towards Davenport.

"The police, Mr Grant."

She turned on her heel, nose in the air. Lisa turned her giggle into a hasty cough.

"Sorry to bother you, Mr Grant but there's been a murder nearby and a witness said that on Friday night there was a light on in one of the downstairs' windows. Were you by any chance working late that night?"

"I often work late, Sir and do I get any thanks for it? No I..."

"So it was you on Friday night?"

"Yes it would be me that night and every other night that week!"

"When did you leave, Sir, on Wednesday night?"

"I can't remember that. It's over a week ago."

"Try, please."

Looking extremely annoyed, the man thought. He pushed his glasses up from his nose.

"I was never later than 8.30. I like to get back home in time for the nine o'clock news. Is that any help?"

"Did you by any chance see anybody in the road out there?"

"Nobody."

"Which way did you go?"

"I drove in the direction of Floors Road."

"Past the large house?"

"Yes. Either early bedders or out. The house was in darkness, apart from one light in the roof."

"In the roof?"

"Well, attic then."

"Thank you Mr Grant. I won't keep you any longer."

Giving a big sigh, the little man went back through the swing doors, glaring at Lisa as he went.

Davenport thanked her for her help. She looked at her watch and began getting her things together. He was glad that it was a small factory as it seemed that a mini avalanche poured out of the building just after he had left and by the time he had switched on the engine of his car, the car park was empty, apart from two cars, no doubt those belonging to Mr Grant and Eddie Rankin. With the manager away, the staff were taking advantage and leaving exactly at closing time. Davenport waited for a few minutes then put the car into gear and drove slowly out of the car park. He turned left, drove to the house at the end of the road and pulled up.

It was a youngish man who opened the door.

"Yes can I help you?"

"DCI Davenport."

Davenport showed his ID card. He was not invited in.

"I think we've told you all we know about this murder, Inspector."

"Maybe. I've just been told that there was a light on in your attic room on the night of the murder when your parents were out. Were you at home, Sir?"

"No I wasn't. As I told your young constable, I stayed overnight at a friend's house."

"So, the light in the attic?"

"I imagine Dad or Mum must have gone up for something and forgotten to put the light off. We're expecting some relations to stay quite soon and we'll need all our bedrooms including the attic room."

Davenport thanked him and got back into his car.

CHAPTER 21

As soon as Jackie Hobbs got through the swing door, her cool demeanour vanished. As Davenport had thought, she was not wearing even a thong as that item of her clothing was nestling in the jacket pocket of her deputy manager.

On the evening Davenport had questioned the caretaker and Alan Grant about, she and her boss had been having sex in his office on the first floor. It was the first time they had used their workplace for this activity. She had telephoned him at home and he had pretended to his wife that the alarm had gone off in the factory and, being the most senior man still in the country, he would have to go across the city. Jackie had been waiting in the car she had borrowed from brother, on the main Glasgow Road, as arranged. He had pulled up behind her and got into her car as this way the car would not be recognised should anyone see it. She had parked in the road through the estate. He had a master key so no alarm had gone off and they were confident that the caretaker would be reading or even dozing in his room. Ian McAllister relocked the back door. Although it was summer, it was a dull night, and his room with only one small window was quite dark.

With only the light from the car park shining in, they had wasted no time. On the way up the stairs, he had put his hand up her skirt and fondled her buttocks. She had stroked him in return and both were hot for each other by the time the door was shut. In minutes she was standing in her lacy thong, the wonderbra that thrust her pert breasts towards him and black stockings and suspender belt. His wife had denied him sex for so long that he almost climaxed on the spot. He moaned and, pulling her over to his desk, he swept papers off it and shoved her on her back across it. He tugged down his boxer shorts and then in one swift movement, pulled down her thong and thrust himself inside her. Luckily she had been as needy as himself and they came together and lay panting heavily until he withdrew and let her stand up.

At that moment they had heard footsteps in the corridor outside and he moved silently to lock the door. They stood in silence as the footsteps faded away and the caretaker went down the steps at the other end of the corridor. The fear of discovery had excited them both and he moved to her and this time he fondled her breasts which were full and youthfully thrusting towards him. He took off the bra and bent to lick her nipples which hardened under his lips. She went down on her knees and took him in her mouth. Sensing his imminent orgasm, she pulled away and he grabbed her and pushed her against the wall. He knelt this time and licked her till she came to the same peak as himself, then inched himself into her, teasing her. He withdrew and she pleaded with him. Once again he refused to go fully inside her until she almost screamed at him in her need. He plunged fully in and she arched her back away from the wall.

When it was over for the second time, they dressed and he listened carefully before unlocking and opening the door. He had put the light on briefly to check that they had left no evidence of their visit for the cleaner to find, then they had crept downstairs and, seeing the light under the caretaker's door, tiptoed to the outside door, unlocked it and were soon back in her borrowed car.

"Jackie. That was great. Thank you."

"And thank you, Ian. You were great too."

She had driven him back to his car on the main road.

Every day since then they had come to work early and he had contrived to meet her in the cupboard outside his office and had delighted in just removing her thong and knowing that it was in his pocket. If he met her and there was nobody about he would put his hand up her short skirt and fondle her. He took great pleasure in knowing that she was wearing no panties, especially in meetings where there were other men. They had waited behind one evening and had sex once in the same cupboard but they had almost been caught by Alan Grant as they were leaving.

Now Jackie had to see her boss, to let him know that there had been a murder that first night and the police had interviewed Eddie Rankin and Alan Grant.

"Come in!" he shouted.

Ian McAllister looked up to see Jackie in his doorway and as always on seeing her in her clinging dress, felt himself harden.

"Shut the door, Ms Hobbs."

She did this and he came across the room and, pushing her against the door, felt up the short skirt of her navy dress. She could feel herself getting wet and so could he.

"Ian. Stop please. It's too dangerous right now."

He moved away from her, his erection straining against the material of his trousers.

"You're right. Sorry. Can you wait behind tonight? I've told Nancy I've to work late."

Jackie now remembered why she had come to see him.

"There's a problem, Ian."

"What is it?"

He looked alarmed.

"That first night when we came here, there was a murder in the road outside the factory. The police have been here asking questions."

"And why does that concern us?"

"You know we saw someone when we were walking to the car."

"Yes, a youngster walking away in the opposite direction from the one we were going in. So?"

"We should tell the police."

"Oh no, we can't do that, you little fool. We'd have to explain why we were there at that time."

"It could have been the murderer."

She had bridled at the 'little fool'.

"I don't care. I've got more to lose than you remember. My wife mustn't find out, Jackie."

His voice was wheedling.

"You do want us to continue seeing each other don't you, darling? I'm going to Paris for a few days in a few weeks' time and I thought you could plead illness and come with me. Five star hotel with a spa and time to enjoy each other."

Jackie looked uncertain. The two evenings spent in his room had been very exciting. He went down another avenue.

"Look Jackie, we saw a youngster. He'd probably been seeing his girlfriend for some sex in the bushes."

"He certainly looked small. If it hadn't been for the time, I'd have thought it was a child," said Jackie.

"Not a murderer, anyway."

"Paris, did you say?"

McAllister smiled.

"Yes, Paris and what do you say to me buying you some expensive jewellery?"

"Oh Ian, yes please."

"And no more talk of speaking to the police. Promise?"

"I promise. I can stay tonight. Mum's going to be late home herself."

Pulling her towards him, he kissed her, their bargain sealed.

CHAPTER 22

Penny had trawled through Moira Findlay's phone book. She had gone through A to L and so far had only come upon distant connections, people who had met Moira on holiday for example or people she had been at school or college with. None of these had seen her recently. As she expected, there were lots of entries under M. She sighed and looked at her watch. It was nearly 12.25 and her stomach had been rumbling for a while. She and Salma and Frank took it in turns to go for lunch together, leaving one of them on duty. She wondered where Frank was right now as he had left his desk some time ago.

Hearing footsteps in the corridor, she looked up as DS Macdonald passed the open door.

"Ma'am," she called out.

Fiona Macdonald stopped and looked in.

"Yes, Penny?"

"Would it be OK if I went for lunch in the canteen? I don't know where Frank has gone."

"I met him coming back from the toilet and asked him to go a message for me. He should be back soon. Are you missing Salma?"

"Yes ma'am, I am."

"Well I don't see any reason why you can't have lunch with Frank when he gets back. He shouldn't be long. I'm here to man the fort."

"Thanks Ma'am. Is it OK if I go back up to Floors Road first then? We didn't get anyone in at one house, folk called Henderson. I think they were on holiday over the murder time but I'd better see if they know Moira Findlay."

Penny drove quickly up to Waterfoot. Through the glass door she could see that the mail had been replaced by two suitcases. The door was answered on the first knock. A young woman stood there. Penny showed the photograph and asked if she had ever seen this woman.

"Oh yes, I've seen her before. She walked past me one evening when I was helping my husband in the garden."

"Are you sure it was her?"

"Yes, positive. She looks quite like my sister. At first I thought it was Eileen."

"What direction was she going in and when was that?"

"It was the day before we left for Greece. It must have been the 8th of June. She was going up the way, away from the main road. What's happened? She looks dead."

Grateful for a witness who had a memory, Penny informed her that the woman had been murdered in the Keel Estate. She thanked her and remembered to warn the woman against having mail delivered while they were away.

She went back to the station and informed DS Macdonald. Frank arrived back shortly afterwards and Penny told him that they could both go for lunch. The canteen was busy but by the time they had collected trays and lined up to choose their meal, there were a few empty tables to choose from, all unfortunately messy ones. Penny asked the girl behind the serving counter for a wet cloth and wiped one clean. She and Frank sat across from each other. It was a large police station, divided into sections and they tended not to know other members of staff though Frank often chatted up the prettiest of the constables from other areas when he got the chance.

"Hi, Frank."

One slim blonde constable called across and Frank called back, "Hi, gorgeous."

Obviously having a girlfriend was not stopping him from giving the ready chat-up line, thought Penny.

"How is Sue?" she asked now and Frank had the grace to blush.

"She's fine, Penny."

"How's your sorting out of catalogues going?"

"OK but it's very boring. Hope the murder enquiry hots up soon. What about you? Any luck with the phone calls?"

"None. To wait for some to call back to as they weren't in but all the others were casual acquaintances. I've reached L."

"Rather you than me."

They were quiet for a while, eating their lunch, then Frank asked Penny about Gordon. He noticed her rosy cheeks go even redder than they were usually and could not resist teasing her.

"Oh ho, Penny Farthing. Getting serious is it?"

"A wee bit," replied Penny, always honest.

She looked at her watch.

"Time we went back to work."

Half way through the Ms, Penny spoke to a Mrs McDuff who turned out to be Moira's aunt, her mother's sister, who lived in Aberdeen.

"PC Price you said. Is Moira in trouble?"

"I'm afraid to have to tell you that's she's dead, Mrs McDuff. I'm trying to contact people like yourself. I..."

"How did she die?"

"I'm sorry to have to tell you that she was murdered, a week last Wednesday."

"Murdered! Oh how awful. Thank God her parents are dead and don't need to know that."

"Are you her nearest surviving relative Mrs McDuff?"

"Yes, I suppose I am now that Dave and she split up about a year ago. They've been apart for about 18 months I think. The poor girl took depression but last time I heard from her she was better."

"Where did she work?"

"In a school called Greystone Academy. She's… she…was a lab technician there."

"What about her ex-husband?"

"He taught there. Chemistry, I think. That's where they met but he changed schools and I don't know where he went. I'm sorry. Do you know who killed Moira?"

"No, not yet. Sorry. Can you tell me why they split up?"

"No one else for either of them, she did tell me that so I don't know."

Penny thanked the woman for her help, promising to let her know when the funeral could take place. She continued with the Ms but got no more relevant information.

At 5.30, feeling all phoned-out, she put a line under her last person. Only the Ts-Zs to do but she was what her old granny would have called 'wabbit'. She went along the corridor. DS Macdonald's door was open and there was no one in the room so she continued along to the DCIs room. The door was shut and she could hear voices so she knocked.

"Come in," called her boss.

She went in. Davenport was seated behind his desk and his DS was across from him. Both nursed coffee mugs in their hands.

"Yes, Penny?"

"Sir, I've reached the Ts in the list of Moira Findlay's contacts. There was only one helpful person, her aunt, a Mrs McDuff who lives in Aberdeen; her mother's sister. She told me that Moira worked as a lab technician in Greystone Academy, that she was depressed after her husband left her. He didn't leave her for someone else, according to her aunt and Moira wasn't seeing any one else either."

"Yes, her doctor told me about the depression. Did you find out where her ex-husband worked?"

"He used to work in the same school as a chemistry teacher, she thought, but he moved after the break-up and she didn't know to which school. I haven't managed to get everybody in, Sir and there was nobody answering at the house of someone called Findlay which will, I imagine, be a relation of her ex-husband who will probably have his address and know what school he's now working in."

"Thanks, Penny. Get off home now and if you're phoning Salma, tell her I was asking for her. Would you take the Findlay number and try it from home after 6pm please. Claim for the call of course."

"Tell Salma I'm thinking of her," said Fiona who had remained silent throughout the conversation.

Penny went back to her room where she collected her jacket and hat and switched off her computer. Frank was just doing the same and the pile of catalogues on the floor by his desk had shrunk considerably. Penny had picked up Frank in the morning and he was glad that they were able to leave at the same time or else he would have had to walk through to Pollokshaws Road for a bus to Shawlands.

As they drove home, Penny asked him about his plans to buy a car.

"You were going to buy a car ages ago, Frank. What happened?"

"Don't much fancy having to shell out every month, to be honest."

"No one does but I'd hate not to have a car now. I suppose you let Sue drive when you go out together."

"Well, it doesn't seem to bother her. She doesn't drink much and says she doesn't mind having soft drinks when we go out."

"Is she still driving her wee red Corsa?"

"Yes."

By this time they were pulling up outside Frank's house where he lived with his parents and two of his brothers. Frank thanked Penny who said she would pick him up in the morning again. She drove off and was soon parking round the back of the block of flats where she shared a first-floor apartment with Alec. Instead of going in the back entrance, she walked round to the front and crossed the road to the small Tesco. It was her turn to make dinner and she needed potatoes. Her meals were very plain but Alec seemed to enjoy them. After dinner she was going to finish the Skinner novel that Gordon had lent her and hopefully have an early night.

Her meal over, Penny took out her mobile. She didn't have a land line yet and didn't want to use Alec's although he would not have objected.

The phone was picked up after only two rings.
"Hello."
"Hello, Sir. My name's PC Price and I'm calling to ask if you are related to a David Findlay who used to be married to a Moira Findlay."
"Yes, I'm Dave's father. What's the matter?"
"I'm afraid that Moira's been murdered, Mr Findlay. I need to ask your son if he would identify the body, as her nearest relative lives in Aberdeen."
"Dave's back living with his mother and me. He should be home soon. Will I get him to call you?"
"Let him get used to what's happened, Sir and phone me at the station in the morning, first thing."

Penny gave the name of the station and her department's number and rang off after telling

Mr Findlay senior that they had no details to give as yet. She rang her mother and was invited, with Gordon, for dinner the following Friday evening.

CHAPTER 23

"Well at least you have the victim's name now, Davenport."

Knox sat as usual in his large chair behind his rosewood desk. He always wore full uniform and, as he looked like a bulldog, having hardly any neck or with what was his neck encased in double chins, Davenport found him a comic figure. Knox was always florid in complexion and looked as if he was about to have a stroke or heart attack. On his right side sat Solomon Fairchild whose face, in contrast, was pink and cherubic. His bald head was shining under the lights.

It was seldom that both men interviewed him at the same time and the chief constable was now explaining why.

"I'm going down to London tonight. I have an important series of talks to attend and I'm actually giving one myself."

He threw out his chest as he said these last words and Davenport caught himself picturing the man inflating and then bursting like an overblown balloon. He had to cough to cover up his amusement and nearly lost in this attempt when he caught Fairchild's eye, as Solomon was also trying to hide a grin, not very successfully.

"Yes, I'm doing a talk on dealing with the press."

This was almost too much as Knox was notorious for his bad handling of the Scottish press. He tended to tell them that the case was nearly wrapped up when it was nowhere near finished.

Davenport managed a shaky, "Good for you, Sir," managing not to look at the assistant chief constable as he spoke.

"So Davenport, Mr Fairchild will be overseeing your new murder case. I've told him that you need to have your nose kept to the grindstone at times. Remember the public need to see their police force successfully apprehending wrongdoers, especially murderers. Now, who's in the frame for this murder?"

"Sir, we've only just found out who the murdered person is!"

"See what I mean, Solomon?"

Knox's impatient look was turned to his subordinate.

"I'm sure Charles will get this case solved as expertly as he has the other murder cases he's had to deal with since he came to us, Sir."

"Humph!"

"Why don't Charles and I adjourn to my room now and let you get on with that speech you were writing when I came in."

Fairchild was rising to his feet as he spoke and Charles rose too.

"OK. Now I'll be back next Friday. I'm taking the chance to see my son and his family while I'm there. Hope this case will be solved by then. See yourselves out."

Back in his own room, Fairchild unloosened his tie and took off his jacket, motioning Charles to do the same.

"Tea or coffee, Charles?"

"Coffee please, Sir."

Fairchild rang through to his secretary and asked her to bring two coffees and some biscuits. He took a seat by a coffee table at the window and motioned Charles to take a seat. They chatted about their families. Fairchild had two grown up children and was always interested in hearing about Pippa. Charles doubted that Knox even knew that he had a daughter. The door opened and Sheila, Fairchild's secretary came in carrying a tray. She smiled at Charles.

"In need of this, Mr Davenport?"

He grinned back. She set the tray on the coffee table between the two men and went back to her own desk outside. Fairchild offered Charles the milk and biscuits then sat back in his chair.

"Right, Charles. Tell me about this latest murder."

Charles told him that the woman was called Moira Findlay, that she had an ex-husband and possibly a new lover. They were going through her address book and phone book and had come across an aunt in Aberdeen who was the one who'd put them on to the husband.

"She worked in Greystone Academy, Sir. We'll interview any friends there and we've found an old school friend in the address book. She'll be spoken to as well and of course the ex-husband. There was a light on in the factory which is near the crime scene but that turned out to be a worker doing overtime and he left too early for the time of the murder. There was a light on in the nearest house although the occupants were out. It was probably just a light left on, according to their son who lives with them. It's all been quite plain sailing, except for finding out whom she was meeting that night, if anyone."

"Any other reason she might have been where she was found? Where was she found anyway?"

"In the Keel Estate, Sir. It's called that because of the small factory there. It makes turn-tables, very expensive ones I believe. The road through the estate goes from one quiet road to the main Glasgow Road. She was going towards the main road so she couldn't have been using the estate road as a short cut to her home as she'd have been quicker simply walking up the main road in that case. I think she must have been meeting someone in one of the back roads and was going home, as her house is across the main road. Do you want to know the state of the body, Sir?"

"No, I've read the stuff in the two folders you left with Mr Knox. What you've said seems logical, Charles. Probably meeting a lover somewhere, though I wonder why he couldn't have run her home."

"That puzzles me too, Sir," said Davenport.

"Mr Knox seems to favour someone who was frustrated, wanted sex, then found he couldn't rape the woman and had to make do with ejaculating over her dead body," said Fairchild.

"It's possible, Sir."

"More coffee, Charles?"

"No thanks, Sir."

"Any way I can be of help in this case?"

"We're one member of staff down right now, Sir. Sergeant Din lost her mother and has compassionate leave till Monday at least. We could do with another constable till she comes back."

"Her father's dead, isn't he?"

"Yes, Sir. She and an elder brother are in charge of the family now."

"So you want someone from another department?"

"I'd be grateful, Sir."

Fairchild walked to his desk and picked up his phone. Charles thought how this angelic-looking man had his finger on the pulse. He doubted if Grant Knox would have even recognised Salma, let alone known about her father.

"Roger… Solomon here. Look, send Fraser Hewitt down to Davenport's area will you…till Monday at least. Thanks, Roger. I owe you one."

He came back to his seat.

"That's fine. Roger Dickson will send Fraser Hewitt, his latest recruit. He's more intelligent than he looks. He looks about twelve, poor guy. Put your Penny Price in charge of him. She'll keep him right. Lovely lass that."

"Yes, she is. I'm really lucky with my department."

"How's young Selby shaping up? He's not the best time-keeper in the world is he?"

"He's got his act together, Sir. On time now and much more tidy."

"How does he get on with Salma? I heard that he gave her a hard time at first."

"Do you have CCTV cameras trained on every department, Sir?" Charles laughed in admiration.

"No, I just chat to people. You'd be surprised at how much I get to know."

He grinned.

"And how's the lovely Fiona Macdonald? I believe you and she are taking the same time off in the summer."

Charles felt himself blushing. Really, the man was unbelievable!

"I wouldn't want this broadcast, Sir but we' re going away together, with my daughter.

How did you suspect that we were friends?"

Charles put emphasis on the word 'friends'.

"You know how Alfred Hitchcock is always in his own films, in a bit part. Well I blend into the background like that, often in The Railway Inn."

This mention of their favourite pub, explained a lot. This was where he and Fiona often went for lunch. He had never seen Fairchild there.

"Don't worry, Charles. Your secret's safe with me. I'm glad Miss Macdonald is happy in her new station. It was unfortunate what happened to her at her last place. Now to get back to the case, keep me informed if anything interesting turns up. Meanwhile, is there anything you want me to tell the press or do you want it kept under wraps for the present?"

"What do you think, Sir? Should we ask if anyone saw a woman walking along Floors Road on her own that night? Or should we wait a few days?"

"Leave it too long and Joe Public might forget what they saw. I think maybe it might be best to inform Noel Brown of The Herald. He won't dramatize it and I'll try to fend off the tabloids if they come sniffing about."

"Thanks, Sir."

"Well, if that's all, Charles, I'll let you get back to the chalk face."

Fairchild rose. Charles did too. They walked out into the corridor together, both taking time to thank Sheila for their coffee. Solomon stayed with Charles till the lift arrived, then they shook hands and parted, Charles feeling elated at the thought of Fairchild being the captain of the ship, at least until Monday.

CHAPTER 24

"Another policeman came here? What on earth did they want this time, Robert ?"

"Calm down, Dad. He'd been told that there was a light on in our attic room on the night of the murder and wanted to know if someone had after all been at home."

"I hope you told him we were all out."

"Of course I did. I told him we'd been expecting Aunt Jean and Uncle Harry and the cousins for a few days and that either you or Mum must have left the light on in the attic bedroom. OK!"

The older man went to the door of the lounge and called to his wife. He had poured out her pre-dinner sherry and when she came in, beautifully dressed as always, he handed it to her. His son was helping himself to a whisky from the bar which was kept in a small room off the lounge. He had poured the same drink for his father.

"Lorna. We had another visit from the police last night."

"What for this time?" Her shrill voice was not in keeping with her appearance and her husband winced. When had she lost the pleasant soft voice she had had when they had married? Probably about the same time as she had found out about his most serious affair, he thought. She had been so busy with the children and so tired every night, that their sex life had suffered and he had sought this elsewhere. She had forgiven him the first time, with his secretary, Joan and had admitted that it was her fault as well as his. She had tried to be more willing in bed but he felt that she merely submitted rather than took part and she had a morbid fear of becoming pregnant again which was ridiculous as she had gone on the pill immediately and she also insisted that he wear a condom.

He had cheated on her again and she had almost found out when he had inadvertently left the receipt for a bracelet for Janet, his latest secretary, in his trouser pocket.

"Another affair? How dare you. I've kept my side of our bargain!"

Even the word 'bargain' made her response to his love-making seem like a business deal!

"Who was this for?" she had demanded, holding up the offending piece of paper.

"You of course, darling," he had replied.

"Well, where is it? Why haven't you given it to me. This was bought two days ago."

"It's getting altered. Your wrist is so slender."

"And what are you buying me jewellery for? It's not my birthday, or our anniversary?"

He remembered now that her voice had been shrill for the first time.

"Do I have to have a reason for buying my wife jewellery?"

He had had, of course, to buy another bracelet from the same shop and had had the sense not to buy the exact replica in case she saw it on Janet's wrist at the firm's Christmas party.

He had escaped that time, and he should have learned from it but Janet was so compliant, so utterly feminine that he had continued with the affair.

He remembered the day when she came to him with her news.

"I'm so sorry, so terribly sorry but..."

"But what, Janet? Please don't say you're wanting us to stop seeing each other!"

"Oh no, never that my love but..."

"Come on. You can tell your Cookie anything."

"I'm pregnant."

He knew, when he was delighted at the news, that he was not merely having a fling with his secretary. He wanted her to have their child and would have asked his wife for a divorce had Janet not persuaded him not to.

"I can cope alone, darling as long as we keep seeing each other," she had said. "I'm sure you don't want to be kept from seeing your sons."

Things had gone on as before, except that he had set Janet up in a small, modern flat and hired his third secretary. His daughter was a joy to him and everything had gone along well till that day fourteen years ago.

"Mr Cook. The police are here to see you," his new secretary announced. It was about nine o'clock on the morning of Monday 11th December, 1985. He had come out of his sanctum to see two solemn-faced constables standing in the office.

"Mr Cook. Sorry to have to bring you bad news but Miss Janet Frew has been killed in a road accident. You were in her dairy as the one to be contacted in an emergency."

Somehow he had got through the morning then he had thought of Lily who always went home for lunch from the nursery she attended. She was four years old. Throwing over his shoulder the information that he had something to collect, he had driven quickly to the nursery school, where luckily he was known by the woman in charge, and taken Lily into his arms. He could vividly remember the confrontation with his cold wife. He had arrived home in the middle of the afternoon with a bewildered Lily and one suitcase. Lorna had been hosting a bridge party and he had taken Lily up to a small, unused bedroom, brought her a glass of milk and a biscuit and stayed with her until the bridge ladies had left. They had gone downstairs, hand in hand and he had confronted Lorna in the lounge where she was tidying up.

"This is Lily...my daughter."

She gasped.

"Your what?"

"My daughter, Lorna. There's no easy way to do this so I'll be blunt. You were correct a few years ago. I was having an affair. We had Lily. Her mother died today in a road accident. She will be staying with us now."

"Keep your whore's child? Never!"

"It's your choice. Either she comes to live with us or I go to live with her in Janet's flat which is mine anyway. Are you willing to go through a divorce and give up your comfortable life style? Could you bear the scandal?"

He knew he had been cruel and at first she took her revenge on Lily, treating her with dislike. Their sons loved their little half-sister however, and eventually the youngster's winning smile and happy nature, worked its magic and she became an accepted member of the family, loved by the boys and tolerated by Lorna.

Lily had left school and gone to Strathclyde University and then Jordanhill College. She was now living in Carluke, teaching English at a school there and living in a flat with her new boyfriend, Jim. 'Living in sin', Lorna called it when she mentioned her adopted daughter which was seldom. Lily was like her mother had been, warm and caring and so happy.

His thoughts came back to the present.

"He'd heard that there was a light on in the attic on the night of the murder and, as I had said that we were all out, he wondered why there was a light on. They were told that we'd been preparing for Jean and Harry and the kids coming and had probably left the light on by mistake."

"Cheek of the man, doubting your word. You're an important lawyer and prospective member of parliament, for goodness sake!"

It was another unpleasant trait he had noticed in her over the last few years, this snobbish way of referring to him, especially pronounced now that he was going to stand for parliament at the next election. Snobbery and a tendency to see everything in terms of money, had been absent in her nature when he had first known her.

"Go and see what's keeping Mary with the dinner please," she said now to Robert, and her husband wondered how many women of her acquaintance had a cook and housekeeper coming in most days.

Their son returned to tell them dinner would be served in five minutes.

"Just time for you to change out of that working suit, darling," she said. Richard had hoped for once to have avoided this ritual of changing for dinner but it was not to be.

Ten minutes later, the three of them were seated at the large dining room table. Conversation was stilted as it usually was. Robert, unlike his brother, Neil had not followed their father into law but ran an estate agent's business in Shawlands. His mother thought this job demeaning and seldom, if ever, asked him about his day. The fact that he had divorced his eminently suitable wife, Claudia, was just another bone of contention between them and he could hardly chat about his new girlfriend whom he had met at the gym and who was a lowly shop assistant.

"What do you think of someone being murdered almost outside our front door?" his father said.

"Wonder who it was, Dad. I...

"Not the best subject for mealtime," his mother reprimanded them and they went quiet again.

The rest of the meal progressed in a cold silence.

CHAPTER 25

When Penny arrived at the station on Friday morning, Bob told her that a David Findlay had phoned her about half an hour ago. He had left his number so she immediately rang him back.

"Mr Findlay? PC Price here. Sorry I wasn't here when you rang. Yes, your father told me you were divorced from Moira. When did you last see her?"

She spoke to him for a short while then hung up and went along to the DCI's room. The door was open as it usually was and her boss was busy writing at his desk. Hearing her footsteps, he looked up and invited her to come in.

"Sir, that was David Findlay, the dead woman's ex-husband, on the phone. He last saw her about three weeks ago when he went up to collect something from their house."

"Did he say anything else?"

"I asked him to come in here to talk to us and he said he would come in later if that suited. I said it did. He finishes school at 3.30 so should be here just after 4pm if nothing crops up to prevent him. Was that OK, Sir?"

"Quite right, Penny. There are maybe things he won't want to talk about on the phone. I think their problem was their lack of children. What school does he work in?"

"He's in Braehead Secondary, Sir. He's the chemistry principal. Mrs McDuff told me that bit though she didn't know what school he was in. I got that from him a minute ago."

"Would you get in touch with Alison Jones and ask her to come in too, say at about 5pm, if that suits her. I think you've still got the last of the phone book names to go through. Yes?"

"Yes, Sir. I'll get onto that right away."

Penny spent the rest of the morning on her phone but all she got of interest was an item under W, Westwood Clinic. She rang the clinic, explained the situation and was put through to someone who called herself Sister Conway.

"Under normal circumstances, Constable I wouldn't be able to divulge any facts about a patient but as Mrs Findlay is deceased I can tell you that she had been sterilised in....2001."

Thanking the woman, Penny rang off. She finished the telephone book quickly, there being only one number left under Y and Mrs Young had been an elderly friend of Moira's mother and had lost touch when her friend died.

"It must be a very old phone book. I haven't heard from Moira for over twenty years," said the quavery voice. Why are you phoning me?"

Penny felt bad having to tell her that her old friend's daughter was dead. She left out the fact that Moira had been murdered, hoping that the old woman would not read newspapers very thoroughly.

"Well don't bother giving me the funeral arrangements if that's what you were calling for. I try not to go to those now. It's getting too near my own."

"That's OK, Mrs...Miss...Young."

"Miss Young, my dear. I lost my fiancé in the war."

Saying she was sorry, Penny rang off.

Once again she went up the corridor to Davenport's room. This time he was on the phone but motioned to her to take a seat.

She heard him say, "Thanks, Martin. I'll see you later then."

He replaced the receiver and smiled at Penny.

"Martin wanted to know when to have the body ready for inspection. I told him later this afternoon if the ex-husband was agreeable. Now, what about Alison Jones?"

"She finishes work at 5 pm, Sir so will be here about 5.30pm."

"Any luck with the other entries in the phone book?"

"Moira Findlay was sterilised nine years ago, Sir. There was a clinic entry under W."

Davenport looked thoughtful. He pulled on his left ear lobe and then ran his fingers through his thick, brown hair and, getting up, motioned to Penny to follow him. As he passed DS Macdonald's room, he knocked and shouted, "Incident Room as soon as possible."

Frank was coming back from the canteen. He had a young man with him. Had it not been for the uniform, Davenport thought, he would have assumed it was a schoolboy here on work experience. He wracked his brain swiftly and came up with the surname.

"PC Hewitt?"

"Yes, Sir."

The lad blushed up to his ears.

"Good to have you on board. I see you've met Frank. This is Penny Price."

Penny smiled at him. Fiona Macdonald had caught up with them.

"And this is DS Macdonald. DS Macdonald this is Constable Hewitt who's been lent to us until Sergeant Din returns."

"Pleased to meet you, Constable Hewitt," said Fiona, smiling at him.

"Thank you, ma'am."

"Right team, into the Incident Room," said Davenport.

Penny saw Frank and the young man exchange glances and realised that her colleague had obviously told the new recruit about their boss's 'team' habit. She frowned at them. Frank grinned back but young Hewitt looked guilty. They all sat down, facing Davenport.

"We've had the usual response to The Herald's request for anyone who saw Moira Lindsay in Floors Road but the only one of any interest was from a Kevin Johnstone who lives on Glasgow Road and took his spaniel out for its last walk. He said that he saw a couple in a car in Floors Road. Said the windows were steamed up and he nearly banged on the window because he was fed up with this kind of disgusting behaviour."

"Spoilsport," muttered Frank.

"Moira Findlay's ex-husband is coming in today and so is Alison Jones, her friend. Penny found out from a clinic that Moira had been sterilized. I wonder if this was why they divorced. The Dr told me that he got the impression that David wanted children but Moira didn't. If she'd kept the sterilization from him, he would be understandably annoyed. It's really important for this case when it was that he found out."

"You mean he could just have discovered that and killed her because of it, Sir?" said Fiona Macdonald.

"Well, he could have met her, had a row and she taunted him with what she'd done and he saw red and killed her. He divorced her for a reason about a year ago and that was probably when he found out for the first time."

"Why the love bite, the one which was made after death, Sir?" asked Penny.

"To make it look like a lover's quarrel, perhaps."

"No, Sir," said Fiona, "There were already some bites before she died so he didn't need to make new ones."

"And why would he ejaculate over the dead body, Sir?" asked Frank.

"Who knows? It turned him on perhaps, seeing her dead. Or he could only treat her like a woman once she was dead, hence the love bites and the ejaculation."

"She was quite small, Sir. Could he not have overpowered her and done those things to her alive?" offered Frank.

"Maybe he was smaller and frail. I don't know," replied Davenport.

"Why bite off her ring finger?" asked Fiona.

"If it was Findlay, maybe he did it in rage over their sham of a marriage and wanted his ring back," suggested Penny.

The questions and answers were flying back and forward and Fraser Hewitt was beginning to look like a spectator at Wimbledon as he looked from one to the other of his new colleagues.

"It seems that there are possible reasons for everything," said Davenport.

"Why would they arrange to meet in the Keel Estate?" asked Fiona Macdonald.

"Could her dead body have been brought there?" a quiet voice spoke. Four pairs of eyes swivelled towards Hewitt.

"Ben Goodwin - he's head of SOC, Fraser - said the grass was flattened where there had been a struggle. I'll have to ask him if it could have been flattened by a body being pulled across it. Well done, son. Let's look at things from that angle."

Davenport thought for a minute.

"David and Moira Findlay arrange to meet for some reason. She taunts him again with the fact that she never could have had a baby after being sterilised. He is incensed with rage and strangles her. They've come to their meeting place in his car. He puts her body in his car, takes it to the secluded estate road and pulls it through the hedge. He wants to make it seem like an attempted rape so he gives her a love bite..."

"He is suddenly turned on by what he has done and ejaculates over her dead body. It doesn't ring true, Sir, and how did she get the earlier love bites?"

Fiona looked apologetically at her boss. He smiled ruefully.

"Sorry, I got a bit carried away but I think we should still run the idea of the dead body being dragged there past Ben Goodwin. Yes?"

"I agree," said Fiona. "Do you want me to contact him?"

"Yes, please."

"Any other avenues to explore, folks?"

"Maybe Alison will have remembered some other man in Moira's life," said Penny.

"We could talk to some of her school colleagues," said Frank.

Davenport smiled at him.

"Right. here's the plan for today. DS Macdonald, you interview David Findlay when he gets here. Tell him we want him to identify the body and if he's willing to do it today, phone Martin. He's half expecting someone to come today. Drive Findlay over there. I'll wait on and speak to Alison Jones when she gets here later. Frank, Penny and Fraser, you get over to Greystone Academy and interview as many staff who knew Moira as you can. I'll phone the headteacher and prepare him or her, ask for an interview room to be set up for you today and tomorrow."

They all bustled off.

DS Macdonald returned with the news that Ben Goodwin had ruled out the body having been dragged there as there was no flattened grass on the road side of the hedge.

"He said that the body was definitely dragged upright through the hedge, Sir, as there were pieces broken off high up."

"Bang goes that theory then. Tell the others for me please, Fiona."

CHAPTER 26

"I've got an appointment with a DCI Davenport," said the man. He was dressed in a brown cord jacket, with crisp white shirt, maroon tie and brown trousers and was looking decidedly nervous.

Bob at the desk, picked up the phone, spoke into it, and then directed the man up the corridor to the end door which was open. As he walked up the corridor, he could see a woman rising from a seat behind a desk. As he reached the open door, the woman came forward, hand outstretched.

"Mr Findlay? DS Macdonald. Good of you to get here so promptly. Please take a seat."

David Findlay sat down and cleared his throat nervously.

"I was told I'd to see a DCI Davenport."

"I'm his second-in- command, Sir. He's interviewing someone else right now."

The man nodded.

"As you know, Mr Findlay, your ex-wife's body was found last Friday. She'd been murdered, rather brutally I'm afraid. I need you to tell me anything that might help us find her murderer."

"I really can't think of anything. We've been separated for about a year and a half... irreconcilable differences. I wanted kids and Moira made it clear that she didn't."

"You hadn't discussed this earlier in your marriage of...how many years, Sir?"

"About ten years. I just assumed that she would want children, I suppose and we were using contraception at first. Moira was on the pill. Like most young couples we wanted some time to get our house organised, share some good holidays, that kind of thing."

"So how did you discover that she didn't want children, Sir?"

"I mentioned one night that maybe she could come off the pill and she said then that she would if I would use something."

"And that was it?"

"Yes."

"So you knew nothing of her visit to Westwood Clinic?"

The young man's face went red then the colour receded leaving him white-faced.

"Well, Mr Findlay?"

"I think I knew about that," he mumbled.

"You *think* you knew? Either you knew or you didn't."

"Yes, I knew," he said sullenly.

"So why not tell me that right away?"

"I thought it might give me a reason for killing her. You know, you might think I got very angry and lashed out at her."

"And did you?"

"I got very angry when she told me but all I did was walk out. I didn't kill her. I didn't. Surely I was right to be angry. She'd pretended about being on the pill when all along she'd been sterilised. She'd even had had me wearing condoms to keep up the pretence of her eventually wanting kids."

"Very well, Mr Findlay but in future don't keep things from us. It makes us suspicious. How did she manage to have an operation without you knowing?"

"I went away for three days with some pupils about five years ago. I guess she must have arranged it for that time."

"Now, when did you last see Moira?" asked Fiona.

"About three weeks ago when I went up to the house to see if I'd left my passport there. I hadn't needed it since I left and when I did want it I couldn't find it."

"Going away, Sir?"

"Yes. I'm going to Greece with...Jane. She's my girlfriend," he said defiantly.

"From before or after the split up, Sir?"

"After. I met her at my new school and I didn't move schools till last August."

"Did you find the passport?"

"Yes. It was still in our holiday folder in the filing cabinet."

"And what did you talk about then, Sir?"

"I told her I was going on holiday and she asked if it was with a woman and I said yes but I didn't tell her who it was. Teachers and folk who work in schools always know someone who knows someone else and I didn't want her nosing into our business."

"Did she tell you if she had anyone else in her life, Sir?"

"Oh yes. She seemed delighted to be able to tell me that she had also met someone."

"Before or after?"

"She said after but who knows."

"Did she mention a name?"

"Sandy was what she called him. She didn't mention his surname and I wasn't interested enough to ask."

"Did your wife have any hobbies?"

"Why is that important?"

"She must have met this Sandy somewhere. I take it that there were no Sandys or Alexes or Alexanders at your last school where she still worked?"

"Not while I was there but he could have arrived in August, I suppose."

"Hobbies, Sir?"

"She played badminton at Eaglesham church on Tuesday evenings. She went to church there sometimes. She went out for a meal with two old chums from her university days but only once a year... oh and she saw Ali quite often, usually on Saturday afternoons when I was at football matches."

"That would be Alison Jones, Sir?"

"Yes."

"Anything else?"

"She mentioned something about a book club that day I went to the house. Think she had just started going. I got the impression that she was trying to show me that she had a busy life which didn't include me."

"Any names?"

"Just one: "The Curious Incident of the Dog in the Nightime."

"I meant any names of people who went to the club, Sir."

"Oh, sorry. No, no names but I got the impression from something she said that it was a mixed sex group. Yes, she said the books had to appeal to men and women."

"Can you think of any reason why she wasn't reported missing, Sir?"

"Well if her new man murdered her he wasn't likely to let you know she was missing, was he?"

"And if he wasn't the murderer?"

"Then no one tried to get in touch."

"Not even the school she worked in?"

"Yes, that's odd."

"Finally Mr Findlay, where were you on Wednesday evening, the fifteenth of June?"

"A week ago last Wednesday?"

The man took out his diary.

"I met a friend for a couple of pints in '1801'."

"Where's that, Sir?"

"At the corner of Pollokshaws Road and Haggs Road."

"Thanks. Then?"

"I was there till about 9 pm then I went home."

"Were your parents in?"

"Dad was in bed with flu. Mum was out at a church guild meeting, I think."

"Did you look in on your father?"

"No."

Fiona got to her feet and the young man rose too.

"Thank you, Mr Findlay. Please leave your address and phone number at the desk. I'll catch you up and take you to the city mortuary."

"Mortuary?"

The man had gone pale.

"Did no one tell you that we needed you to formally identify your wife's body?"

"No."

"She has no other next of kin except for an elderly aunt in Aberdeen, Sir. I hope you have no objection."

"N...no."

David Findlay walked off down the corridor to the desk where he gave his address and phone number to Bob. By the time he had finished, Fiona Macdonald had joined him and they walked out of the station together.

"Where do you stay, Sir? We're going into Glasgow. Would it be handier for you to have your car or will I bring you back here."

"I live in Pollokshaws, with my parents. I'll go with you."

The drive took about fifteen minutes, the roads being quite quiet in the lull leading up to rush hour. Most of the traffic was going in the opposite direction..

Martin Jamieson was waiting for them, Fiona having apprised him of their estimated arrival time. He shook hands with David Findlay and expressed his condolences then took him and Fiona to the room where they kept the corpses of recent, unexplained deaths. He walked across the room to a large freezer, opened it and, selecting the bottom handle, pulled out a metal tray, holding a covered body.

David Findlay shivered.

Martin uncovered the body and Moira's ex-husband looked for the last time at his partner of ten years.

"Yes that's her," he said, turned away quickly and went outside. Fiona thanked Martin and said, laughing, that she hoped she would not see him again soon.

Once back at the station, she thanked David Findlay for his cooperation and went off to her own room, shedding her jacket before going to the end room which she had used to interview David Findlay as it was bigger than her own small office. Davenport was back in residence and looked up at her approach.

"Well, any further forward, Fiona?

"Her boyfriend's name was Sandy and it seems that she could have met him at work, at Eaglesham church, at badminton there on Tuesday evenings or at a book club which she had recently joined and which had men and women members. She saw Alison Jones most Saturday afternoons. She might be able to fill in some blanks."

"And his whereabouts on the night of the murder?"

"With a friend till 9 ish then home: father in bed, mother out."

"So no real alibi for after 9 then."

"That's right. He didn't look in on his father."

"And did he identify the body? How did that go?"

"He wasn't happy doing it but he didn't shed any tears either. I think that relationship was well and truly dead. Charles, why did her school not report her missing?"

"Yes, that's odd isn't it? Will you give them a ring tonight before you leave, please? It's nearly time for my interview. Get off home after that, my dear."

"I think I'll write up my report of the interview first, Charles. I prefer to get it down in black and white as soon as possible."

When Fiona phoned Greystone Academy, it was to find that Moira had had an appointment at hospital for a minor operation on the Thursday and when she did not come in on the Friday the school secretary had phoned her house and no one had answered.

"Is something wrong with her?"

Fiona had explained briefly. She rang off. Charles was passing her room, so she called out to tell him why the school had not reported their lab technician missing.

"So that was the phone call where the caller withheld their number I suppose," she said.

"Probably."

He blew her a kiss which she blew back.

CHAPTER 27

Alison Jones was a slim, strawberry blonde, in her thirties, Davenport judged. She had come straight from work and looked extremely elegant in her black suit and pale blue blouse. As she walked in front of him to his room, he appreciated her shapely legs enhanced by high-heeled black shoes. Whatever she did, it surely it did not involve standing all day!

He invited her to sit down at his coffee table rather than across from him at his desk. She was not, after all, a suspect in this case. Woman friends did not murder each other in lonely fields.

"Thanks for coming, Mrs...Miss Jones."

"It's Miss. Please not Ms, I'm not a manuscript."

Her laugh was pleasant and she seemed totally relaxed, in spite of the place and the reason for her being there. She unbuttoned her jacket, revealing a generous chest.

"No one good enough for you? Either that or the young men of today must be blind," Davenport risked a compliment, hoping that her comment about Ms meant that she was not a rabid feminist and would not bite his nose off.

"Thank you kindly, Sir. I was engaged once but discovered when the chemistry wore off that I didn't much like him and I've been a bit scared of relationships since then."

"Would you like a tea or coffee, Miss Jones? It's not canteen stuff."

"I'd love a coffee, black please, no sugar and if it's not against police protocol, please will you call me Alison?"

"Certainly...Alison."

Davenport busied himself with his coffee percolator and handed her a cup, taking one himself but adding milk and one sweetener. He sat back down. Alison's cheerfulness had dissipated all of a sudden. She looked upset.

"The policewoman who rang me, told me what happened to Moira. When was she killed?"

"On Wednesday 15th of June. Her body wasn't discovered till the Friday."

"Who found her?"

"A local woman out for a walk."

"I'll not ask how she was killed. I'd rather not know. Is that cowardly?"

"Not at all."

"How can I help you?"

"Alison, what I want from you, if possible, is a name for Moira's new man. I know it's Sandy something."

"Macpherson. She met him at church originally and he persuaded her to go to the church badminton club and to a book club up near where they live."

"Do you know where Sandy lives?"

"Not his address I'm afraid but I do know that he lived in the same road as Moira, Riverside Road, in Waterfoot. Further down the road I think because she waved in the direction to show me once when I was leaving her house. He works as a nurse in the Southern General...no wait a minute...I think Moira said he was now in the new Victoria Hospital."

"Were they just friends, Alison? Or was there more to their relationship than that?"

"I'm sure it had gone beyond that but only recently," she ventured.

"Can you think of any reason why she might have been walking home through the estate near her home and late in the evening?"

"Well she told me that Sandy and she had agreed not to go to each other's houses in case neighbours spotted them. Maybe they met somewhere near there, in a quiet layby perhaps."

"And why would that matter, them being seen together?"

"Sandy is separated from his wife and didn't want to jeopardise his standing in a divorce case. His wife had left him for another man and Sandy was citing this man as correspondent. Witnesses seeing him with another woman might have made things messy."

"So he could have met her near the Keel Estate but why would he leave her to walk home alone? Surely he could have driven her through that lonely road and let her off somewhere safer and I can't imagine why she wouldn't take her own car to their meeting -place."

"Moira didn't drive, Inspector. David did the driving. She got a lift to work from a woman in Eaglesham who works in the same school, even before the split-up."

"Unusual for a woman her age not to drive," Davenport mused out loud.

"She kept meaning to take lessons but she loved faraway holidays and they had to save hard for those. I suppose she felt she couldn't afford lessons right now."

"Is that one of the reason why she didn't want children, her love of far flung holidays?"

"Oh, you know about that!"

"Yes. David, her husband told us earlier today."

"She'd been sterilised some years ago and Dave found out. He was furious. She said he'd looked murderous...sorry, bad word to use... don't think Dave could have ever been violent. More like Moira attacking him in an argument rather than the other way round."

"So she was the quick-tempered one?"

"Yes. We've had many an argument, Inspector. Moira was quite opinionated and always fought her corner fiercely."

"Did she ever mention any fights with her new man?"

"No, Inspector. They were still at that sickening lovey-dovey stage. I was sick hearing about how marvellous Sandy was, how caring, how understanding of her not wanting kids. Well, he had two of his own already so it was easy for him to feel like that, wasn't it?"

"Anything else you can think of, Alison? Anything that might help us to find her killer?"

"Just that he must have been a strong guy. Alison would have put up a fight, I'm sure of that."

Alison's voice wobbled a bit. She took out a paper hanky and dabbed at her eyes.

"I'm sorry. I just wish she hadn't lain there for two days. It makes it seem as if no one cared about her enough to report her missing. I should have phoned her to ask about the hospital visit but I knew we could chat about it on Saturday."

"What was the visit for?"

"She'd been having some pain in her foot and they suspected plantar fasciitis. Think they were doing an x-ray."

"You weren't to know."

"No we didn't phone each other very often, just met at the usual place on Saturday afternoons."

She seemed to brighten a bit.

"Well, thanks for coming, Alison. If you can think of anything else just get in touch and leave your address and phone number at the desk on your way out, please."

Alison Jones rose to go. At the door, she turned.

"Is there any word of a funeral yet?"

"No, not yet but we'll let you know in plenty of time."

As the woman went off down the corridor, high heels clicking, Davenport's mind turned to something she had said about children, that Sandy didn't mind Moira not wanting kids because he already had two. This was something he and Fiona had never discussed in their conversations about their relationship. OK it was platonic at the moment - almost - being restricted to kisses and hugs, but if things were to get more physical he would need to know where she stood on the children front. Pippa, his daughter, was such a blessing and he was more than happy to have no more kids but would Fiona want at least one of her own and if she did, would he comply with her wishes and do it willingly?

He gave himself a mental shake, picked up the phone and dialled Martin's mobile number. Personal things could wait.

As he had expected ,when he apologised for disturbing him at home, Martin said that he wasn't at home yet, as an interesting body had been presented to him.

"Martin. There was nothing about Moira Findlay having had an operation in your report."

"Yes there was. Wait a minute till I retrieve my dictaphone message to my secretary."

Silence.

…"and she had had a sterilisation operation about four to five years ago…"

"Did you hear that, Charles?"

"Yes, I did but I don't remember reading about it. Hang on while I get the report."

Another silence.

Davenport read out the salient paragraphs. There was nothing about an operation.

"Sorry, Charles. Maria must have skipped that part for some reason. Not like her; she is usually very efficient."

"It doesn't really matter, Martin. Two people have told me about it today and I just wanted it confirmed."

"I shall get Maria to type this out again and send you a revised report. OK?"

"Thanks Martin. Now get home to that poor wife of yours."

Martin laughed and hung up.

CHAPTER 28

Penny was in a rush. She had not got home till after 6pm, having gone to see Salma after her interviews at Greystone Academy.

"Penny! How lovely of you to come," Salma said. "Come in."

Penny had been taken into the cosy lounge, decorated in shades of red and grey. She knew that Mrs Din had just had the room redecorated as Salma had told her about the discussion she, Shazia and their mother had had about the colour scheme. Salma had favoured more subdued colours but Shazia and her mum had wanted their favourite red to predominate and she had been outnumbered. Certainly, the crimson curtains gave the room warmth, Penny thought now, seeing it for the first time. She perched herself on the new settee, patterned in red and grey and smiled at Shazia. Salma introduced her brother who apologised for not having managed to talk to her at the funeral or afterwards.

"I did try to speak to everyone but it just wasn't possible. Nice to meet you now, Penny. Salma's talked a lot about you."

"All bad probably," said Penny, laughing.

She had known that the atmosphere in the house would be sad but had the sense that she had interrupted something serious as no one else even smiled.

Forthright as ever, she asked if everything was OK.

"Is something wrong? Apart from the death of your Mum, of course," she said looking embarrassed.

She saw Shahid shake his head but Salma glared at him and looked inquiringly at her sister.

"Yes Salma, tell Penny. See what she thinks," said Shazia.

"D'you remember me telling you that Shazia wanted to leave home a while ago?"

"Yes."

"Well her friend has asked her again, just before Mum died and Shazia thinks this is the right time to do it."

"And I..."

"Don't say anything, Shahid. Let's see what Penny thinks," said Salma, smiling at her friend.

"Well maybe it is the right time to make a break, that is if Salma feels that she can cope with Rafiq without Shazia's help."

"He's old enough now to not need much looking after. He's nearly eleven," said Shazia. "And Salma will have Farah here too."

"How do you feel, Salma?" asked Penny.

"That's what I was asking when you arrived," said Shahid.

"To be honest, I envy Shazia but there's no reason why all of us girls should be kept in the family home. Hopefully by the time I want to leave, Rafiq will be old enough to stay with Farah."

"As head of the family, I think that Shazia should stay here until she marries and you too, Salma," Shahid said, a bit pompously, Penny thought.

"And who's going to arrange the marriages? You, Shahid?"

"Naturally."

"Have you forgotten the free life you led until recently?" demanded Shazia, angrily.

"Shahid," said Salma quietly. "I have no intention of having a marriage arranged by you or anyone else. I'm very sad that Mum died so suddenly but, having no parents, I feel set free to choose my own husband."

"Me too," said her sister.

"I'm going to get my uncle to talk to both of you," said Shahid angrily.

"Do that Shahid and I'll say the same to him as I have to you."

Salma's voice was quiet but determined.

"Now, Penny. Tell me about what's been happening at work."

Still arguing, Shahid and Shazia left the room.

Penny had brought her up to date and then, looking at her watch, jumped to her feet.

"Have to go. Gordon and I are going to Mum's for dinner and I've still to buy wine and some chocolates."

The journey back across to the South Side had taken a bit longer as many people were going home from work, then she had had to dash into Morrisons in Newlands, where she grabbed two bottles of wine, one red and one white and a box of truffles which were Jack's favourites.

She rushed about the flat, running a bath, laying out her clothes and talking to Alec about their plans for the weekend. It was Alec's turn to provide the weekend meals and Penny told him that she would be in the following night as Gordon was on the emergency rota.

Trying to relax in the bath, she heard her mobile ring and shouted to Alec to answer it for her. It was Gordon, saying that he would be about an hour late and telling her to go to her Mum's without him and make his apologies.

"He says to start the meal and just put his aside to be reheated. He's used to that," shouted Alec through the bathroom door.

Dressed and ready, Penny rang her Mum to give her the news. As she had expected her mother was completely unfazed and said that the meal could be easily postponed and would Penny tell Gordon to ring her when he was leaving work. Penny did that and then made her way to her Mum's house. Jack was at the window of the front room and opened the door for her, giving her a big hug as usual. Penny handed over the wine.

"I brought red and white as I didn't know what we were having, Jack, and make sure Mum gets at least one truffle, gutsy."

At this point her Mum came into the hallway and Penny got another hug.

"It's a chicken dish that only takes half an hour, same time as the potatoes, so there's no panic about when Gordon gets here. Come on into the lounge and Jack will get us all a drink."

Penny had walked over to her Mum's house as it was quite near her flat, so she asked for a white wine spritzer.

"That's white wine with lemonade, Jack," she told him.

"Cheeky! I do know that," came the reply from the drinks' table. "I'm not a complete dinosaur."

When they were all seated, drinks in hands, she told them about the funeral and about the conversation she had recently had at Salma's house.

"I hope that Salma and her sister can stand up to their uncle the way they did to Shahid," said Penny.

"You hear such things in the news," replied her mother, "Asian girls being murdered by their own relatives to stop them marrying someone unsuitable."

"Surely that's a rare event, though," said Jack, seeing Penny look frightened for her friend.

"Fancy Shahid being so...so...Muslim," said Penny, "especially after the kind of life he's been living in London. It's so hypocritical of him to turn traditional now."

"Well it happens, Pen," said Gordon later after he had been regaled with the story. "A girl in my class at school seemed very Westernised. She went to uni, then on to teach and never wore the burka but as soon as she got married she started wearing it."

They were back sitting in the lounge after having finished their chicken meal which had been followed by Penny's favourite, her Mum's pavlova, trimmed with strawberries. They sat now with coffees and Penny remarked on the new decor in the lounge. Her Mum and Jack had decided that when Jack had time, he would repaint every room in the house to celebrate their new life together and Mrs Maclean had bought new furnishings for the first room which had been the lounge. The beige curtains with bright orange swirls and the orange coloured cushion covers added warmth to the pale coloured walls.

"Very modern, Mum. I heard the other day that orange is this year's black."

"Eh?" queried Gordon. "What does that mean?"

"Just another way of saying that orange is this year's favourite colour," Penny told him.

"When I was younger than you are now, pet, I bought a purple midi coat as purple was that year's colour and of course it dated my coat as the next year the colour was a lime green," said Margaret Maclean.

They all laughed and the talk turned to Gordon's emergency pet.

"A man came in just before we closed to say that a dog had been knocked down outside. I went out and brought it in and we operated to try to save its leg. I wanted to wait till he regained consciousness, poor wee chap."

"Is he OK?" Penny asked anxiously.

"Yes Pen, a happy ending for you. He had a collar on with his address attached to it so I rang his owner who was very relieved and raced down. Seemingly the wee fellow took off when a bigger dog went for him in the park and he just ran and ran and they lost sight of him."

"What about you, Penny?" asked Jack.

"Well your namesake, a Mrs McLean, spelt differently, just Mc, not Mac, found a body about ten days ago..."

"Yes I read about it in The Herald. Youngish woman wasn't she?" Jack asked.

"Well young to you maybe," joked Penny. "Mid-thirties. I thought they put folk down at that age."

"Cheeky monkey. Didn't you bring your daughter up to respect her elders and betters, wifey?"

"Wifey ! Don't you dare call me that Jack Mclean. She knows to respect those who deserve respect, don't you love?"

It was a cosy, informal evening and Penny and Gordon did not leave till after midnight. Gordon had not had anything alcoholic and he drove Penny the short distance to her flat, giving her a goodnight kiss that made her feel warm and glowing, before he left for his own home. She would have invited him to come in but he had already said that he had to be at the surgery early the next day. They arranged to meet for lunch, locally, on Sunday. Penny wanted to go to church with her Mum and had told him she would be able to get there for 1pm. As she went upstairs, she thought how lucky she was to be able to choose her boyfriend and hoped that Salma, and Shazia too, would insist on that same freedom.

CHAPTER 29

Sunday arrived and with it a problem for Davenport. He had left the station before his constables had come back from their school interviews on Friday and he wondered now whether he should call them in today or leave their reports until Monday when Knox would be back and breathing fire at his DCI for not having sewn up the case in his absence.

He rang Fiona who answered a bit breathlessly.

"What were you doing? Steamy session with your lover?" he said lasciviously.

"Oh yes. In the shower. He was wonderful."

"Would he part with you for the afternoon?" Charles asked.

"Wait and I'll ask him."

She shouted, "Claude is it OK if I leave you this afternoon, darling?" and heard Charles at his end inquire sweetly, "Euphemia, my love, can you bear to be without me this afternoon?"

Fiona laughed heartily and he joined in.

"Aren't we daft, Fiona? Just as well our colleagues can't hear us."

"So, Charles is it just me you want to come in to work or is it everyone?"

"Well, I need someone to go to the Victoria to see Sandy Macpherson and I want to hear what the young ones found out at the school. I'll have to report to Knox tomorrow and you know what he'll think if we've taken the weekend off and don't have answers for him."

"OK then. I'll phone Penny. You get in touch with Frank."

"That's right. You take the easy one, DS Macdonald. She's always willing to give up her free time."

"Maybe not now that she's got a new boyfriend."

"Oh has she indeed?"

"Yes, a young vet called Gordon Black."

"Penny Black! I like it."

"Don't say that to Penny, Charles. Frank spotted that one and he's always teasing her about being a rare, old thing."

"There's the young guy Fraser too. He went to the school with them."

"Right, I'll get his number from Bob and phone him too."

"Thanks, Fiona. Tell them two o'clock."

Charles left the hall from where he had been phoning and went into the kitchen where Pippa was drawing on the table in the midst of the breakfast debris.

"What's the point in having a daughter if she doesn't do the washing up?" he asked.

Pippa looked up indignantly.

"Why would a boy not have had to do it?"

"Oh, feminist already!"

"What's a feminist?"

"What do you think pet?"

"Well female means a woman so it's something to do with a woman."

"Good. A feminist is someone who thinks that men and woman should be equal in everything."

"So they should. That's what I told Ronald when he said girls should cook and clean."

"Ronald? Do you still see him?"

"Only on Fridays. He comes up from the secondary to see me in the playground after school. Auntie Linda doesn't get there for me right away on Fridays 'cos that's her whist day."

Pippa had made friends with Ronald when she had first gone to her new primary school. Older than his classmates, having been kept back for a year, he had tended to bully them till Pippa had arrived and managed somehow to tame him. He had gone up to secondary school in August, the school obviously thinking he was ready for the move and Charles had assumed he had lost touch with Pippa.

"Did you put him straight then, pet?"

"I did, Dad. I told him that when I got married, my husband would have to take his turn at things like cooking and washing."

"I give in."

Charles filled the basin with hot water and Fairy liquid and started on the breakfast dishes. A minute later, Pippa was by his side with the tea towel.

"Thanks, pet. Now, have you planned anything for today?"

"Well I told Kathy I would go to her house if you didn't need me for anything."

"When?"

"About 2. She goes to Sunday School and has her dinner when she gets home. Dad, could I go to Sunday School with her one Sunday?"

"Of course, pet. Which church does she go to?"

"That big one on the main road. Will I phone her and tell her I can come at 2?"

"Yes and let me speak to Kathy's Mum or Dad."

Charles spoke to Mrs Bryce who agreed that it was OK for him to drop Pippa off about 1.25.

He reached the station to find that everyone was there before him, even Frank who was not noted for his punctuality. That young man looked at his watch.

"Sorry, PC Selby. I know I'm late. Sorry everyone. Had to get Pippa organised first. Thanks for coming in at such short notice. I want to know first of all how the three of you got on at the school."

"The headteacher was a bit of a sourpuss," said Penny. "We asked if we could speak to the staff about Moira Findlay and he said that we couldn't do it till after school finished. I said that you had called and he said yes but he hadn't realised that we were just going to turn up. He hadn't had time to set up a room for us. He said he was a very busy man."

"He said that we probably only needed to see the science staff, Sir," added Frank.

The new recruit spoke up.

"I told him that in a case of murder, it was imperative that the police be given cooperation and as soon as possible."

"He looked at Fraser and Fraser just looked back at him and he agreed to tannoy for any member of staff who knew Moira Findlay well to come to the office as soon as possible."

Penny looked in admiration at the young man and he blushed under her gaze.

"I heard my DCI say that once when I was with him," he said. "I hope that was alright, Sir."

"It was very alright, young Fraser," Davenport congratulated him. He noticed that Frank was looking a bit disgruntled.

"Frank, who did you talk to?"

"I spoke to Harry Richards, head of Chemistry. He said that Moira had been having some pain in one of her feet recently and had a hospital appointment on the 16th of June. When she didn't come in on the Friday, he just assumed that she had been kept in for some reason and the office would let him know when she was due back."

"Penny?"

"I spoke to a girl in the Physics department. She was quite friendly with Moira and had met Sandy once. She had been going to Moira's for a meal after school one evening and when they got out of her car, Sandy had been getting out of his further down the road, by the flats, she said, Sir. Moira introduced them and told this woman, Pauline Lawrie, that he was her new boyfriend."

"Fraser?"

"I saw a young woman who lives in Eaglesham. She teaches History and gave Moira a lift into school every morning and took her home most evenings. Moira paid her every month. This woman, Elaine Smith, said that Moira was full of chat about her new boyfriend. Said Moira had been very down after her marriage broke up and that she had been off work for some weeks with depression."

"Did she not wonder why there was no Moira waiting to be picked up on Friday morning?"

"No, Sir, same as the office. She just assumed that Moira had been kept in hospital and hadn't managed to phone her. She rang Moira in the evening, got not reply and assumed that she was well enough to be out with her boyfriend or still in hospital.

"That would be the call I listened to," said Fiona. "Oh and I checked the diary. The V in Thursday's space would be Victoria."

"Did any of you get names of any other people whom Moira was friendly with?"

"Just Alison Jones, Sir and we knew about her," said Penny.

"Elaine Smith said that she'd gone out with someone briefly before Sandy but it didn't last long," added Fraser.

"Pauline said that Moira seemed almost over keen to meet a new man, to show her ex-husband that she wasn't missing him, she said. Pauline mentioned her talking once about a younger man but his name was never brought up again and she didn't talk about him again."

Penny looked at her notes.

"Pauline said, 'Moira talked once about meeting a young man at a bus stop when she was coming home from visiting Elaine Smith.' That's all Sir."

"No one else came forward?" Davenport asked.

"No, Sir. Frank offered to come back to the station so he drove Fraser and me home then came here…"

"...but you and DS Macdonald weren't here, Sir so I just went home," added Frank.

"Thanks, Frank. That was good of you. Sorry you all had to come in this afternoon instead."

Davenport walked to the flipchart. He had written Moira Findlay's name at the top of a blank page and now he wrote underneath:

Sandy Macpherson
David Findlay
Young man at bus stop
Other man before Sandy
Someone living near the murder site

"What do you mean by the last one, Sir?" asked DS Macdonald.

"Someone in one of the houses I suppose I mean, or someone else, apart from the man I spoke to, staying late at the factory."

"So what now?" she asked.

"I want someone to go to the Southern General...no the new Victoria. Sandy's moved hospitals recently, and someone to go to Riverside Road, to the houses at the bottom of the road..."

"The ones we didn't need to go to when we went there 'cos we found out where Moira lived and got her name?" asked Penny who found it difficult to keep quiet for long.

"That's correct Penny. Ask around for Sandy Macpherson. We should find him either at work or at home this afternoon. Now who wants to volunteer?"

"Me. I'll volunteer," said Penny at once. "I'm free today. Gordon's at work."

"I'll do the other one, whichever Penny's not doing, Sir," said Fiona. "Let the two men have the rest of the afternoon off. Show them the women aren't afraid of hard work, eh Penny?"

"Yes ma'am."

Penny grinned at her boss.

"Which do you want to do ma'am?"

"I'll take the hospital then and you do Riverside Road."

"Tell him to come into the station tomorrow, whenever it suits his job," said Davenport.

Frank and Fraser looking delighted, they all made their way out of the station.

CHAPTER 30

"Come down," Lorna shouted. "That's Neil's car now."

She opened the door and went out onto the slabbed area containing tubs of flowers which had been prepared for her by Rouken Glen Garden Centre. They had chosen this new house for a number of reasons, one of which was that it had comparatively little garden space for such a large house. She had never liked gardening and her husband was too busy at work and had little time for it.

The doors of the black, gleaming Lexus were opening and she moved forward to greet her favourite son and his perfect wife and two lovely children.

"Neil, darling, how great to see you and you too, Martha. Hello, Katherine and Christopher. Come and give your grandma a big hug."

The serious-looking girl, aged eight, came straight over and gave the requested hug, followed by a little replica of Neil, aged six, who did the same. They were impeccably dressed, Katherine in a sundress of white cotton decorated with red flowers and Christopher in a pair of navy shorts with a white short-sleeved shirt.

They were just about to enter the house when another car came along the estate road and pulled up. Out got Lily and her partner Jim, both wearing denims and tee-shirts. Lily's blonde hair was caught up in a ponytail. Her father looked at them ruefully. He loved Lily dearly but wished she would just once make an effort to please her stepmother.

"Lily, my love. So pleased you could manage for Sunday lunch," he said now, moving to give her the bear hug he had managed to avoid giving his daughter-in-law whom he deemed a cold fish. His wife threw him a dirty look which meant trouble for him later, he knew.

"Give Martha a hug," she hissed at him as they went into the house behind their visitors.

Robert rose from his seat by the log-burning fire. It was cool for late June and he had been enjoying the heat from it.

"Lily! Hi love."

He hugged his sister.

"Afternoon, Martha."

He shook her hand.

Martha took the vacated seat. She always looked as if she needed warmed up, Robert thought, and fatted up, he added to himself. She was far too thin.

He caught his father's glance and they grinned at each other. The two children were politely shaking hands with Jim. Lily ignored their hands and gave them both a hug.

"Drinks folks? Martha?"

"Dry sherry, please."

"Lily?"

"D'you have beer, Dad?"

"I think so." He knew he had, having bought some the day before. He knew that his wife who disliked anyone drinking beer, especially women, would not have bought any.

"Jim? Neil?"

"Beer, thanks," said Jim, smiling at him.

"Scotch and soda," said Neil, a man of few words.

"What about you, my dear? Sherry too?"

"Of course," his wife answered.

As they both left the room, he to get the beer from the fridge and she to see the cook about dinner, the others were taking various seats except for the two children who wandered over to the window.

"If you hadn't bought that disgusting stuff, they'd have had to take something more suitable."

"They're our guests. They should be able to have what they want, Lorna."

The doorbell rang, cutting off the argument. He went to the door.

"Mother-in-law! How lovely to see you."

"Pay the taxi please."

She swept majestically past him into the hall. Even at ninety she was brisk and formidable. Like her daughter, she had once been warm and friendly but after her husband had left her when she was in her late sixties, she had become bitter and unreachable.

He paid the taxi driver, asking him to return about six o'clock, then stood by the door, the look on his face and the slump in his shoulders showing his dejection at the thought of the hours to come, surrounded by his mismatched family. He squared his shoulders, turned into the house and shut the door just as his wife's shrill voice called to him to come in and get the drinks. She had brought the cans of beer and had brought out two large glasses and was handing them to Lily and Jim.

"I hope you don't mind using a glass, James," she said sweetly.

"Mother, you know...." began Lily.

"No problem, Mrs Cook," Jim smiled at her. "Please call me Jim."

"I don't like shortened names, James. Sorry. Christopher and Katherine, come into the kitchen and choose a soft drink for yourselves. Robert, get my mother's martini and lemonade please."

The two children followed her obediently.

"Are they always so perfect, Rob?" Lily muttered to her brother.

"'Fraid so, Lil. Not natural, is it?"

"Martha always looks as if she's got a poker up her back," Lily added and Robert had to stifle a snort of laughter.

"Dinner's ready."

Their mother was back in the room.

"Martha, please go in with your father-in-law ; Lily, go in with Christopher ; Katherine go with Robert ; mother go with Neil ; James you may take me."

The little procession made for the dining room, Lily sending Jim a sympathetic glance and getting a cheery smile in return.

Dinner proceeded. A tureen of vegetable soup was brought in by Mary, the cook, followed fifteen minutes later by a large roast which was placed in front of father, at the head of the table. He was handed his utensils by Mary and started his carving.

"None for me thanks, Mr Cook," said Jim.

The conversation stopped abruptly. Lorna Cook looked askance at her guest.

"Mother, I phoned you last week and reminded you that Jim's a vegetarian," said Lily." I presume you've got cook to make him something different."

"I certainly have not. I assumed that out of politeness your young man would take what he was given."

"No problem, Mrs Cook. I can take some vegetables and potatoes," Jim tried to keep the peace.

"No, Jim. That's it. I'm not having you being insulted. You think you're so polite and correct mother but you're just a snob. Come on, Jim, we're leaving. Sorry Dad."

Mr Cook rose and followed them into the hallway.

"So sorry, Dad, she's just impossible. I came this time. I wanted to see..."

"It's OK Lily.," broke in her father. "I'm sorry too. Sorry, James, I can only apologise for my wife."

"Don't worry, Mr Cook."

"Richard."

"Don't worry, Richard. Maybe another time and remember you're always very welcome at our house."

He waved them off, shut the door and went back into the dining room with a heavy heart.

His mother-in-law was talking. He caught the end of her sentence "...expect from someone who works with cars."

"There's nothing wrong, Grandma, with someone who works for their living, at something ordinary. My girlfriend, Patsy works in a newsagents' shop."

Robert was angry.

"I don't want to hear about your…floosy, Robert. How you could leave that nice Claudia I'll never know."

Robert got up and left the room. They heard his footsteps going upstairs.

"I'm sorry, everyone. Let's get on with the meal and try to forget the bad manners we've been treated to today."

Lorna Cook was at her icy best and her mother shot her a sympathetic look. The meal progressed. After the dessert, the women and two children went into the lounge, leaving the two remaining men to have brandy and cigars at the table. When they had finished, they went upstairs, coming down about half an hour later with a calmed-down Robert who invited Christopher to come into the games' room where he would give him a lesson in playing billiards.

"Tell grandma about getting the class prize this year, Katherine," said her mother and the little girl was included in the conversation for the first time.

At six o'clock, the hoot of the taxi horn signalled the end of the family get-together. Richard Cook got his mother-in-law's fur jacket, helped her into it and escorted her out to the waiting car.

"Time you did something with that daughter of yours, Richard. Little Katherine could teach her a thing or two about manners."

"Yes, mother-in-law. I hope you get home safely."

The taxi drove off.

"Old witch," he muttered under his breath.

His son and family were in the hallway.

"Goodbye, Neil. Goodbye Martha. You must come again soon and bring our delightful grandchildren."

Lorna Cook smiled benignly at the two children and nudged her husband who went into his wallet and produced two ten pound notes which he gave to Katherine and Christopher. They thanked him politely.

"Thanks Uncle Robert, for the game," said the little boy.

"No problem, Chris."

"...topher," said Mrs Cook.

"It's OK Grandma. I get called Chris at school."

"There's hope for you yet," thought his grandfather as he waved them away.

CHAPTER 31

Salma was glad to be back at work. She had met Penny in the canteen for their usual hot drink and had told her about the fraught atmosphere at home.

"After you left, Shahid went over to my aunt and uncle's house. Uncle Fariz came straight back with him and they brought Auntie Zenib too, luckily."

"Why luckily?"

"Well Uncle Fariz got very angry with Shazia and me. Told us we had to listen to our brother who was now the head of the family. I reminded him that Shahid had not been the perfect Muslim while he lived in London so what right had he to make us conform now."

Salma, usually so calm and peaceable, was upset and still, Penny could see, angry.

"And did your aunt help?"

"Yes, thank goodness. They never had any children but I think she'd have been more…I don't know what to call it…more modern, I suppose, with daughters if she'd had them. She told my uncle that it was unfair to expect Shazia and me to live the way we would have if we'd been living in Pakistan. She said she was sure both of us would meet nice Muslim men one day, and to leave us alone now."

"Did he give in to her?"

"Yes, he usually does. She makes his life hell if he doesn't!"

Salma laughed.

"Enough of me. What's been happening here?"

Penny told her that she had been back to Riverside Road to try to find Moira Findlay's boyfriend and that DS Macdonald had gone to the new Victoria Infirmary to do the same thing.

"Who found him?"

"I did. Look, we'd better get up to the department. I went straight home afterwards so nobody except the DS knows what happened and she'll only assume I found him when she didn't."

They were soon all settled in the Incident Room, Frank just having time to send Salma a sympathetic smile.

"Right, team. Update on Sandy Macpherson. DS Macdonald drew a blank at the hospital. He wasn't on duty on Sunday but was due back today… if you didn't have any luck, Penny."

"I got him, Sir."

"What happened and did he know about Moira's death?"

"Yes, Sir, he found out on the Wednesday, a week after she was murdered. He didn't ring her before as they weren't meeting at the weekend because he was on duty in the evenings and she was busy, seeing Alison on the Saturday afternoon and something else, he couldn't remember what, on the Sunday afternoon."

"So he tried to call her when?"

"On the Monday. He wasn't particularly surprised not to get her. Thought she might be out with Alison as they sometimes did their grocery shopping together then. He tried again on Tuesday evening and began to get worried so he rang her school on Wednesday morning and they told him."

"Didn't he read anything in the paper when we asked for help in finding out who she was?"

"I asked that, Sir and he said he didn't buy a paper and there hadn't been anything on the TV about it."

"Fair enough. Did he say anything helpful?"

"He said that David had probably done it. Bit of jealousy there I think, Sir."

"Did he give any reasons why Findlay might have done it."

"He said that Moira had told him about David being extremely angry when he found out about her having been sterilized. He said she was quite afraid of her ex."

"Any incident in particular?"

"He said that David was due up to collect his passport and some other papers and that Moira didn't want to see him. Sandy had offered to be there when he came but she had said no, that might make him worse."

"But, Sir," said Fiona. "Didn't Mr Findlay say that she was almost taunting him about her new man and how busy she was socially?"

"Yes he did. And Alison Jones said that Moira was the boss. Someone wasn't telling the truth."

"My money's on David Findlay being the liar, Sir," said Frank. "What good would Moira get out of lying to Sandy about him?"

"Might be wanting to make herself seem fragile and dependent on him," said Fiona. "Some women like to be thought vulnerable."

"Anything else, Penny?"

"No, Sir."

"Did you tell him to come in here as soon as possible?"

"I did, Sir and he's coming in this afternoon after he comes off duty at 12."

Frank and Fraser and Salma were grouped round Penny's desk. Frank had introduced Salma and Fraser on the way down the corridor and was intrigued to see the young man's face flush.

"She's not for you, Fraser, Salma I mean. She'll be back in that hijab thing, married to another Paki and trailing round six kids before very long," had been Frank's words to the young PC when Salma had gone on ahead of them..

"Excuse me saying so, Frank but you really shouldn't say Paki. They don't like it."

"Why not? I was listening to a programme the other night on TV and people from Kurdistan are called Kurds and people from Turkistan are called Turks so why can't we call people from Pakistan, Pakis?"

"Simply, because they don't like it."

"I've been called Jock down in England and I don't moan on about it."

"Well if all Scots hated that, then people would have to learn not to call them that, wouldn't they… and anyway I have a girlfriend already."

Penny came up to her desk at this point and Frank, not wanting her to know that he had been racist again, kept quiet. He liked Salma very much now but it had not cured him of his rather bigoted view of other Muslims.

"Did you have much trouble finding Sandy Macpherson's house, Penny?" asked Salma

"I went to Mr Galbraith's house first but it seems that he only knows people with dogs and Sandy turned out to have a cat. Mr Galbraith's going to keep Amigo by the way, unless some member of Moira's family wants him."

"Good," said Frank who had taken a liking to the friendly collie.

"I went across the road to the family I'd spoken to before and they didn't know the name either, so I went to the semi-detached house before the flats and at the second one, the woman there knew him."

"How come so few people knew him?"

"Think it's probably his job. He works odd hours so he's often in bed when other people are up and up when they're in bed. Also he turned out to be living in one of the flats at the foot of the road so he had no garden and people tend to get friendly over the garden fence."

"So he lives in a flat," mused Salma. "How was it that Moira got to know him again?"

"At church, then at church badminton," said Frank.

"He'd seen her at church and liked her but knew that she was married and so was he. David came along occasionally. Then he heard that they had separated and his wife left him, so he plucked up the courage - his words - to invite her to badminton and the rest, as they say, is history."

"Did they never meet in each other's' houses?" asked Salma.

"Not once. He had never been inside her house and she had never set foot in his," replied Penny.

"So where did they meet?" asked Fraser.

"Sandy would take his car to somewhere quiet nearby and she would walk there, or he picked her up on the main road and they went into town or across to the West End. Occasionally, if his shifts allowed, they would go to the pictures in the evening."

"So what happened on the night of the 15th of June?"

"Tell me what happened on the evening of the 15th June, Mr Macpherson."

Davenport sat cross his desk from the young man, thinking that the name Sandy suited him well with his sandy-coloured hair and thin, ginger moustache.

"I'd rung Moira at teatime. I wanted to see her. We hadn't met for a few days. We normally went somewhere quiet or the opposite, somewhere very busy where we wouldn't be noticed."

"Why was that, Sir?"

"Well, I'm going through a divorce. My wife left me for another man and I'm citing him so I don't want to jeopardize my case and Moira didn't want David to know in case he didn't like it and tried to harass us. So it suited both of us."

"Yet we were told that she had taunted him by mentioning a new lover when he came to her house to collect something."

The young man looked bewildered.

"Who told you that?"

"David Findlay."

"Ah that explains it. He would say that, wouldn't he? She was frightened of David, Mr Davenport. I know that."

"So to come back to Wednesday evening, the 15th. What happened then?"

"We didn't have much time as I had a shift at 10.30pm so we arranged that I would meet her in Floors Road."

"When?"

"At about 9. She walked through the estate. It was a nice night to start with though it rained later. We sat in the car and…well we…"

"Made love, Sir?" Davenport tried to help him out.

The young man's sallow skin flushed rather unbecomingly. The colour clashed with his hair.

"Not fully… you know what I mean."

"You did some heavy petting?"

"Yes. Then I realised that it was after 10.00 so she got out. I said she should walk home by the road but she said she preferred the estate way. I watched her in the rear mirror and waved out the window as she turned into the estate road."

He took a deep breath.

"Where exactly was she found?" he asked.

"Not much further on than that, Sir, just past the first big house and before you come to the factory."

"Did he...was she..."

"Raped, Sir? No she wasn't but she had lots of love bites on her neck."

Again Sandy Macpherson looked embarrassed.

"From me, Inspector."

"One at least was given after death, I'm afraid."

"What kind of sick pervert gives a dead body love bites!"

"Someone who is impotent perhaps, who can't get it on with a live woman. I don't know but we will find out, I promise you that, Mr Macpherson. Now, let's summarise what you told me. Moira was with you until about 10.00. She was alive when you left..."

"You think I might have killed her, don't you?"

"Everyone is a suspect in a murder case, Sir, until proved otherwise."

"I didn't kill her. I loved her, Inspector."

"Yes, Sir. Well, thank you for coming in so promptly."

Davenport rose to signal that the interview was over. Sandy Macpherson got up and went to the door.

"Please leave your address and phone number at the desk on your way out, Sir," Davenport told him.

"So he could have murdered Moira that night," said Fraser.

"Yes or her ex-husband could have killed her," said Frank, looking a bit resentful at Fraser for having an opinion.

"Why would he kill her then and not when she told him about the sterilisation?" Fraser persisted.

"How do you know that?" Frank demanded.

"I read Salma's reports and her copies of everyone else's reports. Hope you don't mind, Sergeant but I thought I'd better be up to date on the case."

Salma smiled at him to show that she did not mind.

"Clever clogs. You got a degree in fast reading then?" said Frank sarcastically.

"No, in English."

"A degree in English, Fraser," said Salma. "Which university? My sister did English too. How old are you?"

"Twenty-two and I went to Strathclyde."

"So did she and she's the same age. Her name's Shazia...Din of course."

"I remember her. Good-looking girl but not as pretty as you."

Frank snorted.

"Got a degree in flattery too?" he said, quite nastily, Penny thought. She decided that the conversation should be changed and smartly.

"How long will you be with us, Fraser?" she asked

"I expect I'll go back tomorrow, now that you've got Sergeant Din back."

Almost on cue, DS Macdonald appeared in the doorway.

"Fraser, the DCI says you can go back to your own department now. Thanks for your help while Salma was away."

As she turned to go, she caught the expressions on Frank and Salma's faces. Frank seemed delighted and Salma, disappointed.

CHAPTER 32

"Thanks, Martin. I'll inform her next-of-kin. Did anything else transpire under closer examination?" asked Davenport.

Martin Jamieson had rung to say that Moira's body was now available for a funeral.

"Well she had an enlarged kidney but nothing dangerous. The other one was OK but nothing more about her killing. As I told you already, there had been sexual activity but not penetration. Some love bites on her shoulder were made prior to death; another two were made afterwards. I still think the murderer had large hands, Charles and the finger was bitten straight though in one bite."

Davenport rang off. He found the phone number of Mrs McDuff in Aberdeen and called her. He told her that Moira's body was now available for burial or cremation.

"Oh it'll be a burial, Inspector Davenport. Her parents are buried in Glasgow. I don't know what the lassie wanted herself. I don't suppose she'd thought about it. You don't when you're young.

Me, now, I've got it all written down, hymns, Bible reading, the lot."

"Right, Mrs McDuff. Do you need any help from this end?"

"Could you give me the number of your Co-op. funeral parlour? That would be a help."

"Wait a minute."

Charles put down the phone and took his telephone directory from one of his desk drawers. He found the number, scribbled it down and picked up the phone again. He gave Moira's aunt the number and asked her to let him have details of the funeral once she had arranged it all.

"I'll either come myself or one of my colleagues will attend."

"Moira's folks are buried in Linn Cemetery so she'll join them there. I've no idea if they'd reserved a layer for her or not. Still it doesn't matter. They'll not be able to chat to each other, will they?"

A cackle of laughter came down the phone.

"No relatives to contact, Mrs McDuff?"

"No, her parents have been dead for some time and she was an only child. I didn't have any children and I was her mother's only sister. Her father was an orphan so no family there. Should I invite her ex-husband, Inspector?"

"I would think so. I'll be seeing him and her current young man. Do you want me to tell them and her friends once I have the details?"

"I'd be very grateful."
Davenport rang off.

The expected summons from the chief inspector did not come in the morning. Davenport wondered whether or not to contact him or just be relieved to have extra time to get on with the case.

He called his team into the Incident Room after lunch.

"I want you, Frank, to go to the Victoria Infirmary and ask when Sandy Macpherson arrived on the evening of Wednesday 15th. Check too that he didn't leave till his shift was over."

"Salma, you get over to Greystone Academy and speak to Elaine Smith, Head of History. She mentioned Moira talking about seeing a younger man, briefly. See if she can give you any more information about this man. I'll ring the headteacher so that he'll be prepared for you coming this time."

"Penny, you go up to Keel Park and ask for the caretaker, whichever one it is that's on at 5pm. Tell him that another light was seen briefly in an upstairs room and ask if it could have been him.

Ok folks, off you go. Penny, if your reports are up to date would you continue with your filing cabinet work. No point in going up to Keel Park till near 5pm. DS Macdonald, will you come to my room and let's talk over what we have so far."

Frank and Salma walked off down the corridor together, Frank whistling, "The Skye Boat Song." Penny bringing up the rear, grinned. It was a while since Frank had been given anything to feed his hopes that the DCI and the DS might start a station romance and imitate Flora Macdonald and Bonny Prince Charlie.

Unaware of why Frank was whistling that particular song, the two people concerned went into Charles's room and shut the door.

"Coffee, love?"

"Yes please, Charles."

As he busied himself with his percolator, Charles voiced his thoughts.

"Moira's husband, David Findlay, could have gone up to the estate and murdered his ex-wife."

"How would he know she was there?"

"He could have followed her from her own house. If he was, as she suggested, unhappy about another man in her life, he might have been watching for them to get together, to get proof."

"But he has another girlfriend."

"Maybe, maybe not but anyway that wouldn't stop him being jealous if he's the jealous type."

"Or something could have gone wrong between Sandy Macpherson and Moira and he killed her in his car, drove to the estate road and dumped her body, biting off her finger before leaving," Fiona voiced her own idea. "We'll need to get Ben to check both their cars."

"Good thinking, batwoman."

"I'm not just a pretty face."

He came over with her coffee, laid it on the desk and gave her a kiss on the cheek.

"No you're certainly much more than that."

She flushed and picked up her cup hurriedly, to cover her confusion. He took pity on her and collecting his own cup, he sat down across the desk from her.

"I think I'd better call Knox and get it over with."

He picked up the desk phone and pressed in the numbers.

"Miss Sharp. DCI Davenport here. Is Mr Knox available? Oh he is, is he? Thank you."

He punched in some more numbers.

"Sheila, Charles Davenport here. Is Mr Fairchild available? ...thanks...Hello Sir, Davenport here. I was expecting to be sum....called up to come to see Mr Knox but his secretary says he's not back yet... Thursday...Yes the case is going along fine. We have two possible suspects...her ex-husband and the new lover but we're also following another trail to an earlier man she mentioned. Yes, Sir, thank you, Sir."

Davenport put the phone back on its rest and sat back, looking pleased.

"We have another few days, Fiona. Knox isn't coming back to work till Thursday. He's taken some leave to visit his son."

"What do you want us to do now, Charles?"

"Will you phone Ben Goodwin and give him the addresses of Sandy Macpherson and David Findlay. Tell him to get out there and do a test on their cars. I'm going to go to the nearest house, the Cook house. See if they have anything else to tell me as they were the nearest house to the murder. The other houses are a bit too far away, I think, though I'll probably check them in case. Don't expect me back till about 4.30 at the earliest. Oh, did you get the restaurant booked for Saturday night?"

"Yes, booked it for 7.30. You and John get there a bit earlier. I'll pretend to be taking her up to your house."

"Yes ma'am."

He gave her a mock salute, picked up his jacket and went out, leaving her laughing.

He had only been gone about twenty minutes when Bob arrived at her open door with a letter in his hand.

"Miss Macdonald. A wee boy came in with this letter. Said a woman paid him to come in with it. It's addressed to, "The Person in Charge of the

Murder." I went outside but there was no sign of any woman."

Bob put the letter down on her desk and waited, looking interested.

"OK thanks, Bob. You'd better get back to the desk."

Looking disappointed, the middle-aged constable left.

Fiona took two latex gloves from a box on her filing cabinet, put them on and picked up the letter. It had already been handled by the messenger and Bob but she could prevent her fingerprints from obscuring even more of the surface of the envelope. She slipped out the single sheet and read:

TO WHOM IT MAY CONCERN.

I SAW A YOUNG PERSON WALKING AWAY FROM THE FACTORY AREA AT AROUND 10 PM WEDNESDAY 15TH JUNE.

It was printed on a computer, she reckoned. This was not much help, as nearly every home and business had at least one computer these days. So there had been someone else at the murder scene. Walking in what direction, she wondered. She got out her file of the reports written up so far and turned to the interviews conducted by Penny, Frank and Salma. There were two youngsters in the Harris household, two boys, Kenny and Craig. The children in the Fenson house were both too young to be described as being a 'young person' and they would hardly be out on their own at night or indeed even during the day. The Cook house had no youngsters; neither did the house with the elderly, deaf couple, Mr and Mrs Smith.

She tried Charles on his mobile but he was unavailable so she left a message telling him what had transpired and saying that she was going up to Keel Estate to talk to the two boys once they came home from school which would be in about three quarters of an hour as long as they were not staying on for any reason.

She was in luck. Kenny arrived home just as she was getting out of her car and when he invited her in, Craig was coming out of the kitchen with a glass of milk and a chocolate biscuit. Mrs Harris was behind him.

"Hello, Mrs Harris. Back from work already?"

"I don't work, Inspector."

"Detective Sergeant but Sergeant will do," said Fiona smiling.

"I'll try get to a job when the boys leave school but not yet. They've had enough upheaval. How can I help you, Sergeant?"

"It's not you I want to speak to. It's Kenny and Craig."

"Come into the sitting room. Can I get you a tea of coffee?"

"No thanks."

They went into a cosy room which was obviously a family room. A Nintendo lay by the side of one chair; a copy of "To Kill a Mockingbird" was on the settee. The TV was showing 'Deal or No Deal'. Mrs Harris moved across the room to switch it off. They all sat down, the two boys on the settee and the two women on the chairs. The boys looked interested.

"Last Wednesday, when the woman was murdered, did either of you go out again after coming in from Parents' Night?"

Was it her imagination or did Kenny look relieved when he said in unison with his young brother, "No, Sergeant."

Feeling that there was something she should be asking Kenny, Fiona wracked her brain and she ventured.

"Have you ever slipped out without Mum knowing?"

Either this was the wrong question or the older boy had had time to prepare himself because once again the reply was in the negative and neither boy looked at all nervous or guilty.

Thanking Frances Harris who looked perplexed, she said only that a youngster had been seen on that night and left. She drove past the Cook house and saw Davenport's car outside. She arrived back at the station at the same time as Salma. They made their way to their own rooms.

About half an hour later, Davenport called from up the corridor:

"Salma?"

"Yes, Sir?"

"Is DS Macdonald back?"

"Yes and Penny just left, Sir."

"Come down to the Incident Room."

Charles knocked on Fiona's door on his way down.

They entered the room to see Frank who had been in the canteen, already seated, with Salma beside him.

"Frank had just started telling me about Sandy Macpherson, Sir, "said Salma.

"Carry on, Frank," said his boss.

"I saw Sandy's immediate boss, the sister on the ward, Sir. He arrived a bit late that night but they were quiet so she didn't say anything to him as he was very seldom late. She thought he was a bit upset but they're not close enough for her to ask him about it."

"Salma, what about Elaine Smith? Was the head teacher any more cooperative?"

"It was a depute I saw, Sir, a very nice woman who looked at the timetable and said she would cover Elaine's second year class while I spoke to her. She took me to Elaine's room and we spoke in the corridor."

"And this younger man? Any more information about him?"

"She said that Moira had laughed and said she had met this nice, young man at the bus stop one evening when she was coming home from a meal at Elaine's house. Elaine thought that the man had got off at the same stop but wasn't sure why she thought that."

"And how did she know that Moira saw this man again, Salma?"

"Moira had told her a few days later that she had met the same man again and he had asked if he could meet her one night, Sir."

"Why did that friendship, if that was all it was, end?"

"She had no idea. Moira looked a bit embarrassed when she asked how it was progressing so she didn't ask again."

"I wonder if this young man could have turned out to be younger than she thought at first. Could he have been humiliated by her in some way and killed her?" mused Davenport.

Fiona recounted receiving the anonymous letter. She handed it to Davenport who read it in silence.

"Another young person. Wonder why this writer thought the figure was young. His size perhaps or his build and why was she so sure the figure was male?"

"Why won't this informant come forward in person, Sir?" asked Salma.

"Someone up there having a bit of rumpy pumpy and either they or the other person's married," volunteered Frank.

"That would be yet another car unless they were in the one that Mr Cook saw driving away from the area between 10 and 10.15," said Davenport. "Right folks, tomorrow I'm going to call Sandy Macpherson in again for questioning about why he was upset. I'll get David Findlay in again too. See if he can produce someone who can confirm what Alison Jones says about Moira being the boss and not the timid, scared little mouse she made herself out to be to Sandy Macpherson."

"Do you want me to tell you what happened when I saw the Harris boys?" asked Fiona.

"Yes. Sorry," said Davenport. "Luckily I decided not to pay them a visit too or they'd have been complaining about police harassment!"

"The two boys said they didn't go back out that night after they arrived home from Kenny's Parents' Night. Kenny seemed relieved that that was what I was asking about but when I asked if they'd ever sneaked out of the house, he answered no quite happily."

"Sir..." Salma began.

"Are you thinking what I'm thinking, Sergeant Din?"

Davenport smiled.

"Could Kenny have been the young man at the bus stop?" Salma said excitedly.

"And Moira found out that he was a school boy after one night out," added Frank. "He would have been very humiliated if she laughed at him. I know I would have been."

"I think that young man will have to be brought in too, with his mother of course," said Davenport.

"Sir, Ben Goodwin said he would get those cars done tonight, when their owners arrived home from work. I told him that Sandy might have a late shift so he got his mobile number from me and will ring him first to check," Fiona told him.

"Thanks. Now, I'd better tell you what I found out. It's very short and sweet. I found out nothing we didn't know already. All they saw that night was the car driving in the opposite direction. I just wish I knew why they always seem on edge, well she does. I don't think she and her husband get on very well so maybe it's just tension between them. She always speaks sharply to him."

Davenport looked at them, a bit wearily, Fiona thought.

"I'll wait here for Penny to return. See if she has anyone else to add when she asked about that brief light in the factory. Get off home, you lot. See you bright and early tomorrow morning."

When they had left, Charles went to his room. He had the start of a migraine, something he had not had for months. He sat down. The zig-zag lines were slicing the white-painted walls of his room and even though he blinked hard he could not dismiss them. He rested his head in his hands and felt the waves of nausea rolling up in his throat. It was as if an orchestra of discordant instruments was tuning up in his brain and a kaleidoscope of black and white lines was showing in front of his eyes as if he was looking through one of those child's toys which presented the viewer with constantly changing patterns. It seemed important to him that he could remember what that toy was called, as if the remembering of it would chase his headache. Suddenly the nausea became more pressing and he got up, holding his head on both sides and lunged for his small toilet where he emptied his stomach into the tiny wash basin.

"Sir, are you OK?"

It was Penny. Charles felt so bad that he did not care that his most junior member of staff was seeing him like this.

"Migraine. Will you call me a taxi? I need to get home."

"I'll take you home, Sir. Are you well enough to give me directions when we get to Mearns Cross?"

"Thanks. Yes."

Even these one-word answers were making his head reverberate with noise. Shakily, he put on his jacket and picked up his keys.

"Sir, what about your daughter? What about Pippa?"

Davenport took out his mobile. He pressed a button and handed the machine to Penny.

"Ask Linda to keep her for the night."

Penny spoke to his sister who showed sympathy and agreed to keep her niece for the night. There was always a spare set of pyjamas and underwear kept in her house and she would deliver her niece to school the next day. Pippa came on the line and told Penny to tell her Dad to remember to pull the curtains and make his room as dark as possible. Penny promised to do this.

By this time they were in the car park and she led her shaken boss to her car. Trying not to hit any potholes or the sleeping policemen in his road, at any speed, she eventually got him home. He unlocked his door and thanked her, going inside stiffly, his head held very still.

"Pull the curtains in your room and just lie down, Sir," she told him.

"I've got some Migrelev, Penny. I'll take that then lie down and thanks. Drive home safely."

She shut the door quietly and went back to her car where she sat and waited till she saw curtains close in an upstairs room. Some hunch made her ring her detective sergeant who said she would go up later and check on him. Another instinct prompted her to keep this piece of information from Frank the next day.

Charles lay on his bed, fully clothed as the storm raged on in his head, forked lightning, followed by a dull thunder, followed by more lightning He tried to make himself relax then a red mist took the place of the sharp, metallic flashes which had been invading his brain. The mist engulfed him and he sank down into it, welcoming its softness.

CHAPTER 33

He listened at his door, putting his ear to the keyhole as he often did. He could not understand what the others were saying when he heard them but he could tell their moods by the way they spoke. He had been sure that he had killed the hated one but just now he was sure he had heard her voice, raised in anger. Back in the past she had always been angry with him but she had not come near him for some time, not since he had clawed at her face. She had been in his room and he had annoyed her in some way - he could not remember now what it was that he had done - and she had shouted at him and he had, for the first time ever, fought back in the only way he knew how, raking his sharp-nailed fingers down both sides of her face. Blood had oozed from the cuts. Her screams had brought the other two. One had led her away, her hands up to her face, and the other had calmed him down, stroking his long hair and making soothing noises. Her blood was under his fingernails and he had liked the smell.

She had never come back after that day but today he had heard her again and realised that she was not dead as he had thought.

He walked over to the window and looked down. The loved one was coming towards the house. He had not seen her for ages, his blonde angel. He made purring sounds in his throat. He had heard the tiger at the zoo make those sounds when it licked its cubs. He would have liked cubs of his own to love and play with. In his earlier life, there had been a small animal. He had loved to play with it and stroke its black fur but one day he had shaken it in fun and he never saw it again until the day before he had killed the hated one. She was walking with the animal and he had raged that he had never been allowed to see it again.

Now he paced his room, waiting eagerly for the loved one to come but she had not come. He had heard the hated one speaking to her then she had left. He watched from the window. She looked up and saw him and blew him a kiss. Clumsily, he had raised his good hand to his mouth and imitated her action then gone to sit at his table where he had cried for a while, rocking himself back and forward in the chair until he had calmed down. He blamed the hated one for not letting the loved one come to him. He would have to kill her again.

He slid to the floor, reached for the decayed finger which was under his bed and curled himself into a ball, stroking his face with his trophy.

He slept.

CHAPTER 34

As soon as she put the phone down on Penny, Fiona rang the station for the phone number of Davenport's sister as she knew that it was kept there in case of emergencies, Linda Davenport being his next of kin.

Once armed with that, she rang Linda and asked if she or Pippa had the key to the house in Newton Mearns. Linda had it, so Fiona told her she would come over for it as she wanted to go up to Mearns to make sure that her boss was OK on his own.

"More than a boss, I think," thought Linda who knew about the holiday arrangements but had not been confided in by her elder brother.

Fiona took a little time to talk to Pippa who seemed to think she was making a fuss over nothing.

"Dad used to have these headaches a lot, Fiona. He'll be alright in the morning."

"I'm sure he will be but I'll just check."

Fiona let herself in with the key and stood in the kitchen listening. There was no sound. Penny had told her that their boss had been making his way upstairs when she left, so after a quick look into the downstairs room and switching on the kettle, she went up. She knew from an earlier stay which room was Pippa's and which the guest bedroom as she had used it once or twice. The door to the only other room was slightly ajar and there was no light coming from it. She switched on the hall light and went into the darkened room.

There was a moan from the bed and she went over and sat on it.

"Charles, it's me, Fiona. How is it now?"

"Hellish but it'll go. I've taken some pills. It's on its red, dull phase."

"Would a hot drink help the pills begin to work?"

"Maybe."

"I'll be back."

Fiona went back down to the kitchen where the kettle had boiled. She made a mug of tea, putting milk in to cool it a bit and returned to the bedroom.

"Just lean on one elbow. Don't sit right up. Sip this," she said.

Charles sipped then drank a little more. He lay back down. She took off his shoes and unloosening his tie, slipped it over his head. Charles sipped some more tea.

"Stay with me, please," he pleaded, handing her the mug and lying back down.

Taking off her shoes, she lay down beside him.

She woke in the night. It was very dark and she debated whether to go into the guest bedroom or stay where she was. Making her mind up, she got up and slipped out of her skirt and blouse, going back to bed, under the duvet.

Charles woke in very faint light. He moved his head carefully. He remembered the dazzling lights and the searing pain in his head. It had been like being in a fairground, stuck on a roller-coaster with people screaming all round him and his head screaming in pain. This was like the calm after the storm. He felt as if he was in a large, padded, warm envelope, sealed off from harm. He moved and felt as if something was keeping him safe and secure. He wanted to stay like this and he closed his eyes, drowsily. Seconds later, he felt wide awake as he realised that the safe feeling was caused by an arm thrown across his chest. He opened his eyes.

Fiona was lying curled beside him, one arm curving over him. Was he dreaming? She muttered something in her sleep and he realised that it was indeed Fiona. He pulled the duvet slightly off her sleeping form and saw that she was wearing only her bra and panties.

Still slightly bemused from his tempestuous night and without reasoning, he stroked one nipple through the bra. It hardened and she turned on her back, making snuffling sounds. He pulled the bra down over one breast and looked at it, longingly, then pulled down the other side. He stared and managed to touch her only with his eyes. Even so, she seemed to sense this mental touch and moaned and wriggled in her sleep.

"Oh, my love. I want you so much," he whispered.

"Me too," came the sleepy reply.

His eyes travelled to her face. Her eyes were half open and hazy with sleep but she smiled at him.

He touched one breast tentatively. The nipple leapt to meet his hand and the untouched one seemed to thrust itself upwards as if longing for a touch. He ran the flat of his hand over it and heard her groan.

"Are you sure, Fiona?"

"Never been more sure, Charles."

He got out of bed, headache gone and took off the rest of his clothes. He saw her eyes looking at him. They travelled from his broad shoulders to his groin.

"Is that all for me?"

"It is my darling, yours and nobody else's."

He got back into bed, throwing back the duvet. She had taken off her bra and lay in only her panties.

"Sorry they're not more sexy," she said. "I wasn't expecting this when I dressed this morning."

"They're coming off anyway," he smiled at her and suiting the action to the word, pulled them down and off.

"I'm not very good at this, Charles, I'm afraid."

"You can only be as good as I am. Just relax and let me take over."

He ran light, little kisses down her chest, stopping to lick each nipple tenderly and knew by the movement of her groin that she was feeling aroused there as well. He felt between her legs. She was wet for him but he was not finished delighting her yet. Touching one nipple lightly, he bent down and began to kiss between her legs. She parted them and he let go her nipple and moved down the bed till his tongue could find her clitoris. His tongue found the little bud which he touched lightly. Moving further down, he flicked his tongue in and out then pushed it in further.

Her hands were in his hair and she arched her back, her legs trembling.

Sensing that she was about to climax, he withdrew quickly, straddled her and in one firm movement entered her, his greedy cock pushing right against the walls of her vagina. She could contain herself no longer.

"Yes, yes, yes...oh, oh."

Her vagina clenched and unclenched and he felt his own climax building up then it was all over and they were lying gasping, him still on top of her and inside her.

"Thank you, thank you so much," she said tremblingly. "I've never felt like that before."

"Never had an orgasm before? What was wrong with your last man?"

"He said it was my fault. He said I was frigid. That's why he left me," Fiona muttered into his shoulder.

"I told you. You're only as good as the man is. It's a selfish lover who can't please his woman."

"He never did any of what you did...you know with your..."

"...my tongue."

"Can I do something like that for you?"

Her naive question made him start to harden again. She put her hand down and felt him.

"Kiss me there, my love. Let me teach you."

She moved down the bed and kissed him gently then some instinct took over and she opened her mouth and took him inside.

He stopped her just in time and this time he lifted her up and let her take him from on top.

They must have slept and the birds' song woke them. Charles looked at his watch. It was 7.20am.

"I think you'd better get off home, my darling and get changed. I'll phone the station and tell them I'll get a taxi in. My car must still be in the station car park."

"Do you feel well enough to come in to work?" she asked, then realised what she had said after what they had done, and made a rueful face.

"Take that as a rhetorical question, my love," she said.

"Yes, Doctor Macdonald. I think you've healed me but I don't think we can patent the cure."

Fiona arrived at work just on time, going up the station steps behind Frank who said, "I must be early if I've beaten you ma'am."

Penny came out of their room.

"Ma'am, any word about the boss?"

Fiona and Charles had agreed on their story.

"I rang him at home, Penny and he's fine after a good night's sleep."

She felt her face redden and moved quickly away up the corridor to her own room.

CHAPTER 35

Davenport arrived a bit late and went straight to his own room, hoping for a chance to speak to Fiona before their working day began. They had only spoken briefly before she left his house. He felt elated by what had happened between them and he hoped that she had no regrets. He took off his suit jacket, hung it over his chair and switched on his percolator which was always kept full of water. It had just started to bubble when Fiona appeared in the doorway.

"Come in and shut the door," he told her.

She did so and he came across the room and put his arms round her.

"How are you feeling, my love?"

"Probably a bit …silly. We were supposed to be remaining just good friends at least until after the holiday. Surely we could have managed that? We leave in just over a fortnight!"

"You're regretting last night then?"

The disappointment in his voice was almost tangible.

"No, I'm not Charles. It was wonderful and so spontaneous that I had no time to get nervous. I wanted you but dreaded being a failure in bed..."

"...which you certainly weren't!"

She blushed and then went on:

You gave me no time to think. I just reacted and my ghosts have been well and truly laid."

"Well and truly laid, just like you. Nice pun!"

She blushed again.

"Why are you feeling silly then?" he asked, curiously, getting up to pour out two coffees.

"Well it's going to be harder for us not to get physical on holiday now and very difficult to be in the same room and not be able even to touch each other so we were silly to give in last night, don't you think?"

"Maybe but I have absolutely no regrets. I'm sure Pippa will be out of the room on occasion and we can make love then as long as we stay very correct when with her."

She laughed: such a carefree sound that his heart sang.

"Can I pay your daughter to stay away, Mr Davenport?"

"Bribery, Miss Macdonald, doesn't befit a detective sergeant. Now if we've settled all that, when can I see you alone again?"

"Greedy!"

"And insatiable as you're going to find out," he replied.

"Well if you can get Pippa to have a sleepover somewhere, you can come back to my flat after the meal out for Jean on Saturday or I could stay at yours if John takes Jean home."

"Excellent! Right, now we'll have to get on with our work. I've a few calls to make then we can all meet."

He took both cups and she rose and went to the door. His phone rang so she closed the door and went off to her own room.

She removed her jacket, took out her notes on the interview with the Harris boys and began typing them up on her computer. When Davenport passed her room, calling out to his team to meet in the Incident Room, she locked her handbag in her filing cabinet and went after him, meeting Penny, Frank and Salma as they came out of their room.

"Ben Goodwin has just rung in with his results from testing the cars of David Findlay and Sandy Macpherson and there was no evidence of bloodstains in either of the cars. Hairs belonging to Moira were found in both cars but David's car is elderly so they will probably have come from when they lived together and she'd been in Sandy's car recently, actually on the night of the murder," Davenport informed them.

"If either of them had been carrying a bloody finger, there would have been bloodstains, so we can probably rule them both out as the murderer," said Fiona.

"Unless whoever it was, threw the finger away outside the field. We'll have to widen the search," replied Davenport.

"Penny, what happened at the factory? I didn't feel well enough to ask you yesterday," he continued.

"Are you OK now, Sir?" Penny asked.

"Yes, I'm fine. All I needed was a good night's sleep."

"That's exactly what you said, wasn't it ma'am?" said Penny.

It was an innocent comment and Fiona, hoping that her face was not going red, replied that that was indeed what she had said.

"Great minds think alike," quipped Frank.

"The factory, Penny," Davenport reminded her.

"I saw a caretaker who mentioned that he had spoken to you, Sir, a Mr Rankin. He said that he went round all floors a couple of times in the evening but unless any room was open, he didn't go in and he certainly didn't switch on any lights in any rooms. The first floor rooms on that side belong to the deputy manager and the manager."

"The manager's away so it couldn't have been him," said Davenport. "I'd better have a word with his depute and I'll go on to see young Mr Harris after that. Fiona, I want you to talk to Sandy Macpherson. Ask him why he was late at work when he said he'd left in time to get there for ten o'clock. Ask him why he was upset when he arrived at work. Treat him like a suspect, try to fluster him. You know the ropes."

"What about David Findlay, Sir?" Fiona asked.

"Salma, I'm entrusting that interview to you. Take Frank in with you to make it look threatening. Mention that Moira said he could be nasty at times and she didn't want him to know about her new boyfriend. Tell him that he has no witness to the fact that he went home. Tell him he could have gone at 9 pm or after that to watch her house that night then followed her and waited till she was walking home before he attacked her. You've watched DS Macdonald and me in the interview room and it's time you had a go on your own."

"OK, Sir. I'll do my best. Can Frank help out if I need him?"

"Of course he can. Now off you all go. Penny if you've got your reports typed up..."

"Not yet, Sir."

"Well, do that then get on with the filing cabinets when you've finished."

Charles arrived at the Keel factory around eleven o'clock. He was greeted warmly by Lisa, wearing a black frilly blouse with nails painted black to match.

"Hello, Mr Davenport! Come to arrest somebody?"

"No, not yet, Lisa. I want to speak to whoever was in charge on the 15th June."

She looked back in her large desk diary.

"Mr Stewart was away in Holland by then, so it would have been Mr McAllister. Will I get him for you or do you want me to take you up to his room?"

Thinking that it might be an idea to see the room from where the light might have flashed briefly, Davenport asked her to take him up. She came round her desk, slipping into a pair of high-heeled black shoes.

"I take these off when I can. They kill my feet," she admitted, with refreshing honesty. They climbed the stairs together, went through a swing door and halfway along the corridor Lisa stopped outside a door which was closed.

"Mr Stewart likes management to keep their doors open so that they are seen to be available to staff," she said, frowning. "Just as well he's still away."

She tapped lightly on the door and a voice bade them, "Come in."

The man who sat behind the desk was in his fifties, had kept his figure and his hair which was mainly grey with some dark streaks. He looked annoyed at being interrupted and said to Lisa that she should have rung him first before bringing anyone up to his room and would she remember that in the future.

Lisa nodded.

"Mr McAllister, this is DCI Davenport," she said and, turning sharply on her high heels, she left the room.

"Please take a seat, Mr Davenport. He pointed to a chair at the window and rising, came to take the other seat there.

"What can I do for you? I heard about the murder. Nasty business."

"We had a report of seeing two lights on in this building on the night of the 17th Sir. One was in your caretaker's room on the ground floor but the other one could only have been in your room or the manager's and I believe he was away then."

"He still is away. But surely the caretaker must have switched a light on in here or next door."

"He says not, Sir. He doesn't go into locked rooms and he says that both were locked that night."

"How can he be so sure?"

The man sounded irritated.

"I can't think of any other reason why the light would be on, unless I left it on."

"No, Sir, this light came on only briefly, according to our eye-witness."

"Who was this? And was this on the night of the murder?"

"No, Sir it was two nights later and it was seen by the woman who found the body. It's a stab in the dark but I thought if someone was present that night then he or she might have been there on the 15th."

"Staff can stay on if they want to. They don't get overtime but they can accrue flexi- time."

"But why would someone be in your room or the manager's, Sir?"

"I have no idea."

The man was plainly becoming angry. Two red spots had appeared on his cheeks.

"Empty factory, Sir, two members of staff having an elicit meeting perhaps?"

It was another stab in the dark, bringing in this theory of Frank's but it was all he could think of.

"Very unlikely and they don't have keys, Inspector. They could hardly get one of the caretakers to let them in, could they?"

He said this sneeringly.

At this moment, his door burst open and Jackie Hobbs came in, in a hurry. Davenport noted the tight skirt and thought that she was not wearing a bra.

"Ian I...oh sorry, you're busy, I'll come back later."

"If it's urgent, Ms Hobbs, go ahead. I can wait," said Davenport, smiling at her.

"No, no rush," she said and went back out.

"Attractive young woman. Seemed to be in quite a rush, I thought."

Davenport thought the man looked annoyed.

"Jackie's always in a rush."

McAllister wiped the palm of one hand down his trouser leg.

"I see you all call each other by your first names. Very enlightened," Davenport commented.

"Yes, one of the manager's policies," McAllister explained. "Is there anything else I can help you with, Inspector?"

"You haven't really helped me at all, Sir. You can think of no one who might have been very briefly in your room or your boss's on that Friday night and maybe other nights?"

"No, I can't. Now is that all, Inspector?"

"Yes thanks. Don't bother to see me out. I know where to go."

Davenport went back downstairs. Lisa smiled at him again.

"Lisa. I noticed that you called the deputy manager Mr McAllister. Does the factory not follow the modern policy of first names for everyone?"

"Gosh, no. The only people I call by their first names are Jackie and the two caretakers, Eddie and Bill."

"What about Jackie and the manager?"

"She calls him Mr Stewart."

"Thanks, Lisa. Would you call Jackie for me, please. Ask her to come down here."

Lisa got on the phone and asked Jackie to come down to the foyer. When she arrived, she looked harassed and spoke sharply.

"I hope this won't take long. I'm very busy."

"Yes, sorry. Did you manage to see Mr McAllister after I left him?"

"No."

"Well, I'll not keep you long. Is there somewhere we can talk in private?"

Jackie went to the caretaker's room and opened the door. It was empty. They went in.

"Now, Jackie. You seem to be very friendly with Mr McAllister. You called him Ian and Lisa tells me that first names aren't the policy here."

"Yes, we're friendly. No crime in that is there?" she asked defiantly.

"How friendly?"

There was a silence.

"Friendly enough to arrange to meet him in his room some evenings?"

She had a trapped look. Her eyes were wide, like a rabbit's caught in headlights.

"How do you mean?"

"I think it's quite simple, what I mean. Were you having an affair with Ian McAllister and did you meet him in the factory on occasions, in the evening?"

"What makes you think that?"

It was the guilty person's response, answering a question with another question.

"I think you met him here on the night of the murder. I think you saw someone out there and sent us an anonymous letter telling us."

Her shoulders slumped and her pert breasts seemed to lose their firmness too.

"Does Ian have to know all this?"

"I'm afraid so, Jackie. He lied to me and that's not acceptable in a murder case. Now, tell me what happened."

"We met here for the first time on that Wednesday. Ian had his key and we came in by the back door and went up the stairs. It was dull in his room but we didn't put the light on."

"Not at all?"

"I think he switched it on briefly as we were leaving. Maybe to check that nothing had been left for the cleaners to find. I can't remember."

"And you saw someone outside?"

"Yes, just as we got to my car, I saw a young person going towards Floors Road."

"How do you know the person was young?"

"Well, he was small."

"Why do you say he?"

"It was a well-built figure and I just assumed it was a boy."

"Where was your car parked?"

"About halfway between Floors Road and the factory."

"Thank you, Jackie. You did send the anonymous letter, didn't you?"

"Yes. I thought you ought to know. Ian...Mr McAllister was scared his wife would get to know if I told you."

"I can't promise that she won't find out if this comes to court but she might not," said Davenport. "And remember, don't ever keep anything back from the police again," he added.

They left the room and Jackie went back upstairs. Davenport waited, talking to Lisa to give her time to get to McAllister's room, then he made his way back upstairs. Sure enough, the door was open and he heard her say, "I'm sorry, Ian. I couldn't help it. He seemed to know about us because we called each other by our first names."

"Stupid little fool," the man hissed at her. "He was probably just guessing and you fell for it."

Davenport walked in.

"No Sir, not stupid, just honest as you should have been. It was you who was stupid, thinking that we wouldn't find out. Now, tell the truth please."

Jackie slipped out of the room.

The man slumped back in his seat, all his former arrogance snuffed out.

"OK I met Jackie here twice. Once, on the night of the murder and once two nights later. The first night, Jackie rang and said I was needed at the factory, a break-in or something. I can't remember now. The second night my wife went out to her bridge night and the kids were having a sleepover."

"Tell me about this person Jackie says you saw on the Wednesday night."

"It looked like a child. Probably a youngster taking a short cut home."

"Male or female?"

"Male I think."

"Thank you, Sir. As I said to Jackie, you might be lucky. Your wife might not get to hear about this but I can't promise anything. Not that you deserve to be lucky for lying to the police in a murder case."

Davenport did not mention the anonymous letter. The man's ardour for Jackie had probably been cooled anyway without him knowing that. He hoped so, not liking to think of the young girl with this middle-aged man.

He ran lightly down the stairs. One mystery had been solved.

CHAPTER 36

It took Davenport only a few minutes to reach the Harris house. As he had expected neither of the boys was at home, this being a school day. Frances Harris answered the door. She had a yellow duster in her hand and an upright hoover stood in the hall.

"Mrs Harris? DCI Davenport. You've met a couple of my colleagues."

"Yes, Inspector. How can I help you?"

"I suspect that your elder son hasn't been completely honest with us. Don't worry, we don't suspect him of murder but he could help us clear up a few things. Will you bring him down to the station in Govanhill when he gets in from school today, please? Maybe the police setting will convince him of how important it is to be honest with us."

Mrs Harris looked puzzled but agreed to bring Kenny down.

By the time Davenport got back to the station, the interview with Sandy Macpherson was over but

Salma had not yet spoken to David Findlay who had promised to come up after school. The three young ones and Fiona had been to the canteen as they were sitting with plastic cups of coffee and tea.

Davenport told them about getting to the bottom of the anonymous letter and about how the figure seen had probably been a child, a boy, who had been heading towards Floors Road.

"I've asked Mrs Harris to bring Kenny in after school. I think, Salma, that you and Frank should take him on and *I'll* do David Findlay. Kenny will probably be easier to frighten, especially with two of you there. His mother will have to stay in the room too but she seems a sensible woman so I don't think she'll give you any trouble."

Salma looked relieved to be getting an easier person to interview.

"Thanks, Sir, I know that I...and Frank, need to have practice of this sort of thing for our cvs but I admit I'm glad to be questioning a younger person."

Frank shot her a grateful look for including him and she smiled back at him. Davenport saw Penny smile too. She was probably glad that her two colleagues were getting on well. Either that or she was just glad to be getting a break from her sorting of the filing cabinets.

Bob appeared in the doorway of the Incident Room.

"Sir. There's been another call from Mr Knox. He wants to see you right away. I said you were back. Hope that's OK, Sir."

"Oh, Sir, he called just after you left and Bob asked me to let you know." Fiona was apologetic.

"Other things on your mind, DS Macdonald?" enquired Davenport, turning to her so that the others could not see the twinkle in his eye.

"Yes, Sir. I was thinking of my interview with Mr Macpherson. Will I tell you about it now or do you want to wait till after your meeting with Mr Knox… Sir."

She smiled sweetly at him, apparently enjoying reminding him of the fact that he had to see the man he called the Knox lion.

He turned back.

"Meet here after lunch, team. I'd better get off upstairs."

A few days away had not mellowed Knox and he seemed to expect that the case would have been solved while he was away.

"Fairchild informs me that you haven't wrapped this murder up yet, Davenport."

Feeling on a high, with his head clear and his heart happy, Davenport risked a joke.

"When the cat's away, Sir."

Knox glared at him, the veins standing out in his forehead.

"So you've been slacking man?"

"It was a joke, Sir."

"There's no time for jokes, Davenport. Good God man, the public deserves better than this. They pay their taxes and expect results."

"We're interviewing two possible suspects this afternoon, Sir."

This was stretching the truth a little. Davenport thought it better not to mention that one suspect had already been seen as he did not yet know the outcome, though he knew that Fiona would have told him if Sandy Macpherson had caved in and confessed to the murder.

"At least there have been no more murders *this time*," said Knox slightly pacified.

"Yes, I don't think we've got a serial killed on our hands," quipped Davenport.

"God man, are you on something? Why are you treating this case so light-heartedly?"

Knox was turning slightly purple and Davenport wondered what would happen if he said, "because I've just made fabulous love to my DS."

"Sorry, Sir. I had a bad migraine last night and I think I'm feeling a bit lightheaded now that it's gone."

"Well, I'll be keeping a strict eye on things from now on, Davenport. Fairchild doesn't think I need to talk to the press at this juncture but I want to be able to give them some good news at the beginning of next week. Now get on with it!"

"Yes, Sir."

Davenport managed not to salute and got himself out of the room, grinning inanely. Solomon Fairchild was coming out of his room.

"Headache better, Charles?"

Really, the man must have a crystal ball, thought Davenport, then caught himself hoping that the said crystal ball had been in its box last night.

"Yes, Sir, thank you."

"You didn't want the press involved right now, did you?"

"No I didn't, thank you. Just hope we get a lead soon."

"I'm sure you will. You have a good record for murder cases, Charles."

It was a pleased Davenport who met his team after lunch.

Fiona told them that Sandy Macpherson had explained his late arrival at the Victoria, telling her that he had had a puncture in Cathcart Road. He had managed to sort it himself but when his superior had not asked him to explain his lateness, he had not offered an explanation. He had only been fifteen minutes late and had a record for punctuality. Asked if he could prove what had happened, he said he had gone into an off licence to see if he could borrow a hammer to hit a stiff nut with so this alibi would seem to be watertight. He also had the offending tyre in his boot.

"I asked him why he appeared to be upset, Sir. Apparently he and Moira had had a bit of an argument. She wanted him to come to her school's end of term dance and he still wanted to keep their relationship secret. He told me that he hated arguments even though Moira had eventually agreed with him."

At four o'clock, David Findlay arrived. Davenport took him into an interview room complete with tape recording machine. After the usual preliminaries, he looked sternly into Findlay's eyes and began his spiel.

"We've heard from Moira's new man friend that she was quite scared of you finding out that she was seeing someone. Apparently you could be a bit intimidating towards her at times."

"Mr Davenport, I've already said that Moira seemed delighted to be able to tell me that she had a new friend. Ask Ali. She saw us both together a number of times. She'll tell you that Moira was the boss, not me."

"So you say, Mr Findlay. I put it to you that after meeting your friend for drinks you went up to Riverside Road, around 9pm. Perhaps you wanted to confront her with seeing this man friend. She was just leaving, so you followed her, hoping to catch her with Mr Macpherson. You followed her to Floors Road, saw her get into his car and when the windows got steamed up, you got jealous and when she started walking home, you followed her into the estate and killed her."

"I didn't, I didn't! I couldn't kill anything, let alone a person."

"You have no witness to the fact that you went back to your parents' home. Your father was in bed and your mother out till later. Isn't that right?"

"Yes, that's right but I didn't go back out and I didn't kill Moira."

"That's your story, Mr Findlay. You must have hated her for getting sterilised yet stringing you along about getting pregnant at some time in the future and wasting your time to be a father."

"Yes, I did hate her at the time I found out but surely if I'd been going to kill her, I'd have done it sooner?"

"Then you'd have had no alibi, would you?"

"I don't seem to have one now, Sir," the man said ruefully.

"Can you give me the name of anyone else apart from Alison Jones who can vouch for your relationship with your ex-wife?"

"Any of the staff in the science department at Greystone, I imagine. We had a few arguments there and I usually lost."

Davenport found himself reluctantly believing the man. He rose from his seat and switched off the recorder, after informing the machine that the interview had ended.

"Right, Mr Findlay, that's all for now. Just make sure you stay in Glasgow, Sir."

David Findlay rose too and, looking relieved, followed Davenport to the outside door. He stood back to let a woman and young man enter and then ran down the steps to his car which he had parked in the station car park.

Davenport welcomed the newcomers.

"Mrs Harris. Kenny. Come along, I'll show you into an interview room and get Sergeant Din and PC Selby who'll be conducting the interview."

He saw the young lad's face lose the little colour it had when he was shown into the spartan room, easily recognisable after so many TV crime programmes.

"Mrs Harris, you can sit beside Kenny but please don't interrupt. You're only being allowed to be present because Kenny is a minor."

The two sat down and Davenport left.

When Salma and Frank entered, there was no sound in the room. Trying to appear confident, Salma switched on the recorder. She and Frank sat down across from the Harrises.

"Sergeant Salma Din with PC Frank Selby in attendance. Also here, Mrs Frances Harris and her son, Kenneth Harris. The time is 4.27pm, Thursday 30th June. Now, Kenneth, I think you've lied to us about never sneaking out of the house.

I think you met Moira Findlay one night at the bus stop when you were coming home from either your friend's house or from the Boys' Brigade. You got talking. Maybe not the first time but another time when you met her again, you asked her to meet you somewhere. You either sneaked out of the house or your mother was out. You can tell me how it happened. Which was it?"

Salma leaned forward in her chair and Frank stared in as threatening a manner as he could muster at the young man who was clenching and unclenching his hands.

"Well, Kenneth?" Salma said. "I'm waiting."

"I didn't sneak out. That was true. Honest, Mum, it was true."

He turned pleadingly to his mother as if asking her to believe him.

"I believe you, Kenny but it's these people you have to convince."

"Mum went out somewhere, way back in April. She left me to look after Craig. I'd met Moira a couple of times on the bus from Eaglesham. I'd been at my friend's house both times. The second time she'd been drinking, I think, and we stood in the bus stop in the village and she sat with me on the bus. Just before we got off, she...she..."

"She what, Kenneth?" asked Frank.

"She felt my knee, Sir."

"Yes and...?"

"We stood and talked when we got off the bus and I...kissed her. She seemed to like it. I knew that Mum was going out the next night. I asked if I could meet her. She said yes."

"So you met and what happened?"

"We met round the back of the factory. She let me touch her...breasts and she touched me."

The boy was scarlet by this time and almost in tears.

Frank could tell that Salma was finding it hard to remain stern with the boy, as her tone was softer when she spoke.

"What happened then?"

"I...I...came...had what was like a wet dream. She laughed. She asked me how old I was and stepped back from me when I told her my age. She said she wasn't a cradle - snatcher and walked off. I let her go. It was so embarrassing. I went home and got changed. I only saw her once again and I went upstairs on the bus to avoid her. I think she was laughing when she saw me. I'm not surprised."

"You must have felt really humiliated?"

"Yes," he mumbled.

"Did you follow her to Floors Road on Wednesday 15th of June, wait and watch her making love in a car, get really jealous and follow her through the estate and kill her?"

The boy looked as if he was about to collapse. His mother put her arm round his thin shoulders. She appeared to be finding it difficult to keep quiet but she said nothing and Salma admired her strength of will.

"Tell the truth, Kenneth. You're a minor. The court would be lenient with you under the circumstances."

The boy sat up straight and squared his shoulders.

"No, Sergeant. I didn't follow her that evening. I was in the house all the time after we got home from school. It was my year's parents' night. Mum and Craig were there. Maybe they don't count as witnesses but I can tell you I never wanted to see her again, let alone follow her. I wanted to forget all about her."

Salma spoke into the tape machine, ending the interview. She and Frank stood up and Mrs Harris followed suit, nudging Kenny to do the same.

"Come on son, let's get you home. I'm proud of you for telling the truth. It wasn't easy, I know."

She smiled at Salma and Frank.

"I don't know about you but I believe my son," she said proudly.

Salma nodded at Frank and he led Mrs Harris and Kenny back to the front door, Salma going off towards their own room to wait for him to arrive before they went to see their boss.

Davenport spoke to them all in the Incident Room. The names of possible suspects were still on the flip chart. When they were all seated, he put a line through the name David Findlay.

"I feel that he's innocent. He didn't argue when I said he had no alibi, in fact he said it himself at the end. It could be a double bluff but my gut is telling me he didn't murder Moira. I'll ask Alison Jones what his relationship was with his ex-wife but she has already told me that Moira was the quick-tempered one."

"Sometimes it's the quiet ones who turn violent, Sir," said Frank.

"True, Selby. I'm not completely ruling him out. Now, Fiona, you said that Sandy Macpherson had an alibi?"

"Yes, I rang the off licence about half an hour ago and they remembered him asking for a hammer to loosen the nut on the wheel of his damaged tyre. Not something they're usually asked for."

"Salma, what about the young man, Kenny Harris?"

"I felt really sorry for him, Sir. It couldn't have been easy for him to be truthful with us but he was, wasn't he Frank?"

"Yes poor sod...sorry, Sir. Moira Findlay did the chasing. She touched him on the bus and agreed to meet him and when he ejaculated on her touching him, she laughed at him, asked his age and walked off."

"He saw her one more time on the bus and he thought she was laughing at him," added Salma.

"And do you think he was so humiliated that he killed her?"

"No. He was out with his Mum and brother on the night of the fifteenth at the school Parents' Night, then they all stayed in and anyway even if he had snapped and killed her, he would never have bitten off her finger, Sir. He's not a psychopath."

"I think that's the crucial point, team," said Davenport.

"Two of the factory workers were in the factory on the 15th. Frank, you were right, two people having sex, one of them married, the other public-spirited enough to send us a letter, albeit anonymous, to let us know of a youngster being in the road that night. They were both sure it was a boy."

He pulled on his left ear. Penny, sitting on Frank's right, felt his arm raise and, turning slightly in her seat, saw that he was pulling his right ear lobe. She nudged him and he brought his arm down. Davenport had noticed nothing and DS Macdonald who was usually sharp, was sitting on Frank's other side and had not seen him either.

Davenport turned to the flip chart again and scored out the name Sandy Macpherson and that of 'young man at bus stop'. He hovered his pencil over the next person which was 'other man before Sandy.'

"I think the young man at bus stop and another man before Sandy are both Kenny Harris."

"I think so too, Sir," said Fiona Macdonald.

"Macpherson, Findlay and Harris - none of them seem the types to bite a finger to keep as a trophy. Agreed?"

"Agreed, Sir," they chorused.

Davenport circled the last item on the list, 'someone who lived nearby'.

"So we're looking for someone who lived nearby, happened to be out that night, either knew Moira Findlay or just came upon her..."

"This young lad who was spotted?" asked Fiona. "The small figure?"

"Kenny is quite tall," said Salma.

"So we're left with someone who had seen her another time and wanted to kill her or someone who had seen her come along, get into Macpherson's car and possibly make love to him, and had waited and killed her. Alison Jones said he would have to be strong as Moira would struggle and was quite strong. Our witness at the factory said the young person she saw was well built," Davenport went on.

"How about someone who though they were ridding the world of loose women?" said Frank.

No one laughed. History was full of psychopaths who thought they were Godlike and killed prostitutes.

"I do hope not, Frank," said Davenport, "but I'm very afraid that you might be right."

"Doesn't fit a young boy really," said Fiona.

"But it would be good if we could find him. He might have seen someone else. It can't have been Craig Harris if the family was altogether that night. Are there any other boys living nearby?"

Silence.

"Right, Penny, will you telephone that woman who gave Moira a lift to school. See if you can find out what she thought the relationship was between Moira and David. I'll phone her aunt. I need to get a date for the funeral from her and I'll see what she says about her niece's attitude towards David. No use asking David's folks. He'll have had time to speak to them. The rest of you get off home."

Penny rang the school, asking to speak to Elaine Smith and when she came to the phone asked about Moira's relationship with her ex-husband, then she decided to try Pauline Lawrie who had met Sandy Macpherson once. She went up to Davenport's room.

"Sir, the woman who gave Moira a lift, said that Moira claimed that she didn't need to drive as David was a pussy-cat and would give her lifts when she wanted them. I tried the woman who met Sandy Macpherson once and she said Moira had made some comment about always falling for gentle guys. She also said that Moira and David had some ding-dong battles in the school and it appeared that Moira always won."

"Yes, I think Moira was trying to get Sandy to feel sorry for her when she said that she was scared of David," agreed Davenport. "Her aunt said that the times she met David, he was very solicitous towards Moira and Moira treated him quite casually, she thought. It fits in with someone who wouldn't tell her husband about her sterilisation, just went ahead and had it without any discussion."

Davenport looked over Penny's shoulder.

"Did you lot get all that? I thought I told you to get off home."

Laughter came from the corridor and Fiona spoke for the others.

"We were curious and anyway it saves you having to repeat it all for our benefit tomorrow."

CHAPTER 37

At first Frances Harris thought that her ex-husband, Edward, was standing on her doorstep on Saturday morning, then he smiled and she realised by the way his nose crinkled slightly that it was his brother, Bob. That had always been the only way she could tell them apart. She smiled back and stood to one side to let him enter. Her lounge was untidy. She had slept in and not had time to clear away last night's carry-out pizza boxes or wash the glasses she and her sons had used. They had played a game of Trivial Pursuit and the open box was still there, on the floor with some coloured pieces lying on the grey carpet.

"Sorry for the mess, Bob," she said, hurrying in before him to remove some of the debris.

"I'm not Edward, Frances. Untidiness doesn't bother me," Bob laughed, removing a pizza box from the settee and sitting down.

"You've never seen my flat, have you?" he added.

Frances stopped tidying and sat down on one of the seats by the gas fire. No need to put on the fire today as it was a beautiful sunny morning, for once.

"I've been meaning to come long before this," Bob said. "How are you and the boys doing?"

"We're managing fine, thanks. We can't afford things like holidays right now but Edward's been quite generous and I got as much furniture as I needed from the house. I haven't got a job yet as I wanted to be in for the boys coming home from school. I didn't want that to change right away. They've had enough upheaval."

"That brother of mine needs his head sorted, giving up what he had with you all…"

"Uncle Bob! Mum, why didn't you call us?"

Craig was tousle-headed and still in his dressing-gown. He went back into the small hall and called to Kenny to come down.

"Kenny, Uncle Bob's here!"

There was the sound of feet running down the stairs and Kenny joined his brother in the lounge. As usual, he looked smart, although unusually for him, dressed in cord trousers and a casual shirt. They sat down, Craig on the settee next to his uncle and Kenny on the other chair across from his mother.

"Well, you two rogues, what have you been up to since I saw you?" Bob asked.

"I've changed school, Uncle Bob," said Craig.

He noticed that his uncle was looking puzzled and went a bit red in the face.

"I'd been a bit of a fool in the last one so Mum suggested I changed and had a new start."

"Do you like the new place?"

Frances smiled. She knew that she would find things out now.

"Yes. The PE teacher's great. He's made me reserve for the second football team."

"And what about the other teachers?"

"Not bad, except one woman, the French teacher. She's hopeless. Can't keep us in order at all. It's OK Mum. I'm not one of the troublemakers."

He smiled at his mother.

"Any friends yet?" asked his uncle.

"A couple of boys in the same year seem quite nice but I'm not rushing in to make friends yet. At least I haven't met any bullies."

He had noticed his mother looking worried at the mention of the French teacher.

"I'm being good in all my classes, Mum. Honest."

"What about you, Ken?" Bob asked the older boy.

"Kenny's been interviewed by the police," said Craig, excitedly. "He knew the woman who was murdered here a few weeks ago."

"Murdered? Near here?"

Bob looked questioningly at his sister-in-law.

"Yes, in the estate, nearer the other end. Didn't you read about it, Bob?"

"I've been away, in Singapore. I only got back last Monday. How did you know the woman, Ken?"

Kenny, looking a bit sheepish, told the story.

"She doesn't sound a very nice woman, old son. Never mind, you'll meet someone nice one day, someone nearer your own age. No rush. Now, what I came for was to see if you'd all like to come to East Kilbride with me. Thought we could do some ice-skating and some shopping and have lunch if you haven't planned anything else."

"That'd be great," both boys chorused.

"It'll give me the chance to get this place cleared up," said Frances.

"Oh, no you don't. You're coming too. You like to skate, or at least you did when I first knew you."

"Oh Bob, that was about twenty years ago," Frances laughed.

"Doesn't matter. It's like riding a bicycle. You never forget how."

"Come on, Mum, it'll be fun," said Craig.

"OK, OK. You go up and get washed and dressed. I'll give your uncle a coffee while we wait."

Craig shot out of the room and Kenny left too, going back upstairs more sedately than his brother.

"Are you really doing alright, Fran?"

He had always shortened her name, even back in the 1980s when she had met him and his brother.

"Edward was never easy to live with, Bob. He was so critical of me, how I kept the house, how I dressed, the TV programmes I watched, the fact that I read the Daily Record, things like that and there were other women ...but he's your brother. You won't want to listen to me complaining about him."

"Don't worry. I noticed what he did, how he treated you. So does that mean that you aren't too upset by his leaving you?"

"Well it was me who put him out, took him to the other woman this time, so it wasn't unexpected. I imagine everyone else got a shock: the correct, stuffy, Edward Harris having an affair! We kept the other ones quiet when he promised not to do it again."

"Who was she this time? I've never really spoken to him since the split."

"A woman at work. Believe it or not, she's older than me. I've met her a couple of times at works' dances and when I picked Jim up a couple of times. I'd have said a real spinster, though you're not allowed to use that word these days."

"What was the attraction do you think?"

"Well she was always neat and tidy when I saw her. Hair perfect. I can't imagine her in these."

Frances pointed to her denims.

"I never dared to buy these when Edward was here."

"I think they suit you, Fran. You've got the figure for them."

Frances blushed.

"Are you two divorced now?"

"Yes. I'm a free agent again."

At that moment Craig and Kenny arrived back downstairs. Frances checked that everything was off in the kitchen and then grabbed her handbag.

They had a great time in the shopping centre at East Kilbride, skating first and laughing a lot as Bob fell about the rink then settled for watching the rest of them. Frances found her old skill coming back after her first circuit of the rink and enjoyed the carefree feeling it gave her.

"Lunch first, guys?" enquired Bob when they came off the ice, laughing and exhausted.

They made their way to Macdonalds, Craig having suggested this and no one else having a different idea. Bob, helped by Kenny, went for their food and they wolfed in, Frances thinking that Edward would never have put a foot inside Macdonalds. What she had said to Bob was true. He had been a control freak and she didn't miss him, apart from financially.

Eating over, they made for the shops. Frances had been unsure of this part of the afternoon. She expected the boys to want things and she could not afford anything, except necessities but she had reckoned without Bob.

"Right you two. Here's some money. Off you go and spend it on whatever you want."

Craig's eyes shone. He took the money and shot off. Kenny looked at his mother.

"Mum, is there anything I could get that would help you out?"

"No, love. I can afford the necessary things. Do what your uncle said and just enjoy spending it. You can count it as him making up for the times he forgot your birthday!"

Kenny sped after his brother.

"Did I? Forget their birthdays, I mean?"

"I was only trying to make him feel better, Bob. He's too sensitive at times. Yet funnily enough he's the one who still sees Edward and it's Craig who has refused to see him. Craig doesn't want to be a doctor any more. Says his dad made a fool of himself over the nurses. It seems that one of the boys in his last school had been told by his father who works in the same hospital."

Bob looked down at the floor.

"You knew about him too, didn't you, Bob?" she said quietly.

"Yes, Fran, I did. I chinned him about it too. Told him what an idiot he was. It was so odd for someone like him, with his high standards, to play the field as he did."

They sat silently for a while, a companionable silence, then Bob got up to get them both a coffee.

"I always envied Edward," he said, toying with his cardboard cup.

"Envied him? Why? You've got a good job too, lovely car, holidays abroad..."

"He had you, Fran. Did you never wonder why I never married?"

Fran, head to one side, looked at him quizzically.

"I just thought you were a confirmed bachelor. You never said anything all those years ago."

"Would it have made any difference?"

"I nearly called the wedding off, you know," Frances's eyes were misty.

"Why?"

"Edward showed me his not-so-nice side when he decided on the reception venue without consulting my parents and booked the honeymoon without asking me. And..."

"And what?

"I had begun to think I'd chosen the wrong Harris."

Bob picked up one of her hands and held it tightly.

"Are you saying that you had feelings for me, Fran?"

"I am, brother-in-law."

"Ex brother-in-law. Why on earth didn't you tell me?"

"You made yourself scarce every time I came to your folks' house. I hardly saw you from the time we got engaged."

"I couldn't bear to see you with my brother."

He looked down at the hand he held.

"I see you don't wear your wedding and engagement rings anymore."

Bob lifted her left hand and tenderly stroked her ring finger.

"Neither was my choice, Bob. I've never liked them and now they mean even less."

An excited Craig ran into the restaurant. He was carrying three bags. He sat down beside his Mum and delved into one of them, pulling out a red tee-shirt with "You're the Best" written in dark blue letters.

"Mum, this is for you. It'll go with your denims. Doesn't she look smashing in them, Uncle Bob?"

"She does, Craig," Bob said quietly. "What else did you buy?"

"I bought a couple of nintendo games and a pair of trainers. That'll save you some money, Mum. My others are ready for the bin."

Kenny walked in, more sedately, as usual. He too had three bags. He had bought his mother a silver chain with a little silver dog on it."

"Know you'd have liked a dog, Mum. Will this one do?"

Choked by the thoughtfulness of both her sons, Frances could only murmur a thank you.

"What else did you get, Kenny?"

Craig was keen to know. He put his hand into one of the bags. His brother slapped him good-naturedly.

"Hands off. I bought myself some denims. I thought I was getting too like Dad, always wanting to be neat and tidy," he grinned. "And a pair of trainers to go with them. Remember when you asked for a pair, Craig and Dad almost went ballistic? He said they were common and he was furious with Mum when she bought you a pair."

"I remember," said his mother and brother at the same time and they all laughed.

When they got home, Frances invited Bob in for a snack meal and he agreed, saying that it would be a lovely way to round off his day with them.

The boys went upstairs to put away their purchases and Frances confided in Bob that she had been worried that Kenny was going to be like Edward who, in her opinion, always took too much pride in his appearance.

Bob came to sit beside her on the settee. He took one of her hands in his.

"Is it too soon after the divorce for me to ask if you'd consider going out with another Harris?" he asked her.

"No, Bob it's not too soon and you might be another Harris but there the similarity ends, I'm sure."

"Yeuch, Mum. Put him down," said her younger son coming into the room to find his mother and uncle in a warm embrace.

They looked up at him and grinned and he grinned back. She did not need to ask if he minded as his reaction had told her he did not.

"I caught these two old codgers kissing," he informed his brother when he came downstairs.

"So, they're both over eighteen," replied his brother, "but I'm afraid I'll have to ask if your intentions are honourable, Sir," he said to Bob.

The rest of the evening passed happily.

CHAPTER 38

Knox would be sending for him on Monday, thought Charles as he shaved on Saturday morning. Should he have brought his team in today, he wondered. He had been in touch with Ben Goodwin on Friday and asked him to institute a wider search for the missing finger but he would not hear from him at least until Tuesday and it had seemed pointless to make his team miss their weekend as they had had no further leads to follow up. Nevertheless, the chief constable would want to know why they had not been working all out even at weekends to get this case solved. He sighed and Pippa, coming in behind him, asked him what was wrong.

"It's OK for you young lady. You've got six weeks of holiday ahead of you but your poor old Dad's got a murder to solve before he can relax."

"Will our holiday have to be cancelled if you haven't found the person who did it in time?" Pippa asked, an anxious look on her face.

Charles had always tried to be honest with his daughter and he was now.

"I'm afraid so, pet but I really hope to have it all sewn up in plenty of time," he said, smiling and trying to look confident.

Pippa looked happier.

"Dad have you finished shaving yet? Mr Ewing 'll be here for me soon."

"You should have thought of that when you turned over and went back to sleep when I called you," laughed Charles, then, taking pity on her, he wiped foam from his chin and moved out of the bathroom.

Downstairs, he put some bread in the toaster and poured out two bowls of cornflakes. He had tried Special K for a few days but found it tasteless and decided that it would be more worthwhile to cut down his wine and chocolate intake to help him lose weight. At Weightwatchers this week, he had only lost one pound and had to put up with Fiona's crowing over her three pound loss. Having never met the woman who had reported Moira Findlay's murder, he had not known that the friendly woman he had spoken to before and whom he had smiled at again on Thursday, was involved in their case. Fiona had smiled at her too, also not knowing her. She had accused Charles of flirting with the woman, telling him that men were all the same. Once they had got their way with one woman, they moved on to the next. She had made a mock swipe at him and he had sent her a wolfish look and told her he had eyes for no one else.

Pippa arrived in the kitchen, carrying her trainers and crash helmet. Hazel's father had promised that they could ride their bikes this afternoon. He would put Pippa's fold-away bicycle in his capacious boot and take her and it down to Newlands. He and his wife, Sally, were not going away on holiday with Hazel until next Saturday and Hazel had asked if Pippa could stay the whole weekend with her as they would not see each other for about four weeks. This fitted in with Charles and Fiona's plans for Jean Hope's birthday so he had readily agreed.

"Have you packed a bag, Pippa?"

He wondered if he expected too much from his young daughter, being aware that her mother might have done this sort of packing for her but he need not have worried.

"Of course I have, Dad. I've started packing for our big holiday already. Do you want me to do yours?"

"Thanks love but I'll manage for myself. Now do you want more toast?"

She had scoffed her cereal and one slice of toast and marmalade. He always had two jars of marmalade as he preferred lime and she liked shredless orange. He wondered what they would get in the Far East for breakfast.

"I wonder what kind of breakfast we'll get in the hotel?"

"Maybe it'll be rice and stuff," volunteered Pippa.

"Surely they'll cater for all tastes," her Dad replied.

"Well, it's an expensive place isn't it?" said his daughter who had heard him and Fiona discussing finances one evening.

"Yes. I'll have another slice of toast please."

She was sitting waiting in the lounge, reading her latest Chalet School book which she was taking with her in case she had a chance to read during the weekend, when the Ewing car pulled up in the street outside. Hazel got out and ran up the path. Charles opened the door before she could knock and laughed, as she almost fell into the hall.

"Whoa, Hazel. Slow down. It's only a few hours since you saw each other!"

"But I've got so much to tell Pippa, Mr Davenport. Mum wouldn't let me phone last night. She said I could just wait till today."

"Here I am. What is it?" asked her friend and the two went back down the path, talking excitedly.

Ralph Ewing had passed them on the path. He and Charles grinned at each other.

"I think she'll be telling Pippa that I've suggested that we have a few days' camping in the week before school starts back and that we invite Pippa to come along too."

"That would be great, Ralph. It'll save me having to get my sister to look after her for me when we get back. Thanks."

"Right, that's settled then. Now, I'll bring Pippa back early afternoon on Sunday if that's OK. Hazel said that she wanted Pippa to come to church with us on Sunday. Is that OK?"

"Fine. But why the sudden invitation?"

"Oh, Hazel's given up Sunday school. She says she's big enough to sit through church and seemingly Pippa asked if she could try it too. She said she was going to try Sunday school one Sunday with Kathy. I'd better get off. See you tomorrow."

Charles weeded in his back garden, then sat outside and tried his Guardian crossword which was always difficult on a Saturday. Eventually, stuck for three clues and needing his Chambers dictionary, he put the garden seat away and went indoors. He finished the crossword and sat for a while musing about his daughter's sudden interest in religion. She would probably meet people from other religions on holiday which would be good for her too.

At six o'clock, he went for a shower and changed into his best suit which was pale grey, a lemon shirt and a grey tie. He rang Fiona who had just showered and was putting on some make-up.

"When is the table booked for, Fiona? Is it 7.30 or 8?"

"7.30pm, Charles. Remember we said we could play bridge at yours after the meal so I said I would book the table for the earlier time. Also I think older people prefer to eat early."

"I meant to ask you, how do you know Jean won't have already eaten?"

"I said that you were giving us a big supper tonight, since it was her birthday."

Fiona picked Jean up at about 7.15, the usual time for their bridge night.

They travelled in a companionable silence, neither being a chatterer, until they reached the traffic lights at the new Morrisons, then Fiona said, "By the way, Jean, happy birthday. What have you done today? Anything special?"

"No, nothing. I'm too old for doing something special on my birthday."

Jean's laughter held a hint of sadness and Fiona pulled away from the lights before saying that people were never too old for birthdays. At this point she was indicating left and Jean asked where they were going.

"For a special birthday meal," replied Fiona, parking the car and getting out to open the passenger door.

"What have you done?" Jean asked, tremulously.

Taking her friend's arm, Fiona led her into Andiamo's where John and Charles were waiting in the foyer. Fiona whispered to Charles that she had to get some money out of the atm machine and slipped out to the Clydesdale Bank next door. When she returned, the others were seated at their table. Fiona handed her jacket to a waiter and slid into the empty seat.

"Now, Jean, this is our treat and you've to choose absolutely anything. Try not to look at the prices," said Charles, as a waiter brought a bottle of champagne and uncorked it with a loud pop and a small avalanche of bubbles. They toasted Jean, the three of them standing and her sitting, flushed with embarrassment, as other diners joined in the singing of, 'Happy Birthday To You'.

Fiona had ordered a cake and this arrived during coffee, laden with candles which Jean managed to blow out in one puff.

"What a lovely meal. Thank you all for the cake and the champagne too."

"Just trying to get you drunk for bridge," said Charles and John pretended to be annoyed at this attempt to get his partner to make mistakes.

"Are we playing bridge too? Have you not all got better things to do on a Saturday evening?" she asked them, looking especially at her partner John who was always out with some girl or other on Saturdays.

"We have the whole evening for you, my darling," John said now. "Were you not at all suspicious when we changed the day to Saturday?"

"No, I wasn't. I just thought that Fiona and Charles must be busy with their present case and couldn't get off on Friday. And as for you...I thought maybe you'd been stood up!"

This last was to John who looked shocked that she could think such a thing. They all laughed.

The waiter brought their coats and John helped Jean on with hers, Charles doing the same for Fiona. It took only ten minutes to get to Charles's house. When they were seated at the card table, John, Charles and Fiona produced a parcel each. John had bought perfume.

"Chosen by my latest girlfriend, Jean, so I hope it's OK.."

"It'll be perfect John, thank you."

Fiona had bought her a gold necklet and Charles a pair of black leather gloves. Jean thanked them both profusely and the rest of the evening was spent in hilarious, if slightly erratic, bridge-playing.

At eleven o'clock, Fiona glanced surreptitiously at her watch and looking across, saw Charles doing the same thing. They caught each other's eyes and grinned. Jean finished scoring and suggested that they call it a night. Charles had spoken to John and asked him to drive his partner home as he and Fiona had things to discuss about their forthcoming holiday. He was not sure that John was convinced, when that young man winked at him and agreed to be chauffeur.

He and Jean left, Jean thanking Fiona and Charles once again for a very special seventieth birthday.

"Alone at last, my love," said Charles. He shut the door then turned to take her in his arms.

CHAPTER 39

"It's time you showed her who's boss, old man," said Dick Fensom. He sat back in his chair, frowning at his brother.

They were sitting in The Quaich in Shawlands having an after-work drink on Monday and, as usual, Brian was feeling torn in two directions. His brother had always been the dominant one in their relationship and since Brian had married Grace, Dick had been even more demanding of his brother's time.

"That's easy for you to say, Dick but you don't have to live with her. She thinks I should help more in the house and with the kids, especially now that she's pregnant again."

"That's women's work, Brian. You work hard all day and you need some time to yourself or with me. Another drink?"

Brian Fensom agreed to have another drink, though he felt guilty. He knew that Grace got tired easily these days and it had been he who had persuaded her to have another baby. He had always been easily led by his brother and felt pulled apart by the two most important people in his life.

"Why have you never married, Dick?" he asked, as another pint was set in front of him.

"Too selfish, I suppose. Seen what happened to you and didn't want it to happen to me."

"Did you never want children?"

"No, never. They take up all your time as far as I can see."

"I love being with my two," Brian said, realising that that was true. He loved being with Karen and Anne.

"You never give Karen anything. Did you realise that?" he asked his brother.

"Anne's my Godchild so I give her things. Why should I give Karen anything?"

"And you never seem to want to spend time with either of them?"

"What on earth would I do with a five year old and a three year old? They're girls. What do I know about what girls want, well girls their age," he said. "I know what older girls want."

He winked at his brother. Brian still looked annoyed.

"My leisure time's precious. Maybe if you have a boy this time, I'll take more interest."

The beers were beginning to make Brian feel a bit argumentative.

"I'm beginning to think that Grace is right. I do spend too much time with you. I should be home right now with my wife and kids. Have you not got any friends?"

"I've got plenty of friends, thank you very much," Dick said, looking annoyed.

Brian rose to his feet as his mobile rang. It was Grace asking him where he was.

"I was having a quick drink with Dick but I'm on my way home now."

"I don't feel so well, Brian. Please don't take too long."

She did not sound angry, just anxious and Brian was worried.

"Well I guess that was wifie, telling you to get home immediately," sneered Dick.

"She's not feeling so well," Brian said defensively.

"So that's her excuse this time, is it? Off you go then, lapdog."

"Well just one more drink," said Brian, wanting to be away but not wanting to be thought to be under the thumb of his wife.

Dick went to the bar, passing a table of younger men who called out to him to come and join them.

"Later, boys. later," his brother called back.

Twenty minutes later Brian was on his way. Dick had joined the group of young men who now had persuaded some girls to join them. Brian drove fast but carefully, not wanting to be pulled over by police with four pints inside him. As he drew up outside his home, he noticed that the front door was open and, as he approached it, he was met by his neighbour, Frances Harris. She was carrying Karen who was sobbing loudly and Anne was holding onto her skirt.

"Frances, what's up?"

He took his crying daughter from his neighbour and, ruffling Anne's hair, took her hand.

"I'm afraid Grace's been taken into hospital, Brian. She rang me saying that she was in pain and I rang for an ambulance. They've just left."

Cursing his brother, but knowing that it was his own fault for not standing up to him, Brian gave Karen back to Frances.

"You stay with Mrs Harris, pet and help her look after Karen," he said to Anne who nodded.

"I'd better get to the hospital. Which one?"

"They're taking her to Hairmyres. Don't worry about these two. Now that I've seen you, I'll take them home with me and Kenny and Craig will entertain them."

Brian sped off. He reached the hospital in ten minutes and went to the maternity block.

"I'm looking for Mrs Grace Fensom," he said to the nurse at the desk.

"The doctor is seeing her now, Sir. Please sit down."

After what seemed an eternity, a white-coated young man approached Brian.

"Mr Fensom?"

"Yes. How's my wife?"

"She'll be OK, Sir but she's lost her babies I'm afraid. You can see her now but don't stay long. She's exhausted."

"Babies, doctor? Was she having twins?"

"Yes, Sir, she was."

Feeling as if he'd been punched by a heavyweight boxer, Brian approached the bed where his wife lay.

"Grace. I'm so sorry. How are you?"

"We've lost twins, Brian."

His wife's voice was the merest whisper.

"I should have helped you more. I've been so selfish. I know it's too late to undo what's happened but I promise to have my priorities right from now on."

The anguish in Brian's voice was heartfelt. Grace put out her hand and touched his where it was resting on the sheets. He started to cry.

"Can you find out what the babies were? I need to know, Brian," she said.

Wiping the tears from his eyes, Brian rose from the bedside. He came back minutes later.

"Two boys," was all that he said.

CHAPTER 40

Gorilla-like, he swung from his den to a tree. He had watched patiently from his window for some evenings and today he had proved to himself that the hated one was back again. He could see her walking towards him in the distance with the four-legged creature, the black-haired one which she never let him see any more. It had some white in its fur this time, he noticed.

Lion-like he roared. He was sure that he had killed her. He clenched and unclenched his huge hands, then dropped down from his branch. She came up towards where he waited and, keeping in to the side of the road, among the bushes, he followed her. There was no smell from her this time which was unusual. The small black and white creature looked round and growled. The hated one, pushing back black hair from her forehead also turned.

"Kyle. What is it? Come on, there's nothing there."

He heard the sounds but he never could understand the noises humans made.

In the zoo, he had seen the snakes. Now he went down to the ground and, pulling himself along the ground, he slithered clumsily after them both. This way of moving slowed him up and when he got to his feet again, they had put some distance between themselves and him. He hissed in annoyance and once again the small creature looked round, straining on his leash and growling deep in its throat. The hated one sounded scared this time as she tugged on the leash and the creature went with her. He wanted to stroke his friend and was puzzled that it should make sounds that showed it was scared.

His animal instinct told him that he had missed his chance and he flung himself back to the ground and, hissing angrily, made his way back to his tree. At the foot of the tree, he stayed prone on the ground. Time passed and he lay still till a small creature approached. He shot out a hand and grabbed it. One large paw crushed the creature and he heard an outrush of breath as it died. It was the work of minutes to bite off the four small feet. He could carry only two in his one, good hand as he climbed his tree.

Back in his den, he licked the two feet clean and put them under his bed with the skeleton of the finger. He felt good again but he knew instinctively that this feeling would not last. He had to kill the hated one again, so he would watch and wait.

The woman with the dog did not stop till she reached her house. She had seen nothing but had felt frightened in the estate. She wondered whether or not to tell the police.

CHAPTER 41

The windscreen wipers swept their arcs across his car window, sounding their repetitive swish and almost hypnotising him with their monotonous noise and motion. Davenport was on his way to the funeral of Moira Findlay. It had been some time since he had attended a burial and he decided that it always rained on these occasions. His migraine had gone but he feared that this heavy day and the noise of the wipers might start it up again. He was early so he pulled into a bus layby and, switching off his engine, lay back and closed his eyes.

The horn blast shot him awake and he saw in his rear mirror that an angry bus driver was flashing his lights at this purloiner of his space. He switched on his engine and, waving apologetically, pulled out into the road. He glanced at his watch and was relieved to see that he still had time to reach Linn Cemetery.

It was unusual to be turning left instead of right at the roundabout leading to both cemetery and crematorium. He saw in the distance, a cortege, and picked up speed to catch it up. The little procession wound through the cemetery in the drizzling rain, the cars' headlights looking in the gloom like the lanterns of smugglers lighting the way back to the caves in the early light of a sea-misty morning.

The front car came to a halt, the others backing up behind it. A black-suited man got out of the front car and another joined him from the passenger side. They opened the back of the hearse and began to ease out the coffin with its wreath of white flowers on top.

The back door of the second car opened and an elderly woman got out. Her white hair showed her years but she was agile enough and stood waiting for the coffin to be taken to the freshly-dug plot. Davenport knew who she was and was more interested in the other mourners as he always believed that the killer attended the funeral. They had in his last four cases.

Other cars gave up their passengers, about ten in all. Davenport recognised Alison Jones and David Findlay who had come together, along with an elderly man and woman who were presumably Moira's ex-in-laws. Another group he assumed to be from Greystone Academy, two men and two women. Two other men stood alone and Davenport recognised Sandy Macpherson as being the younger of the two. He had remembered, on the way, that Sally Ewing worked at Greystone but he did not see her there. As the mourners moved towards the graveside, he followed them, unfurling his black umbrella as he went.

The minister had come in his own car and manoeuvred himself to the front, speaking a few words to the elderly woman who was presumably Moira's aunt, Mrs McDuff. She went with him to the head of the grave and the others spread out along the other three sides, Davenport between Sandy Macpherson and the other solitary man.

They sang, "Abide With Me" and the minister read from the Bible, the well-loved, "In my Father's house are many mansions" which in spite of the advent of the Good News Bible was always read in the King James version, Davenport had noticed, at funerals.

The committal was short. The rain battered down, making sharp reports on the umbrellas, almost like bullets hitting their targets. When Davenport looked at the other mourners, all he could see were their umbrellas, some brightly-coloured and in contrast to the dark clothes worn by their owners. The coffin was lowered into the gaping hole, the minister and Mrs McDuff threw in a handful of soil each and after a final hymn sung in thin, reedy voices which were carried away in the wind and the rain, the little procession made its way back to the cars.

The minister, after a few hurried words with Mrs McDuff, came forward and told the little group that Moira's aunt would be pleased if they would come to The Redhurst Hotel for a light refreshment. Davenport heard one man from the school group make his apologies. He moved towards his car. Davenport caught up with him.

"Sir, I'm in charge of the murder enquiry and I'm interested in anyone who knew Moira Findlay. Who are you, Sir?"

"My name is Cameron, Hugh Cameron. I'm headteacher of the school Moira worked in."

"Sorry to ask, Sir but where were you on the night of the 15th June?"

"The man went into his breast pocket and pulled out a brown, slimline diary. He flicked through the pages.

"The 15th June? I was at the theatre with my wife and two friends, The Kings Theatre. The production finished just before 10.30."

"Thank you, Sir. I won't keep you any longer."

Mr Cameron drove off, slowly. The people Davenport guessed were other staff of the school, got into the same car and drove off. The funeral car, with Mrs McDuff inside, pulled away next, followed by the minister who was in turn followed by David Findlay's car. Sandy Macpherson stood by his car, looking thoughtful. Davenport went up to him.

"What's the matter, Mr Macpherson?"

"Hello, Mr Davenport. I don't know whether or not to go back to The Redhurst. I think David Findlay and his parents will go back and it might be awkward if I go too. Don't think I will go. Cheerio, Inspector."

He turned abruptly, got into his car and drove off before Davenport could agree or disagree with him. The other solitary man was about to get into his car when Davenport approached him.

"Hello, Sir, I'm DCI Davenport. I'm in charge of the murder investigation. And you are...?"

"Donald Galbraith, Mr Davenport. I'm...I was Moira's neighbour. I seem to have inherited her collie dog, Amigo."

The two men shook hands. It seemed unlikely, Davenport thought, that this pleasant, friendly-looking man had been Moira's killer. That left the ex-husband whom he had discounted and the new boyfriend whom he had also ruled out. Could one of the schoolteachers have done it?

At the hotel there were two little groups at two separate tables, the teachers and the family. Davenport joined the family group.

"Mum, Dad, this is the DCI in charge of the murder," said David Findlay. The three of them shook hands and Mrs McDuff introduced herself too, having only spoken to Davenport on the phone. She thanked him for getting in touch with all those who had attended.

"Did Moira's new young man not come back?" she asked looking round. "I take it that those at the other table are Moira's school friends."

Davenport explained that Sandy had felt that it might make things awkward if he and David both came back and he offered to give her Sandy's phone number so that she could get in touch with him later. She thanked him.

After the refreshments had been taken, the school group came across to the other table and the man introduced them.

"I'm Harry Richards, head of Chemistry and this is Pauline Lawrie from the Physics department and Elaine Smith from History. Our headteacher did come to the funeral but he's leaving for Spain tonight on holiday so thought he'd better get home."

"Thanks for inviting us back. I used to give Moira a lift to school," said the taller of the two women, Elaine Smith.

"Mr Richards, would you give me your phone number please? Are you going off on holiday soon?" Davenport asked the PT of Chemistry.

"No, not till next week but what is it you want? I've got time to talk to you now if the others don't mind waiting for their lift home."

The two women were in no hurry and they and Mrs McDuff moved off to give the two men some privacy.

"I need to ask you where you were on the evening of the 15th of June, Sir," said Davenport.

"Surely you don't suspect me of killing Moira!" Richards exclaimed.

"It's routine, Sir. A question I'm asking anyone connected with her."

"Sorry. Of course it is. Let me see. Oh yes, I was babysitting my sister's two children. They're teenagers and were very indignant about having to be minded. We played video games most of the evening and watched some TV. Their parents didn't arrive home till after 11pm and the two kids were still up. Is that OK?"

"Thank you, Sir."

Davenport smiled at the two women who came across to join Richards.

Mrs McDuff approached them again and thanked them all for coming and they left. Davenport thanked her too and, telling her that he would be in touch when they had news for her, he too took his leave. On the way to his sister's house, he pondered the likelihood of the PT of Chemistry or the headteacher being the murderer and decided that, subject to checking their alibis, he could rule them out. He rang the station and asked Fiona Macdonald to verify the whereabouts of both men on the night of the murder. He had left Pippa with her Aunt Linda, this being the first day of the school holidays and he wanted to take them both out for lunch, something he always did on the first day of the long break.

The murder could wait till this afternoon.

CHAPTER 42

When Charles arrived back at the station at around 2pm, he went straight to Fiona's room where he found her hard at work, typing on her computer. She looked up and grinned at him.

"Complete mutiny while you were away, Sir. The crew refused to do any work. I had to do it all myself."

Charles grinned back.

"Where *are* the layabouts?"

Suddenly serious, she explained that they had had a telephone call from a young woman who lived in Barlae Road, mentioning that she had felt that she was being stalked when she was walking through the Peel Estate the evening before.

"I took the call, Charles. She said that she felt silly reporting it as she could see no one and just sensed the presence of someone or something and that her collie dog had growled a couple of times. She'd read about the murder and had also been questioned by Frank when he was looking for Moira Findlay. I think she was worried that we might think she was a neurotic female or someone looking for attention, especially as she reported having heard strange noises too."

"Such as?"

"One roar and some hissing."

"What did you think?"

"She sounded genuine, Charles, genuine and embarrassed."

"What have you done about it?"

"I sent Penny up to interview her. The woman, Arlene Brown, had an afternoon off because her flexi-time had mounted up, otherwise we might not have heard from her till Monday, if at all. I think she might have persuaded herself she was imagining things if she'd thought about it over the weekend. The others went to the canteen about ten minutes ago for a late lunch."

"Any other news?"

"Just the alibis you asked me to check up. The headteacher and his wife were just about to set off for the airport but gave me their friends' phone number and they were all at the theatre, as he said. Harry Richards' sister told me that she and her husband didn't get home till well after 11pm and her brother was still there. He waited on for another half hour."

"Better have their cars checked, I suppose, just in case."

"Already in hand. I asked Cameron, and his BMW is left on the road. Like a lot of folk, his garage is full of other stuff, so he said. He said he would leave his car keys with his neighbour. I got in touch with Ben and he'll see to that one and Richards' Renault Megane tomorrow."

"Think I might be made redundant if Knox hears of this. Have you left me anything to do?"

"Well, you could shut the door and kiss me."

Charles leapt to his feet and closed the door.

Penny arrived back just after 3pm. Her DCI was sitting at his desk, his door open as usual. He called to her to go into the Incident Room and asked her to call Salma and Frank on the way. The three arrived at the same time as DS Macdonald who had heard her boss's instructions.

They took their seats, Davenport sitting on the front desk.

"Right, Penny, you first."

"It's really odd, Sir. Arlene Brown, who looks quite like Moira Findlay, could have sworn that she heard a kind of roar and then further on a kind of hissing sound in the bushes. Her dog, Glen, another black and white collie, Sir, turned round both times and growled. She walked faster and that was it. Glen lost interest and nothing else happened. She was embarrassed, Sir: said she wouldn't have mentioned it if there hadn't been a murder in that spot."

"Odd. Sounds like a creature, rather than a person. We'll have to ask at the factory and at the houses on the estate if anyone else has heard any strange sounds. Anyone got any possible explanations?"

Silence.

"Right team, here's the other bits of news. Two not very likely suspects, the PT of Chemistry and the headteacher, have been ruled out. They both have alibis. The only other men at the funeral were Sandy Macpherson and David Findlay and we've almost decided that they're innocent as well."

"No other men, Sir? What a poor turn-out," said Frank.

"Sorry, there was one other man: her neighbour, Mr Galbraith. You met him Frank, I think."

"Yes, Sir, a nice old guy. He looks after the neighbourhood's cats and dogs I think. He'd be the kind of man who thought he should attend a funeral."

"So much for my pet theory of the murderer always attending the funeral, eh?" said Davenport ruefully.

"No chance the murderer could be a woman, Sir?" said Salma.

"She'd have to be extremely strong to have managed to strangle Moira who was quite strong herself," Davenport replied.

"Miss Din, have you ever heard of a woman ejaculating?" quipped Frank.

Salma threw him a dirty look then looked embarrassed.

"Sorry, I forgot about that bit."

"I guess we're left with someone who lived nearby. Only one car was seen and that would appear to have been the two lovers escaping the scene."

"Why would someone who didn't know Moira, kill her?" asked Fiona.

"As we said earlier, it could be someone who had seen her meeting Sandy in the car and decided to rid the world of a loose woman."

Davenport did not look convinced by his own suggestion.

"Whatever the reason, it's likely to be someone who often drove through the estate and saw her and who could that be?" asked Penny, her brow furrowed. She pulled on her right earlobe.

Frank started to laugh and changed it hurriedly into a cough.

"Someone from the Harris, Smith or Fensom houses, driving towards Newton Mearns, or someone from the Cook house driving towards Eaglesham?" Fiona questioned tentatively.

"Right then, who have we got?" asked Davenport.

"Smiths first. It's very unlikely that two elderly, deaf old folk would commit a murder. I don't imagine they drive anyway so they would have had to have seen her outside their garden and I hardly think Sandy would stop his car right outside those two houses," he went on.

"And they're not very likely to have gone for a walk through the estate in the evening at their age. How old are they?"

Fiona turned to Frank as she asked this question.

"I'd say in their nineties. What do you think Pen?"

"Yes, I would say so."

Salma nodded her agreement.

"Harrises?" Davenport asked.

"The young lads are too young to drive. Would two youngsters go for a walk for the sake of it?" asked Fiona.

"And if they wanted a bus, they would walk the other way," said Penny.

"Mrs Harris seems eminently sensible, if her attitude to her son being suspected is anything to go by," said Salma. "I don't see her trying to rid the world of a loose woman."

"Jealous of another woman who had a man when she's just been divorced?"

Frank looked a bit shamefaced as he said this. Even to his own ears, it sounded a bit lame.

"Anything's possible but there's still the ejaculation bit, Frank," said Davenport and Salma gave Frank a look that said she was delighted that he had been caught out as she had been.

"Fensoms?" asked Davenport.

"Brian Fensom? Could he have propositioned Moira and been rebuffed?" asked Fiona.

"That's possible," said Penny. "His wife's pregnant and they'd been fighting when we saw them so maybe he's not been getting..."

"...any sex? That's an idea," said her boss. "We'll bear him in mind."

He got off the desk and wrote 'Brian Fenson' underneath his original list.

"Lastly, the Cooks. We'll discount Mrs Cook. That leaves Mr Cook senior and Mr Cook junior..."

"...and there's another Mr Cook. He could have come across from Bearsden that night. Sorry for interrupting, Sir," said Penny going red in the face.

"What about another man visiting the other houses, say Mrs Harris's ex?" said Fiona.

"I think we need to go back to these houses and ask about possible visitors," said Davenport.

Frank groaned then looked embarrassed.

"Sorry, Sir," he said.

"It has to be done Selby and I think tonight."

Davenport looked at his watch. He had heard nothing from Knox today and was really relieved to be off the hook at least until tomorrow.

"It's 4.50. We'll take two cars. I'll take mine then get off home from there. DS Macdonald, you take the other car and the rest of you. I'll see the Cooks and you can all do the other three houses, including the Smiths who might have had a visitor regularly or just on the night of the murder."

He put down his marker pen and walked out. Frank waited until Fiona Macdonald had followed him before rounding on Penny.

"This ear-pulling must be catching, young Penny."

"What do you mean?"

"You were tugging at your earlobe when you were speaking!"

Salma laughed and put her arm round her friend's shoulder.

"Just don't start calling us, 'team'."

CHAPTER 43

It was Tuesday 4th July and when Davenport came in there was a note on his desk saying that he should see Mr Knox at 2pm. Also there was a note, written in Bob's handwriting, saying that Ben Goodwin had reported that the two cars belonging to the schoolteachers were clean. Also he had put his men on to searching in gardens and nearby fields and there had been no sign of the finger.

Charles went despondently to his room, taking off his jacket as he went. He had no more leads to go on, Knox would be after his blood and there were only twelve days till he should be going on holiday. Also, if the murderer had kept the finger, it suggested someone mentally unstable which could mean another murder taking place.

Fiona arrived at his door.

"Why the long face, Charles?" she asked, making sure that no one was nearby to hear her call him by his Christian name.

He explained about the forthcoming interview with Knox and she made a face to match his. He told her about the twelve days and she told him that in a murder enquiry twelve days was a long time.

"Let's round up the team and compare notes about who we saw yesterday," Davenport said. He looked out of his door and saw that the coast was clear for him to risk a quick kiss.

"Saturday night was fantastic, my love but I can't see us getting together again soon."

"No, we can't be like Jackie whatshername at the factory and risk a quickie in your room, can we?" said Fiona looking rueful.

When they were all once again settled in the Incident Room, all with jackets off as it was a very hot day, he told them about his forthcoming visit to Knox. They all groaned, knowing that their boss did not have anything very positive to give the chief constable.

"I'll start," said Davenport. "I saw the older Mr Cook first"

Mr Cook senior had taken Davenport into his study, a pleasant, book-lined room with two leather chairs and a beautiful mahogany desk. He had sat down and invited Davenport to sit too, offering him a cigarette or a cigar which Davenport declined, not being a smoker. Declining the malt whisky was harder but he could not drink on duty or when driving.

"Now, DCI Davenport, what is it this time?"

He was quite genial this time, Davenport noted, gratefully.

"We've had a report of a woman hearing noises as if someone or something was following her yesterday evening when she was walking her dog. Have you ever noticed anything like this, Sir?"

At that moment the study door opened and Mrs Cook came in.

"I hope I'm not disturbing anything private, my dear."

Davenport noticed that the endearment sounded routine rather than affectionate.

"No, the Inspector is asking me if I'd ever heard any strange noises up near here."

"What kind of noises, Inspector?" asked Mrs Cook.

"Animal noises, hissing and kind of roaring, was what we were told," said Davenport, feeling a bit silly and was interested to see the woman glance toward her husband. He turned quickly toward the man and caught him shaking his head.

"Is something wrong, Sir?"

"No Inspector, I was shaking my head because I haven't heard anything like that. There are no cows in the fields though there are sheep occasionally and as for a hiss, maybe there was escaping gas somewhere from the factory."

"What about you, Mrs Cook?"

"I've never heard any strange noises out there, Inspector."

"I did wonder at the time why she said "out there" as if I'd asked her to choose whether she'd heard noises inside her house or outside it," he told his team.

"How could she have heard roaring and hissing inside her house, Sir?" asked Frank sounding puzzled.

"No idea. Unless they've got some illegal animals tucked away and that seems highly unlikely. Maybe I should have asked for a house tour," he laughed.

"I asked if any males ever visited the house and she said only her son from Bearsden. Her other son came in while I was there. He just laughed when I asked him if he'd heard or seen anything odd outside and said, 'What! In bourgeois Waterfoot?' Penny, what about you? You were seeing whom?"

"I saw the Fensoms, Sir, well I saw Mr Fensom as his wife was taken into hospital, yesterday. She lost two babies. They hadn't known she was carrying twins. He was distraught when I spoke to him, Sir but he said he had never heard anything strange and was sure his wife would have told him if she had. His brother comes sometimes but not often, as Grace Fensom and he don't get on."

"Did you ask why?"

"Yes. Apparently Dick Fensom is always keeping Brian late after work, drinking and tries to monopolise him at weekends, playing golf. Apparently he doesn't have any time for his two nieces either."

Looking thoughtful, Davenport added Dick Fensom to his list on the flip chart.

"Frank?"

"I saw the Harrises, Sir. I drew a blank with Mrs Harris and Craig but funnily enough Kenny thought he heard something move in the bushes when he was behind the factory with Moira. He was already feeling very silly so didn't say anything to Moira."

"Did he hear any of the odd noises?"

"He said no to that one, Sir."

"Any male visitors?"

"Mrs Harris blushed, Sir when I asked and said that her husband's brother had come up at the weekend but had never been before."

"What about her husband?"

"He's never been. She won't let him come."

"I guess you drew the short straw, DS Macdonald."

Davenport looked at Fiona and smiled.

"Yes, I got to go to the Smiths," she laughed. "The other three had warned me but it was still tough-going. I asked if either of them had heard anything odd which lead to a discussion about whether or not they believed in God. They didn't and I didn't so luckily that ended that conversation. I absolutely bellowed "Odd!" at them, then they looked offended and told me I didn't need to shout and what did I want to know about 'odd', odd what? So I shouted again, 'Have - you - seen - or - heard - anything - odd - up - here - recently?'"

"And had they?"

"Well they seemed to think it was odd that someone came to ask them about a film recently and kept talking about something red..."

She broke off as Penny and Salma burst out laughing.

"What's so funny, you two?"

"That was the conversation I had with them. It's too involved to explain ma'am but they misunderstood something I said and decided I was asking them about a film," giggled Salma.

"Well apart from you, Sergeant Din, they had seen nothing at all odd and I imagine it would be extremely unlikely for them to hear *anything*, let alone anything peculiar. I asked about visitors and it seems that they have two sons who seldom come to see them."

"So," recapped Davenport, "we have two more possible men to think about. Brian Fensom's brother and the other Cook son whose name is..."

he looked down at his notes "...Neil Cook. He's really Richard Neil but to save confusion as his father's also Richard, they call him Neil."

Davenport moved to the flip chart and added the name, Neil Cook. He also added, 'Smith boys'.

"But Sir, weren't the Cooks across at that son's house on the evening of the murder?" said Fiona. "If so, it would seem unlikely that he would leave them and come all the way across to Waterfoot, even suppose he had met Moira Findlay and for some reason wanted to kill her."

Davenport sighed.

"You're right. I'm not thinking straight."

He rubbed Neil Cook's name off.

"Penny, get on the phone to Brian Fensom. I imagine he's off work right now, seeing to his younger daughter as his wife is in hospital. Get his brother's address, then you and Frank go to see him - Brian will probably be able to tell you when is suitable - and ask him his whereabouts on the night of June 15th. Salma, sorry to ask you to do this but will you contact the Smiths. Hopefully they'll have one of those voice enhancing phones. Ask for the addresses of their sons. Go and see them and check when they last visited their parents."

"What now, Sir?" asked Fiona Macdonald.

"Lunch I think, then I'll have to see Mr Knox. Come on , DS Macdonald, I'll treat you to lunch."

"Thank you, Sir," she said demurely.

The sound of "Bonnie Charlie's Noo Awa" wafted down to them as, having collected their jackets, they made their way to the front door of the station. Luckily for Frank they only recognised the tune and not the words.

CHAPTER 44

Charles and Fiona went to a different place for lunch though it was nearby, at the Busby Hotel.

"A new venue today? Why the change?" Fiona asked as he passed the Railway Inn. It was a difficult manoeuvre getting onto the main road but suddenly the road cleared in both directions at once and he swung the car to the right and then to the left after the railway bridge.

"Well, I told you about Solomon knowing a lot about us, didn't I? What I didn't tell you was that he mentioned that one of his favourite eating places was the Railway Inn."

"Oh, I see. I wonder what he saw. I mean we don't kiss or hold hands in public."

"Probably just the soppy way you look at me."

Fiona cuffed him lightly round his left ear.

"I am never soppy, Charles Davenport.

"Well, look severe now till we see that there are no spies in this place," he replied and they walked into The Busby Hotel, looking every inch the DCI and his subordinate DS. A quick glance round told them that they were the only people in the place.

"It's usually busy here, or it used to be. I'd heard that it had changed hands. Hope the food is OK," said Charles as they sat down.

The food was excellent but halfway through, four teenagers came in and began to play at table football which was an innovation since Charles had last been there. They made no effort to keep quiet.

"Maybe it's the noise that's chased folk," said Fiona, forking the last mouthful of cottage pie into her mouth.

"Let's go, love," Charles suggested. "I don't want to be late for my interview with the lion."

"I think he's more like a walrus with his lack of neck," said Fiona.

The drive back to the station took a little over ten minutes. Going up the steps in front of them was Solomon Fairchild. He stopped on the top step and smiled at them both.

"Changed your watering-hole?" he asked.

"Have you got us tagged, Sir?" asked Charles.

"No. I was behind you on the way up to Busby and you didn't go to the Railway Inn today. Hope I haven't chased you?"

He tapped one side of his nose with a finger.

"Your secret's safe with me."

The three went in together, Solomon going in the direction of the lift, Charles and Fiona to their own rooms. They looked into the main room and saw Salma, Penny and Frank busy at their individual tasks. Penny was at Frank's filing cabinet and had lots of files lying on the floor, Salma was writing industriously and Frank was at Penny's desk with some catalogues.

There was no sign of Knox's secretary when Davenport approached her desk, so he knocked on the man's door.

"Come in," came the sharp reply.

"Hello, Sir. No Miss Sharp today?"

"Off work, with stress. I'm sure I don't know where she gets stress from! Sit down, man."

Davenport placed his manila file on the desk between them, sat down and crossed his legs. He smiled at Knox who did not smile back.

"Well, Davenport, what's the news on the murder front. Any suspects yet?"

"We've eliminated Moira Findlay's ex-husband and new boyfriend as they both have alibis. We've also ruled out two of her male colleagues. It has to be a man because the murderer ejaculated over her so we're now checking on the people who live round that way and their male visitors."

"That'll be the Cooks, the Harrises and the Fensoms," stated Knox.

"Yes, Sir. The two Cook men were both out that night. The son stayed overnight with a friend in the West End. We checked that and his father was in Bearsden with his wife visiting their other son and his family."

"And the Harris boys?"

"Kenny Harris admitted to a very short fling with Moira who stopped it as soon as she realised how young he was. He's a slightly built, though tall young lad and I don't see him being able to wrestle Moira to the ground."

"The younger boy?"

"He said he didn't know the woman and I believe him. He and his brother and mother were all together in the house at the time of the murder. They had all been at Kenny's parents' night, then she gave them supper and packed them off to do their homework. Craig's smaller than Kenny."

"What about Mr Fenson… Brian isn't it?"

"Yes, Sir. He and his wife were at home with their two children."

"Anything else?"

"Well, we received an anonymous letter which turned out to be from a woman who works in the factory. She and one of the men had been having an affair and after seeing each other in the factory late that night, they saw a small person going in the opposite direction."

"Small? Craig Harris?"

"I don't think so, Sir and what motive would he have?"

"Have you run this 'small person' to earth yet?"

"No, Sir."

"Anything else?"

"A local woman reported hearing someone in the bushes the other day. She thought the person was following her and her dog kept turning round and growling. She said she heard odd noises too, Sir, hissing and a kind of roar."

"What have you done about that, Davenport?"

"I've had my staff check with the owners of the nearest houses and, apart from Kenny Harris who heard a noise in the bushes up near the factory one night, no one can remember anything like that although…"

He hesitated.

"Although what man? Spit it out!"

"When I was asking the Cooks, I caught him glancing at his wife. He shook his head but when I asked, he said he was shaking his head because he hadn't heard or seen anything funny."

"So, any more people to be seen?"

"I've sent my team to interview Brian Fensom's brother and Mr and Mrs Smith's two sons. Mrs Harris only had a male visitor this weekend, her ex-husband's brother. Her ex-husband isn't welcome in her home so he doesn't come up."

"Well, you seem to have been busy, I'll grant you that. Is there any way the public could help? Should I talk to the press?"

"I don't think so, Sir. Asking the public if they've heard strange animal noises in the Peel Estate might frighten them or at the other extreme, we might get weird and wonderful animal sightings."

Knox smiled.

"He *smiled*, Fiona, Knox actually *smiled*."

"Are you sure it wasn't wind, Charles?"

"No, he smiled and said to continue with the good work. He said he wasn't too concerned because the story hadn't lasted long in the press and there's been no other murder."

"Fingers crossed that remains the case, eh?"

"True. I've to see him again on Friday afternoon. Where are the others?

"Frank's away to visit Dick Fensom. He has a half day on Tuesdays and was willing to talk to someone today. I didn't need to ask Salma what she said to the Smiths. I could hear her from here. She's arranged to see both sons tonight. Luckily they both live on the South side, one in Shawlands and one in Thornliebank. I decided to let Frank see Mr Fensom alone, Charles, and asked Penny to see one of the Smith men to let Salma get home at a reasonable time. I hope that was OK? I told them both to get home afterwards and tell us what the outcome was tomorrow morning."

"Of course it was. What are you doing tonight?"

"I've got an appointment with a good book. I've never read 'Jane Eyre' and Jean lent it to me a couple of weeks ago. I'm about halfway through and really loving it. What about you?"

"I'm taking Pippa to the pictures to see, 'Marley and Me'."

"Take a box of paper hankies with you. Marley, the dog, dies in the end, I think."

"Thanks for warning me. How are you getting on with your summary of our first murder case together?"

"I've reached the second murder, poor wee William. It's so sad when it's a child who's killed."

"Wonder who that child or young person was that Jackie saw on the murder night," Charles mused out loud.

"No one mentioned any young people living in Floors Road. They were all older people, apart from the one young couple who hadn't any children," said Fiona.

"Why would a child be out so late, alone?" was Charles's next question.

There seemed to be no answer to their questions so Fiona went off to her own room to complete the narrative of William Paterson's murder and Charles got his file on David Gibson out of his filing cabinet, determined to made some inroads into that murder while he waited for Frank to come back.

Frank arrived back at about 4.30. He was not in a good mood and Bob at the front desk decided not to comment on him erupting through the swing doors. Frank stormed up to the room he shared with Penny and Salma. Luckily they had not yet left, so were able to diffuse some of his bad temper before he saw his boss.

"See that Dick Fensom. Thinks he's the bees' knees. Didn't even ask me to sit down. Sat in his big armchair, smoking and smiling and made me stand there!"

"Calm down, Frank. Did you get anywhere with him and his visits to Peel Estate?" asked Penny.

She picked up his hat from where he had thrown it down on the desk she was working on and hung it on a peg.

"He certainly doesn't like his sister-in-law. Says that's why he doesn't go there often. You know, I think he's a poof. I can smell one a mile off."

"Don't talk nonsense, Frank," said Penny.

"Well he's in his thirties and not married."

"Well neither are you. Are you gay?" Penny demanded.

"Of course I'm not!"

"Penny, that young, well, small person seen walking away towards Floors Road. Could it be that Dick Fensom was meeting a child? If he is gay..." Salma hesitated

"A bit far-fetched Salma. Why would he meet a boy up there?"

"To keep it from being near his own home?" Frank chipped in.

"Well, run it past the DCI but I don't think it's likely," said Penny.

Frank, a bit calmer now, went off up the corridor. He told his story to Davenport who did not dismiss it out of hand.

"The DS and I were just talking about the small person. Might be a red herring but we still want to find out who he was. I think I'll call in Mr Richard Fensom and have a word myself. I'll speak to Brian Fensom first and see what he thinks about the homosexual angle. Thanks, Selby. Get off home now. Penny will probably be able to give you a lift as usual if you can wait a wee while. She and Salma are going over that way to interview two other men."

"Right, Sir. See you tomorrow."

Frank whistled as he went off down the corridor but as it was something by the Arctic Monkeys, for once his boss did not recognise the tune.

CHAPTER 45

Penny and Salma drove most of the way across to Shawlands in tandem, then Penny branched off to Tantallon Road and Salma carried on to Thornliebank. She found the street easily as it was just off the main road. The house was a cottage flat and Phil Smith lived in one of the bottom flats. Salma was welcomed into the small lounge and asked to sit down. It was a typical bachelor home, bare of ornaments and with only one picture above the fireplace. The walls were a dirty white and the carpet and curtains self-coloured brown. A large TV sat in the corner. There was one photograph on the highboard and a straggly plant which looked in need of water.

"Miss...Din did you say?"

"That's right, Mr Smith, Sergeant Din," she replied, smiling at this friendly, dark-haired and bearded young man. He had more hair in his beard than on his head, she noticed.

"I believe that your parents live on the Peel Estate."

"That's correct."

"Have you by any chance visited them recently, Mr Smith?"

"Please call me Phil. It's Filbert actually," he grinned. "Mum was determined that her children would have unusual names, having Smith as a surname. My brother is Fletcher and his isn't so easy to shorten, poor sod."

"Right, Phil. Now, about your recent visits to your mother and father?"

"Not as often as they should be but if you've met them you'll understand why, sergeant."

"Not too easy to talk to," she laughed.

"I was last there in May and my visit lasted about twenty minutes. I checked their freezer and said that my sister-in-law would come up with some supplies for them soon and left, feeling grateful that my turn was over."

Salma thanked him for his time. She got up to go.

"I know it sounds silly, Phil, but have you ever heard any odd noises in the area when you were there?"

"If there were any, Mum and Dad shouting would have covered them up," he said. "No. I never heard anything odd up there. Was that not where a woman's body was found some weeks ago?"

"Yes. That's the case we're investigating. Thank you for your cooperation."

Salma looked at her watch. It was just after 6pm. She wanted to be back in time for 7pm to let Shazia get out in time for meeting her friends.

In Shawlands, Penny had met a very different-looking Mr Smith junior. When she had puffed her way to the top flat in Tantallon Road, the door was opened by a fair-haired man.

"Come in, come in. I've told the wife and kids to stay in the kitchen while we talk, otherwise I wouldn't get a word in."

He led Penny into his lounge, a cheerful place with a bright red carpet and gaily-patterned settee, covered by a red throw. Signs of family life were dotted about the room, newspapers, books and video games.

"I just need to ask when you last visited your parents, Mr Smith."

"Why? Is there something wrong with them?"

He looked at her anxiously.

"No, they're fine. It's just that there was a body found up in the estate a few weeks ago. You might have read about it."

"I don't get much time to read but Mary, my wife, did say something about it."

"Well, we wondered if anyone, like yourself, had heard or seen anything unusual when you were visiting."

"Mary goes up more often than I do, I'm afraid. I often work at weekends and they are very difficult to visit being so deaf."

"I know, Sir. I've been to interview them," replied Penny, smiling.

"Mary was up there about two weeks ago, to refill their freezer. Phil, my brother had noticed that it needed replenished. Will I get her in to ask her if she noticed anything?"

"If you don't mind, Sir," said Penny.

Mary Smith, when called, came into the room, looking interested and Penny asked her the same question.

"My ears are usually ringing after a visit to Mum and Dad Smith," she said. "They're a lovely old couple and I get on well with them apart from the fact that I have a plain name and seemingly Smiths should have unusual first names but they are so deaf I have to bellow at them all the time."

"Don't they have hearing aids?" asked Penny.

"Yes but they never will put them in. No, I've never heard anything unusual while there," she added.

Penny thanked them both and left.

Davenport had seen Brian Fensom. He went early in the evening, knowing that Brian would be visiting his wife later.

"I'm sorry to be worrying you at a sad time, Mr Fensom," he said when the man came to the door.

Brian invited him in but did not show him into a room, keeping him in the hallway.

"What do you want to know, Inspector?"

"I hope you won't be offended if I ask you if your brother is homosexual, Sir."

"No, I'm sure he isn't, though…he does seem to hang about with younger men. I noticed that the other evening though there were young girls in the group too. I really don't know what signs there would be. I mean he isn't camp, in fact he's very macho and thinks I'm a wimp. Why do you ask?"

"Well a small youngster was seen on the night of the murder and we're wracking our brains as to why a young boy would be out by himself late at night. The constable who visited your brother thought he might be gay. It's clutching at straws, I know and I hope I haven't offended you."

"Not at all, Sir. Dick isn't my favourite person right now. I won't be seeing much of him in future. My priority's going to be my wife and daughters."

"I'm so sorry about your wife losing her two boys," said Davenport.

"Yes… twin boys. Dick and I are twins, Inspector, but I never guessed that Grace might be carrying twins, unknown to us and to the nurses who'd seen her earlier in her pregnancy."

Thanking him for his patience, Davenport rose to leave as the doorbell rang.

"That'll be one of the Harrises, coming in to babysit the girls for me," said Brian.

Sure enough, it was Kenny Harris, laden with schoolbooks.

"Thanks, Kenny," said Brian, going out into the hall and coming back with a lightweight jacket over one arm.

Brian and Davenport left together and the DCI walked him to his car which was sitting at the front door.

"I hope Mrs Fensom is improving when you see her tonight, Sir," he said.

"Thanks. We're going to plan the funeral of the two babies. It seems that that's what's done nowadays so that parents, especially the mother, can get closure. We've called them after my wife's father and grandfather. I didn't want either named after my father who was Richard like my brother. I'm fond enough of Dad who might be hurt but not right now of Dick, and Grace never liked him."

Brian got into his car and drove out of the estate onto Glasgow Road. Davenport sat in his car thinking for some time, then engaged the clutch and drove off slowly.

CHAPTER 46

"How did the book go? Finished it yet?" asked Davenport, standing on the threshold of Fiona's room, three weeks after the murder.

"Yes, got it read. Didn't get to bed till just before 1am," she replied.

"I haven't read 'Jane Eyre' but I think I saw a bit on TV once. "Does it not have a dramatic ending with a fire?"

"Yes, near the end. Jane has fallen in love with Mr Rochester but after the fire, she finds out that the woman saved from an upstairs room was his mad wife whom he's kept locked up in this upper room for years."

"Now why didn't I think of that? It would have saved me some money on the divorce," her boss laughed.

"Remind me never to get married to you!" retorted Fiona.

He looked suddenly serious.

"On that topic, do you…"

"Sir, sorry to bother you but did you make an arrangement to see Brian Fensom's brother this morning?"

It was Frank.

"Yes, Selby I did. Why?"

"He's rung in to say that he can't manage this morning after all. He'll come in in the afternoon. I said that you would get back in touch as you might be otherwise engaged this afternoon. I hope that was all right, Sir. He's an arrogant ba... sorry ma'am...man so I thought I'd show him that he couldn't dictate interviews."

"Quite right, Selby. Will you tell the others to meet in five minutes, please?"

Frank went off, having given his boss Fensom's phone number.

"Why do I think I'm not going to like this man, Fiona?"

He went on, "I feel that this small person is vital to the case. I wish we could find him."

"Any good asking Mr Knox to put out a request in the press, asking anyone under five feet and living in the Waterfoot, Eaglesham area to contact us?"

"It might come to that but not yet. Go and join the others while I make this phone call."

Penny told them about Fletcher Smith and how neither he nor his wife, who visited her

Smith in-laws more often than their son did, had heard or seen anything unusual.

Salma also spoke of Filbert Smith who had been ashamed of how seldom he saw his parents and had not seen them since May.

"Nothing there then," said Davenport despondently.

"What about you, Sir, with Mr Fensom?" asked Frank.

"Brian and Dick Fensom are twins. Brian resents his brother for commandeering him too often. He says he won't be seeing so much of him in the future. Brian and Grace Fensom are having a burial for their dead baby twins and have named them. Brian was at pains to tell me that he wasn't naming either of the boys after his brother."

"Is Dick homosexual, Sir?" Frank asked eagerly.

"Brian didn't think so, though he seems to have men friends who are younger than himself."

Frank looked disappointed.

"I'm seeing Brian Fensom at 12.o'clock. I had to inform him that it wasn't he who arranged the interview time and that 12 o'clock was the rearranged time whether or not it suited him."

Frank looked a lot happier.

"DS Macdonald, I want you to go up to the factory. Enquire there if any of the staff are noticeably small. Ask for Jackie Hobbs. She's the PR officer there and should be able to tell you.

Speak to Alan Grant who, by the way, is quite small and ask him if he ever heard anything unusual when he was staying late."

Fiona enjoyed her drive to Waterfoot. It was a lovely day with a clear blue sky and she sang as she went. She turned off Glasgow Road into Floors Road, passing the houses which unfortunately had no young people living in them. She passed the spot where a young girl's body had been found a few months ago then turned off left and drove past the impressive home of the Cook family, bringing the car to a halt in the factory car park.

The young woman she had been told was Lisa, smiled at her.

"Can I help you, madam?" she asked.

"DS Macdonald," said Fiona, showing her warrant card. "I'd like to speak to Jackie Hobbs please."

Lisa picked up her phone and in a few minutes another young woman came through the swing doors. Davenport had described her to Fiona: tight skirt, no bra, but this young woman wore a loose-fitting blouse and trousers which were anything but tight.

"Miss Hobbs? Is there somewhere we can talk privately?"

Jackie led her to the small room where she had spoken to Davenport. This time there was a man in residence.

"Bill, would you let us use your room for a couple of minutes please?" said Jackie and a tall man, in his fifties, put down his newspaper and got to his feet.

"No problem, Jackie. Time I did my rounds anyway."

"Excuse me, Sir, are you one of the caretakers?" asked Fiona.

"Yes, I am."

"Do you have to patrol during the day too? We thought that both caretakers only shared a night watch. I'm DS Macdonald by the way. Your colleague met my boss about a week ago."

"Pleased to meet you. The man held out his hand and Fiona shook it.

"Bill, have you ever patrolled the outside of the factory during the day?"

"Well, as I'm a kind of caretaker cum janitor, I get to clear rubbish from the car park too," he grinned. "I really love that part of the job."

"Ever found anything unusual, or seen or heard anything unusual?"

"Apart from Jackie snoring you mean?"

Jackie looked indignant then smiled as she realised he had been joking.

"You know, I did find something rather strange a few months back. It was a paw, think it belonged to a cat. It still had black fur on it."

"Why was that unusual? I mean a cat could have been attacked by something," said Fiona. "Maybe by a fox," she added.

"Yes but why would only one paw be there and it was as if someone had cut it off."

Fiona went still.

"Thank you, Sir. Now, if you don't mind I'd like to speak to Jackie here in private."

The man went out, shutting the door behind him. Jackie was looking puzzled but Fiona did not enlighten her.

"Jackie, you were the one who saw this small person going in the opposite direction. You said the person, probably a man, was small. How small?"

"Well, I'm only five foot four and even though it was in the distance, I would say the person was even smaller than me."

"Under five feet?"

"I couldn't be as sure as that but he was very small for me to have noticed that and very well built."

"Did your ...boss...ever say anything else about this figure?"

"No he didn't. I think I saw the person better than he did as he didn't mention his height."

"Are there any very small people working here, Jackie?"

Jackie thought for a moment.

"I think Alan Grant but he's not well built at all. He's quite thin."

Fiona thanked her and they made their way back to the front desk.

"Lisa," said Jackie, "are there any very small men here?"

"Apart from Mr Grant? No I can't think of any, Jackie. Sorry."

"Can I speak to Mr Grant please, Lisa?" asked Fiona.

Alan Grant, summoned to the foyer, was indignant about being taken away from his important work. Asked if he had heard or seen anything unusual when he had come outside after working late, he said he had not and went back to work, muttering about wasted time.

Davenport sympathised with his constable. He sat across from Dick Fensom in Interview Room 1 and wondered when he had last met a man he had disliked so much on sight. The man had strolled in, ten minutes late and now seemed totally unfazed by his bare surroundings, sitting lounging in the seat.

"We're interviewing anyone who has been in the Peel Estate area in recent weeks, Sir and I believe you sometimes visit your brother, Brian, in his house on the estate."

"I do."

"When were you last there?"

"His kid's birthday, the wee one, Anne or is it Karen? About four weeks ago. Brian'll be able to give you the exact date, no doubt."

"Have you ever met a young boy there?"

He had the pleasure of seeing Dick Fensom caught unawares. The man's eyes widened and he jerked upright.

"A young boy? Eh, no. Why would I meet a young boy up there?"

"But you have met one somewhere else, Sir?"

"It's none of your business."

"Everything's my business in a murder enquiry, Sir."

"Well I've never 'met' any but a consenting young adult, I'll have you know. It's not illegal, is it?"

"So the last time you were in Peel Estate was about four weeks ago and your brother will confirm this, you say. Wait here please, Sir."

Davenport went to his own room and rang Brian Fensom. He confirmed that his brother had not visited them since the tenth of May which was Karen's' birthday

"Thank you, Mr Fensom. How is your wife?"

"She's coming home today and the funeral will be a private one on Friday."

Davenport went back to the Interview Room.

"OK Mr Fensom. You can go now."

The man got to his feet and swaggered out. He almost knocked over DS Macdonald who was coming through the swing door. She looked indignant as he swept past her with no apology.

"I take it that that was Frank's favourite person," she said.

"Yes and a homosexual, as Frank thought. Think we'll keep an eye on him. Maybe alert the police station near where he stays. He said he never saw young boys, just consenting adults but I'm not so sure."

"Will I get the rest? Have you anything to tell us?"

"Yes, I have. Let me get rid of my jacket and I'll join you all in a minute."

Davenport called out to the other three. Frank was doing up his tie as he came out of their room.

When Fiona joined them they were all seated, except her boss who as usual was standing by his flipchart.

"Frank, you were correct about Dick Fensom. Nasty and gay."

Frank looked delighted.

"DS Macdonald, what happened at the factory?" asked Davenport

"The shortest person is the man you spoke to who stays on late, Alan Grant, but he's not well built. He'd noticed nothing unusual at any time when he stayed late. However I met the other caretaker and the caretakers also share day duties, Sir. I asked him if he ever checked outside and he said he had to clean up the car park. Then I queried him about whether he had seen or heard anything unusual and he mentioned finding the paw of what he thought was a cat. I asked why that was unusual as a cat could have been killed by a fox and dismembered but he said the paw was cleanly cut off and still had the black fur on it."

"What on earth are we looking for here, folks?" asked Davenport. Penny caught herself about to pull her earlobe but managed in time to stop herself. Not so her boss, who was pulling at his.

"Someone who strangles with his bare hands, feels sexually aroused by that, then bites off a finger. Someone who also bites off the feet of animals, perhaps?"

"He must be a nut case!" said Frank, disgustedly.

"Could it be a strange animal, Sir" asked Penny. "I mean there were the odd noises, hissing and what seemed like a roar."

"She's right, Sir, an animal is more likely to chew off part of a body," said Fiona.

"Well that's easily checked. I'll phone Martin."

Davenport went off to his own room and returned minutes later.

"No, definitely human sperm," he told them, "and the love bites were made by human lips and the teeth marks on the stump of the finger were human too, if rotten."

"So we're looking for a small, well-built youngster..."

"...or small man perhaps," interjected Davenport. "Sorry DS Macdonald, go on with your summary."

"A small, well- built male, who gets sexually aroused by killing and takes away a trophy body part. This male makes animal noises and has bad teeth."

"Must be lots of them around," said Frank sarcastically. "Sorry Ma'am, I didn't mean to contradict you. You're right of course but it seems so unlikely."

Davenport had been thinking.

"I want you all to read everyone's notes, the typed up ones. Jot down anything unusual however small or seemingly unimportant. Get started on that now and take it home to finish. Sorry if this eats into your free time but I really feel we're getting to the crux of this murder, if we could just spot what's important. My gut tells me that somewhere in our notes is the key to solving this case."

Looking sombre, Penny, Salma and Frank left the room, heading for their computers.

Fiona looked at Charles.

"No one even mentioned lunch. Think we're all fired up now after your speech."

"I'll send down to the canteen for some sandwiches and I'll make you all some real coffee to drink with it," said Charles.

CHAPTER 47

Penny was excited. She had taken her disc home and asked Alec if she could use his computer. Salma had printed off what she had not had time to read, not having a computer at home. Frank had taken delivery of a spanking new laptop recently so he had put all the reports onto a memory stick and gone home with that.

Penny sat in front of Alec's computer and looked at what she had written down since she got home:

"Both Moira Findlay and Arlene Brown were quite small, both were dark-haired though Moira's hair was dyed brown, and both had black and white collie dogs."

She rang Gordon. It was nearly ten o'clock. He was at home and delighted to hear from her but he was puzzled when she asked if he could get hold of a black and white collie dog.

"What for Penny?" he enquired.

"It's important. Can you?"

"Well yes. My sister has one. Not a great deal of white but he is a collie."

"Would you ask her if we can borrow him tonight? I need you too."

She rang off without explaining any more.

"Probably wouldn't agree if he knew what it was for," she muttered to herself as she got changed out of her uniform.

Dressed in casual trousers and a shirt blouse, she opened the door to Gordon about forty-five minutes later. She was correct. When she told him what she planned for them that night, he was not pleased.

"Penny, don't talk daft. If you're right about this and the murderer is only after a dark-haired small woman with a black and white collie dog, you could be in danger."

"Not with you right behind me," she said. "The other two women were alone and anyway no one attacked the one with the dog and I'll have Scout."

She bent down and patted the lovely collie with its shiny black coat and white- tipped ears.

"C'mon, Penny. This is really stupid. I'm sure your boss wouldn't want you to do it."

"He'll only know if it works and then he'll be so pleased, he won't care how we did it." Penny, in her excitement, was beyond being reasoned with.

After almost half an hour arguing, Penny played two trump cards. She remembered her English teacher saying that Lady Macbeth got Macbeth to commit murder by calling him a coward if he didn't and by saying he would do it if he loved her.

"Gordon Black! Are you scared? I'm not."

"No I am not scared."

"I thought you liked me yet you won't help me."

"I do like you. I like you a lot, Penny. You're not being fair."

Penny could sense him weakening and told him that she would do it without his help if he refused to come with her.

That clinched it.

"I'm only coming to protect you but I think you're off your head," her boyfriend stated.

They drove out to Floors Road and parked just past the Z bend in the road where there was a passing place. Penny, wanting to do things the same way as Moira Findlay, demanded that they stay in the car for a while.

"Do we get to do what they were doing?" leered Gordon in fun.

"They didn't have sex," said Penny, blushing in the darkening evening, "just heavy petting."

"I'll settle for that," said Gordon.

He was only making fun of her but suddenly his arms were round her and he was kissing her passionately. She felt herself responding. He was the first man to touch her breasts and she discovered that she liked it, even allowing him to unfasten her blouse and push her bra aside to stroke her bare skin. She undid the top buttons of his shirt and ruffled the hair on his chest. His fingers tweaked a nipple and she felt a strange hot feeling in her groin. She moaned and he unfastened the button of her trousers and eased down her zip, putting his hand inside her panties. She felt a wetness and realised that a response was expected from her.

"Gordon," she whispered. "I won't go the whole way but I do want to do what you want me to do."

"I won't go the whole way, Penny. Trust me."

He guided her hand down to his zipper and she pulled it down and felt inside. Soon she was rubbing him as he showed her how to. Minutes later she felt something build up inside her groin, then she could hear herself saying, 'Yes' over and over again as something seemed to burst inside her and a wet stickiness flooded her panties. She lay back in the car seat, her chest heaving. She had stopped touching him and now she did not want to continue with that. He seemed to understand and zipped up his trousers.

"Enjoy that, Penny love?"

"Was that an orgasm?"

He laughed.

"That's my Penny, blunt and to the point. Yes, that was an orgasm."

"I can see why girls go the whole way without meaning to," she informed him. "Thank you for letting us stop there."

She pulled up her trouser zip and suddenly seemed to realise why they were there. The car windows were steamed up and she rubbed the one on her side and looked out. It was getting quite dark now.

"Right, Scout!"

The collie who had been asleep in the back seat, sat up. Penny got out of the car, opened the back door and attached his lead to his collar. Scout came out happily and began to sniff round the car.

"OK, Gordon, I'll walk up past the house and the factory. You follow me but try to keep into the side."

Penny, with Scout by her side, walked up to the entrance to the factory road. She noticed as she passed the Cook's house that it was all in darkness. She was just approaching the entrance to the factory when she heard a noise, a rustling in the bushes on her right hand side. She stopped. Looking round, she could make out Gordon's shape behind her. She walked on and had just passed the factory entrance when she heard another noise, not a hissing or roaring but what seemed like a kind of chatter, a kind of 'chee, chee, chee' sound. She stopped again. Scout's ears were straight back and he started to whine.

"Who's there?" Penny called out suddenly.

In the bushes there was a heavy breathing, then the sound of feet running behind the bushes.

Frozen in shock, Penny stayed motionless then started to run, hampered by Scout who was pulling in the other direction. Gordon ran up to her.

"Are you OK?" he asked.

"Yes, get him!" she shouted and, thrusting Scout's lead at him, made off again in the direction of Floors Road.

When he caught up with her, Penny was staring up and down that road.

"I can't have missed him. I can't have," she said. "Where could he have gone?"

"What about into that garden?" said Gordon pointing to the Cook's house.

There was no gate and Penny went into the garden. Gordon followed her and they walked round the house, finding nothing. Scout was happily following them now.

"Look, Scout knows he's gone," Penny said, in a disappointed voice.

They walked slowly back to the car, looking round them as they went.

Back in the car, Gordon asked Penny what she would do now.

"Will you tell your boss what happened?"

"I'd better tell him. He's bound to be furious. I might have scared the man away," said Penny bravely. Gordon put his arm round her and hugged her tightly.

CHAPTER 48

As he always did, as it grew dark, he opened his window and peered out. He could see very well in the dark and preferred it to the light of day when he usually slept. He had fewer visitors since he had started biting and scratching when they tried to clean his room. He let one keeper partially dress him each morning, consenting to wearing trousers only. From an early age he had refused to wear shoes as he liked to be able to grip the branches with his long toes. He liked his animal smell though he knew that the hated one did not. She had once taken him into the garden and used a long snake - like thing to shoot water at him. He had grabbed it and shot water back at her and her dark hair had gone limp. She had screamed and one of the others had led him back to his room and towelled him dry. He had hated his smell that day and had rolled in some earth that night.

Now, as he looked into the distance, he saw the car again. It was nearer to him this time and again he could not see in the windows which were misted up. Patiently he sat and waited, wondering if it was once again the hated one in the car. As it got darker, the door opened and someone got out and seconds later the dark-haired animal got out too.

He jumped onto the window-ledge and from there to his tree. In seconds he was on the ground and following the hated one. Her smell was strong again this time. It made him feel aroused as it had done the night he thought he had killed her. The animal looked round and whined which upset him as he knew he could love it and he would never hurt it. He tried to talk to it in the chattering language he had heard the monkeys at the zoo use but the animal did not talk back. Instead the hated one stopped and made an angry noise. He was scared. He was always scared when she was angry as there had been times when she had hit him.

He scampered back towards his home and heard footsteps pounding after him. The animal was coming after him too, pulled by the hated one. Then another figure joined them. He reached his tree and climbed skilfully up it, knowing instinctively to remain in the branches rather than go any further.

He looked down as they moved beneath him. The smell was even stronger now that there were two of them. The animal was wagging its tail now. He was glad that it was no longer scared. Then the two others moved away. He watched as they got back into the car and drove off. Quickly, he slithered down the tree and waited. A red creature, the same size as the loved animal, approached him but he let it pass as he felt an affinity to it. Minutes later, a smaller creature stopped and stared at him. He shot out his good hand and closed it tightly shut. With a tiny scream the creature breathed its last.

Back in his room, he added the white tail he had torn off to his cache under his bed. He felt content as he smelled the blood on his hand but he knew this feeling good would not last.

He had to kill the hated one. He had to.

CHAPTER 49

Davenport was livid. He had welcomed Penny into his room early on Thursday morning and smiled at her as usual. He had asked her to sit but she had remained standing.

"You did what?" he shouted, then very quietly, "You did what?"

This was worse than if he had kept shouting at her. Penny quailed but stood her ground though she wanted to run down the corridor and out of the station.

"I know it was stupid, Sir but..."

"Stupid! It was criminally insane, you little fool! You could have been killed!"

Down the corridor, Fiona, sitting at her desk, listened aghast as Davenport tore into Penny with a voice that could have stripped paint. This was a side of him she had never seen and she felt for her subordinate though she realised that Davenport must have good reason for his scarily threatening manner.

Further on down the corridor, Salma and Frank also listened. Penny had come into the station, her usual rosy cheeks white, with bags under her eyes from a sleepless night. She had refused to tell them what was wrong and had gone up the corridor right away, just stopping to remove her hat and leave her bag.

There was the sound of Davenport's door closing.

Behind it, Penny stood twisting a handkerchief in her fingers and trying not to cry.

"So, let me get this right. You went up to the murder scene late at night, for what reason exactly? Give me the details now."

"I read in my notes that Arlene Brown had dark curly hair and remembered that she was small like Moira Findlay. Both had a collie dog which was black and white."

She stopped and swallowed. Her mouth was dry.

"Go on, Constable Price."

"I thought that I looked quite like both of them and thought that if …if I went up to Peel Estate at night with the same kind of dog, the murderer might try to… might try to…"

"…might try to murder you. What a great idea!"

Davenport's voice dripped sarcasm.

"And how were you going to stop this man from murdering you, may I ask? Had you thought of this? I mean you're slightly built and our mystery man is well built and has already successfully killed a woman who by all reports was stronger than you. Come on, tell me the master plan."

"Gordon was with me?"

"So he's an idiot as well! You're well- matched."

"I made him do it, Sir. I said I would go on my own if he didn't come."

"I see, and, being a vet, he no doubt could provide the dog. Was this a sick dog he was supposed to be caring for?"

Penny was indignant.

"I would never have used a sick dog and he wouldn't have either. It was his sister's dog."

"That makes all the difference. Did she know that she was putting her pet into danger or did you both just omit that part?"

Penny was silent. She looked down at the floor and felt a tear slide down her cheek.

"And it didn't go as planned, I take it? You didn't manage to wrestle this murderer to the ground, tie him up and bring him in with you this morning?"

"No, Sir," said Penny, in a whisper.

He sighed.

"Sit down, Penny and tell me the bad news."

He pulled a paper handkerchief from a box on his desk and handed it to her. She sat down, looking even worse now that he was being more gentle towards her.

"We stayed in the car for a while."

Two spots of red appeared on Penny's cheeks.

"I took Scout and walked into the estate, past the Cooks' house, Sir. As I was approaching the factory, I heard a weird noise from the bushes on that side of the road. It was a chattering sound, like monkeys make. Scout tried to pull me to the other side of the road. I shouted "Who's there?" then I heard a scampering sound in the bushes. I tried to run after him but Scout was trying to pull me in the other direction so I didn't get after him as quickly as I could have. Gordon heard me shouting and crossed over to see if I was OK, instead of chasing the man."

"Naturally" said her boss.

"By the time we got to Floors Road, there was no sign of him and we checked in the garden of the Cooks' house too."

"So you lost him, Penny."

"Yes, Sir," she replied in a tiny voice.

"And he now knows we're after him."

"Not necessarily, Sir. I could just have been someone taking my dog for its last walk before bedtime."

Penny's head came up and she said this in a stronger voice.

"Well, Constable Price, this is what happens now. I send you home. You're suspended from duty as of now. I'll try to keep this from getting to the chief constable's ears. By rights, I should report you to him or to Mr Fairchild. Mr Fairchild is a kindly fellow who might want to let you off but it wouldn't be fair of me to put him in that position. However it's only fair to warn you that I will tell the chief constable if I have to secure my own position. Is that understood?"

"Yes, Sir."

Penny said the last almost in a whisper. She looked as if she had been punched.

"Collect your things from your room. Do not talk to Selby or Sergeant Din. The fewer people who know what you did, the safer it is for both of us. Understood?"

"Yes, Sir."

Penny got to her feet shakily. Just before she opened the door, she turned to face Davenport.

"I really am sorry, Sir. I know now that what I did was stupid but at the time I thought I was being helpful. I'll understand if you have to report me."

She walked quickly to the room she shared with Salma and Frank, grabbed her hat and handbag then fled down the corridor to the sound of Frank shouting after her, "Penny what is it? What's happened?"

He and Salma both rushed to the door of their room just in time to see the outside doors swing shut. They looked at each other in shock.

Davenport stood at his door, witnessing Penny's flight and her colleagues' astonishment.

"Incident Room, everyone. Now!"

When they had gathered in front of him, he cleared his throat.

"I've had to suspend Constable Price. I can't tell you why and please don't try to find out. Just believe me when I say that not knowing is better for her and for me."

The other three sat amazed. Frank's mouth had opened but no sound came out.

"Right, I want to know if you came to any conclusions after your reading yesterday and last night. DS Macdonald, you first."

"It struck me that both Moira and Arlene Brown had the same kind of dog. I'm afraid that was all, Sir."

"Salma?"

"I noticed that both women were quite small, Sir and both dark-haired. I didn't think of the dog thing."

"Frank?"

Frank was looking mutinous and had to be brought back to the present by his boss repeating his name, more sharply.

"Selby!"

"Can we help Penny in any way without knowing what's happened...Sir?" Frank asked, the Sir coming a bit delayed for the first time in ages.

"You can help her by helping to get this case solved. Now did you or did you not notice anything in the reports?"

"I wondered if, as everything seemed to happen around the factory and the Cook house, the man had come from one of those places."

"Right. Thanks everyone. I was drawn to the fact that a light was spotted in the attic of the Cook house.

"They explained that though didn't they?" said Fiona. "Something about relatives visiting."

"It was Mr Grant one of the factory workers who saw the light and the Cook son, the one who lives at home, said that his Aunt Jean and Uncle Harry and his cousins were coming and that the attic bedroom would be needed and that someone must have been getting the room ready and had left the light on," said Davenport.

He thought for a minute.

"I'm going to phone the estate agent's in Kilmarnock Road. Get on with your tasks while I'm away."

He went off to his room. Fiona went to her own room. She knew that Salma and Frank would want to discuss Penny and she did not want to be part of their discussion. She had to be loyal to Charles, though, like them, she was curious about what had happened.

As soon as she had left the room, Frank almost exploded.

"What on earth has Penny done, Salma?"

"I don't know. She's such a good person. I can't see her doing anything to warrant being suspended."

"Neither can I. I'm going to phone her."

"You can't do that. The DCI said that it was better for Penny and for him if we didn't know. We have to trust him, Frank."

Mutttering, Frank walked off to their room.

Davenport had phoned Robert Cook at his work and asked him for the address and phone number of his brother in Bearsden. Armed with this, he went into Fiona's room and closed the door.

"Look love, I'm going to tell you what happened with Penny but you mustn't tell the others. Promise?"

"I promise, Charles."

"The silly little idiot tried to smoke out our murderer by going up there last night with a collie dog."

Fiona gasped.

"She'd realised, as you did, about the dog and, as Salma did, that both women were small and dark-haired as she is. She threatened to go alone if her boyfriend didn't go with her so the poor sod went."

"What happened?"

"She heard a chattering noise in the bushes, asked who was there and the man, if it was a man, ran off in the direction of Floors Road. By the time she dragged the scared dog in that direction, the person had vanished. Her boyfriend came to see if she was OK before following after her. They lost the person."

"Oh, Charles. She could have been killed."

"I know. I should by rights tell either Solomon or Knox. Fairchild would be sympathetic but would have to act. I don't want to put him in that position and Knox would probably have her removed from the force."

"Surely not, Charles."

"I've suspended her to keep myself clean but I don't want upstairs to find out because they'll want to know why she's been suspended. If they did find out what she did and I'd done nothing, I could lose my job. I could plead ignorance; say I thought suspension by me was the right approach. I would look stupid but might escape losing my job. What do you think?"

"I think you've been very kind to Penny. I'm very fond of her but what she did was so wrong and you must protect yourself."

"I'm hoping that if we catch the murderer, this need never come out. Am I being naive?"

"As long as it's kept between ourselves and Penny, it might work. Can you trust her not to tell the other two?"

"If we solve the case and I tell her to come back, I'll tell her if I find that she has told the others, I'll have to tell Knox. That should do it."

"What now?"

"I'm going across to Bearsden. I've a question to ask Neil Cook and I want to see his face when I ask it. Apparently he always goes home for lunch. Will you man the fort here?"

"Of course. I'll not let on that you've told me and I'll reinforce what you said about it being better that we don't know. Will that be OK?"

"Good idea."

Neil Cook had not yet arrived home when Davenport reached his house but his wife Martha showed them into their tastefully furnished lounge to wait and brought him coffee in a dainty cup patterned with roses. There were school photos of two children on the piano so he asked about them and this kept them occupied till they heard a car pull up in the forecourt of the large detached house.

"Hello, Martha. I'm home," called out Neil Cook.

"I'm in the lounge, dear," she called back.

He entered the room and looked surprised to see a stranger waiting there.

"DCI Davenport, Mr Cook," said Charles.

They shook hands and then they all sat down, the two Cooks on the settee and Davenport on a chair.

"It may seem a silly question, Mr Cook but I'm trying to work out dates and I want to know when your Aunt Jean and Uncle Harry and your cousins arrived at your parents' house."

"What? They haven't come up for ages, years, about five years, I think. Is that right, Martha?"

"They haven't stayed with your parents for much longer than that, Neil. They stayed with us the last time they came, remember?"

"Why didn't they stay with your parents, Mr Cook?"

Neil looked at Martha. They both looked uncomfortable.

"I think you'll have to ask my parents that, Inspector," said Neil.

"I'm asking you, Mr Cook. This is a murder enquiry remember."

"Neil's mother didn't really like Jean, Inspector. It caused some unpleasantness the last time they stayed. She didn't think that Jean was good enough for her family."

Neil smiled at his wife and she smiled back.

"My mother is a difficult person to get on with, Inspector," he added.

It took Davenport about forty minutes to get back to the station. He had done a lot of thinking on the way across the city. He contacted the main office and asked for a search warrant made out for the Cooks' house in Peel Estate then he went to his room, closed the door and had a cup of strong coffee.

Fiona, seeing him close his door, changed her mind about going in to see him as he obviously needed some time on his own.

It was well into the afternoon before his search warrant was delivered. He put on his jacket, opened his door and called to his DS to follow him which she speedily did. He looked into the main room as he passed. Frank and Salma were working at their various tasks.

"DS Macdonald and I are going up to Peel estate. Look after things here please, Sergeant Din."

"Yes Sir."

On the way up Charles told Fiona what had transpired at Neil Cook's, that the elder Cooks and their other son had lied about the visit of their relatives and that that had made him suspicious about the light in the attic room.

"Why lie about a light being on when they were all out, Fiona?"

"Someone else in that room, maybe."

They were at the traffic lights at Muirend. She turned to him. She looked excited, he noted.

"Remember what I told you about the book I was reading - 'Jane Eyre' - Mr Rochester kept his mad wife in the attic."

CHAPTER 50

It was Mrs Cook who opened the door to them this time, as they had expected. Both Mr Cooks would still be at work, even though Davenport had had to wait for his search warrant. She looked decidedly annoyed at seeing them there.

"Are you coming in?" she asked ungraciously and stood back to let them enter.

Once in the lounge, Davenport remained standing, while Fiona took a seat on the settee.

"You may wish to call your husband or your son, Mrs Cook as I intend to pay a visit to your attic."

The woman gasped and her face paled, then she seemed to recover her composure.

"Why on earth do you want to look in our attic? It's simply an extra bedroom."

"Where your brother and sister-in-law stayed recently?"

"Yes, that's correct."

Her usual haughty demeanour had returned and she sat down on one of the armchairs, crossing one leg elegantly. She was dressed in a tweed skirt and a blouse with a string of pearls round her graceful neck. As usual, her beautifully styled hair was swept up with one curly tendril artfully escaping at the side.

"It's odd that your son didn't know anything about that visit, Mrs Cook."

"Robert was the one who told you they were coming in the first place," she said.

"I meant Mr *Neil* Cook, Mrs Cook. Did you perhaps forget to tell him the story you were spinning us?"

"I'm going to phone my husband, Inspector," she retorted and, getting up, went into the hallway. They heard her voice, then silence and the phone was put down. She came back into the lounge.

"My husband says I'm to say nothing till he gets here."

Luckily, it was only twenty-five minutes before they heard the car pulling up outside as the silence was beginning to put a strain on the three people in the lounge. The outside door opened and shut then Mr Cook had joined them.

"Now then Davenport, what's all this about our visitors? I don't think we told Neil that his aunt and uncle were coming. They were only staying for a few nights after all."

Cook laughed.

"So he wasn't to see his cousins either then? Odd that, when the last time they came, it was Neil and his wife they stayed with. However, if there's nothing wrong, you won't mind showing us into your attic bedroom, Sir, will you?"

"Only if you have a search warrant, Inspector. This is an infringement of our rights."

Every inch the lawyer, Cook made a final show of dominance.

"Here it is, Sir," said Davenport, handing over the missive.

Cook's shoulders slumped.

"Lorna, I'm afraid it's all over," he said, putting an arm round his wife. Her face had paled again but she stood up looking defiant. If anything, Fiona thought, she looked relieved and the look she turned on her husband was almost warm.

"You take them up, dear," she said.

"Call Lily at work. I think she might be needed," he replied.

They climbed the wide stairway to the first floor then in single file, like Indians, they climbed another, narrower, stair. Cook stopped outside the only door. He listened at the door. There was silence. A key was sitting in the lock. He put out his hand then turned to Davenport who was immediately behind him, with Fiona bringing up the rear.

"I can only warn you that this might be nasty. I'll go in first. You wait here."

Suiting the action to the word, he turned the key and slipped inside, closing the door behind him. There was silence then noise erupted as if there was a menagerie behind the door. Davenport had stepped back instinctively, almost standing on Fiona's toes. From behind the door came a roar, then some loud hissing. They heard Cook speak in placatory tones. There was another roar and the sound of something heavy hitting the door. The door opened and Cook slipped through, shutting it behind him.

"I'm afraid that you'll have to wait until my daughter gets here, Inspector. She works nearby, in East Kilbride. She won't be too long."

He led them back downstairs and offered them a coffee. It was obvious that the man was distraught so Davenport agreed, for his sake if for no one else's. Mrs Cook must have anticipated this request, as she emerged from the kitchen with three dainty cups.

"Perhaps you can tell us who or what is behind that door upstairs, Sir," Davenport asked.

Cook looked at his wife. They both sat down, holding hands, on the settee. Davenport and Fiona took the remaining chairs.

"It began on the 15th of June 1977 when my wife had a multiple birth. We had only expected one child and I was thrilled to be told by my mother-in-law that she had heard the nurse tell Lorna that she had 'another' beautiful baby boy. I was thrilled. It took some time before we were called in but Marjorie, my mother-in-law, explained that the placenta sometimes didn't come away immediately."

He stopped, unable to continue. His wife took up the story.

"I had given birth to three boys, Inspector. The first two, Robert and Neil, were beautiful baby boys, Robert weighing just over 7lbs and Richard just under 6 lbs. The third baby should have been the smallest, coming last but he was over 9lbs and not a beauty. We named him Leslie. We'd been going to call a girl Lesley."

Her husband took over from her.

"Leslie seemed quite ordinary except for the fact that he had red hair. That in itself was not impossible with two dark-haired parents."

He looked at his wife.

"Lorna was dark-haired and curly and I, believe it or not, had a head of thick dark hair. No, what was strange was that Leslie had red hair on his arms and chest. We kept having that shaved off but it only grew back thicker than ever. To say that he was slow to walk and talk would be litotes. He never learned to talk at all and still just makes noises or chatters like a monkey. He can walk and did, when he was younger, but now he tends to crawl or kind of lope."

Fiona reacted to that, raising her eyebrows at him and Davenport knew that she was thinking of the reports of unusual noises.

"We took them all to the zoo once when they were about three," continued Mr Cook. "Leslie was absolutely fascinated by the animals, particularly the lions, the chimpanzees and the snakes. When he imitated their noises we were happy, thinking that he was reacting normally but he didn't want to come away from the zoo. He made frightening noises while the other two simply came away quite happily. We bought them all ice-creams and Leslie was the only one who couldn't hold his. One of his hands is deformed, having only two fingers and no thumb."

"We only ever took Leslie out once after that, to the seaside at Troon. He was terrified of the water and then some children laughed at him and made fun of the way he walked," said Lorna Cook.

"Neil and Robert were angry with the children and chased them off. They love their brother but no one can cope with him the way his step-sister, Lily, can," added Mr Cook.

"He hates me," said his wife. "I'm afraid I smacked him quite often, trying to get him to do things normally. He was about seven years old the last time I lost my temper with him and slapped his face. Lily was nearly four. When he put one arm… he has very long arms… round my neck, it was Lily who took the other hand, his deformed hand and spoke gently to him. He almost choked me before she persuaded him to let go and from then on he went berserk whenever he saw me. I haven't seen him since he turned nine, Inspector. Ricky and the boys saw to his needs."

She began to cry; long wracking sobs which seemed to come from her soul. The warm tears seemed to unfreeze something inside her and she put her head on her husband's chest, saying brokenly:

"Oh, Ricky, I'm so sorry, so sorry. I left you to do it all."

"Come on, Lorna love. I understood and I had Neil and Robert to help me... and Lily of course."

Davenport waited while they consoled each other then he coughed gently to remind them that they were not alone.

"Sorry, Inspector. As you will imagine, Leslie was not able to be educated. As he got older he wouldn't allow us to put any clothes on him except an old pair of jeans. He won't accept new trousers either. The other children watched over him as they all grew up but naturally they began to leave home. I used to wait till one of them came to visit us before taking Leslie out for fresh air."

"Did he stay in his room?" asked Davenport.

"We had to lock him in, eventually. He didn't grow tall but he grew very strong and his arms also grew. Then one day he got out. He was in the garden unbeknown to us when some young children passed on their way home from school.

He went over to the wall apparently and they saw him and burst out laughing. He grabbed one of them. They all screamed. Luckily I was at home for some reason and I ran out and managed somehow to get him to release the boy. The boy's father came to complain and I promised that it wouldn't happen again. He said his son had described a monkey-boy and I managed to persuade him that his young son was exaggerating. It didn't happen again but some dogs and cats went missing and we found some animal parts in Leslie's bedroom."

"So we moved here, Inspector, to this remote house. Things were going well till you came to the door a few weeks ago."

"Did you suspect your son, Mr Cook?"

"Not at first. He wouldn't let us in to clean his room any more so we saw nothing suspicious to show that he had been out but you showed us the picture of the dead woman and we recognised her as someone who walked her collie dog in the estate. We used to have a black and white collie, Inspector, till Leslie shook her too hard and ruptured her spleen."

"Leslie always got very upset when he saw a dog like ours," said Lorna Cook. "I never said anything to Ricky..."

"...and I never said anything to Lorna but I guess now that we both had our fears from that moment on."

The doorbell rang and Richard Cook got up to answer the door.

"Oh Lily, so sorry...we need you...I'm sorry. It's Leslie...He..."

"What's happened, Dad, tell me. Is he hurt?"

The petite blonde was obviously scared.

"There's no easy way to tell you this, pet. Leslie's killed a woman. He won't let me near him. I'm afraid we need you to calm him down."

CHAPTER 51

As deer in the Scottish Glens sense the start of the shooting season and move into the hills, so he sensed danger. Going down on all fours, he felt under the bed for his lucky finger and held it close. Fearful, he held it too tightly and the finger bone snapped. Angrily he crushed what remained in his huge paw. He began to pace from door to window and back again, then his ears flattened against his head. He had heard footsteps, footsteps of three people coming up the stairs. He stopped at the window. Should he go to his tree? Should he go under his bed? He had been indecisive for too long. The door was opening.

It was not the hated one. He felt relieved till he smelt the strange smell of two unknowns and, reacting to danger in the only way he knew how, he roared and leaped at the man in the room, claws curled. The man jumped aside just as he hurled himself at the door and tottered to the side He heard the retreating footsteps. He listened at the door and felt safe again.

Some time passed. He bent over and pulled a small foot from under the bed and sniffed it. That made him feel better but he knew the good feeling would not last as long as the smell from the finger would have done. He curled up on the floor in his straw, the foot clutched in his good paw. Last night he had missed the hated one again and once again he had failed to connect with the small animal which for some reason feared him. The good feeling was going again as he thought of his failure last night.

Weariness overcame him and he slept in the straw.

He awoke to another knock at his door and was about to roar when he realised that the voice belonged to the loved one, his blonde angel. He had missed her so much. The door opened slowly and she stood there, smiling down at him. He got to his feet and opened his long arms wide. With a sob, she ran into them.

CHAPTER 52

Lily had argued with them all.
"I know that I can calm him down but what then?"

"Do you have any tranquillisers for him?" asked Davenport..

"Nothing works. The doctor has tried them all."

Richard Cook sounded weary.

Fiona Macdonald gestured to Davenport to come into the hall and he went with her.

"What is it, Fiona?"

"If the poor soul is more animal than human, could a vet have something stronger?"

"I can ask them. He is their son after all."

They went back into the lounge.

"Would you be willing for a vet to try a tranquilliser?" he asked Leslie's parents.

"What have we to lose, Lorna?" The man looked at his wife in appeal. "If it kills him, that will save him from being incarcerated for the rest of his life."

"Go ahead, Inspector." Lorna Cook agreed with her husband.

Davenport went into the hall. He rang Penny at her home. A dull voice answered.

"Penny. I need your boyfriend here. Immediately. With a strong tranquilliser."

He listened.

"Are you in any position to ask questions?"

He listened again.

"After what he was party to last night, I don't think he's in a strong position to refuse. Tell him I'll take the blame if anything goes wrong."

He made one more phone call, to Martin Jamieson, requesting him to bring a stretcher and some sedatives.

He went back into the lounge.

"Someone will be here shortly. Tell me, why did the light go on so briefly that night?"

"Leslie doesn't like the light. He prefers the darkness. He can see very well in the dark so I can only imagine that he hit the light switch by accident. Whatever the reason, he will never be able to tell us."

There was a sob from Lily.

"What will happen to him, Dad? Surely they won't put him in prison?"

"I imagine they'll put him in a psychiatric hospital, in a locked ward," replied her father.

"But that's cruel. You know how he loves being outside."

"I know, Lily, but he can't be left at large if he's going to kill people."

The woman turned to Davenport.

"If we kept his window locked, could he not stay here?"

"He could break out somehow," Davenport answered.

"And if I refuse to help?" she countered angrily.

"Then we'll have to shoot a tranquillising dart at him without comforting him first. Whereas if you are with him, at least he will feel loved in his last free minutes."

Mrs Cook motioned to Lily to come out into the hall. They were there for about five minutes and Richard Cook looked very surprised when his daughter came back in and immediately agreed to do what Davenport had asked. Lorna came in minutes later and he sent her a look of gratitude.

They waited in an uncomfortable silence, until the bell rang. It was Gordon Black with Penny.

"I thought that I told you that you were suspended, Penny," said Davenport, rather sadly.

"You know what I did, Sir and I think I know what you want Gordon to do and I don't imagine that you want that broadcast either," said Penny bravely, her head held high.

"True," he said ruefully. "Touché."

He explained to Gordon what was going to happen. That young man looked rather reluctant so they had to explain what Leslie had done and why he couldn't be allowed to remain in the house.

"Don't come up with me. He'll smell strangers," said Lily. "Give me about ten minutes and then you come up by yourself," she said to Gordon.

She opened the door slowly and there he stood with his long arms open wide. She went into his arms and he hugged her very, very gently. She moved with him over to the bed and they both sat down. When he was with her, he became almost human and chattered softly to her. Though she could not understand what he was trying to say, she knew that he was showing her affection and her skin crawled at the thought of what she was doing. She was betraying him yet it had to be done. He seemed to sense her unhappiness and patted her head very softly with his good hand. She lay down and he lay down next to her, putting one long arm across her chest as if to protect her. They had done this before and he fell asleep quickly as she had known he would.

The door opened slowly and very quietly. Gordon crept in, his syringe at the ready. It was the work of seconds to inject the sleeping creature. He stirred briefly then his body slackened and Lily came out from the shelter of his arms. She was crying quietly.

Downstairs, Lorna Cook spoke.

"Please, Mr Davenport, can I have a minute with my son before you take him away? I need to make my peace with him after all the years he has hated me."

I'm sorry, Mrs Cook. I can't allow that," said Davenport.

"Don't you see, Inspector, I made him what he was. I gave birth to him and I made him hate me. That women he killed, looked like I looked years ago when I mistreated him. Do you want me to live with that guilt for the rest of my life?"

"Go on then. Five minutes only."

She passed Gordon and Lily on the stairs and they heard her open the door of the attic room. Lily sobbed again and Gordon put his arm round her, drawing her into the lounge and handing her over to her father who put both arms round her.

Lorna Cook came back down just before the allotted five minutes, just as the doorbell rang. It was Martin Jamieson and two of his men with a rolled-up stretcher.

"Upstairs, Martin, in the attic. He's on the bed. He should offer no resistance."

Martin and his men climbed the stairs. In the lounge, Lily looked at her stepmother who gave her a tremulous smile.

A clatter of footsteps announced Martin who erupted into the lounge.

"Charles. You are right. He will not offer any resistance. He is dead!"

"Dead?"

Davenport turned to Gordon.

"Don't worry, Gordon. I'll carry the can for this. He obviously didn't need as much tranquilliser as you thought."

"I don't think you'll have to take the blame, Charles," said Martin. "Unless you stabbed him twice. There are two stab wound in his chest and the knife is still sticking out from the second one."

There was a sigh as Lorna Cook fainted.

CHAPTER 53

They were in the Incident Room. It was July the 6th. As usual Davenport stood at the front with his team in front of him. He took a cloth and wiped the flip chart clean.

"Case over, folks. I've made an appointment to see Mr Knox. He will delighted to know that we found our murderer."

He smiled at Frank and Salma.

"Like you two, there are some things he will never know and I ask you to just accept that."

Frank glowered and mumbled something.

"Penny and I will be very grateful to you, Selby. Between these four walls, she and I could be out of a job if some things about this case come to light. Do I make myself clear?"

Salma smiled at him.

"Yes, boss. Very clear. I understand and I'm sure that Frank will too when he's had time to think about it."

Penny, looking very serious, touched Frank on the arm.

"Please, Frank. The DCI is right and I'm going to add that Gordon's career could be on the line too if certain things were to be found out. It'll be safer for both of you if you aren't told some things."

Davenport smiled round, then went on.

"What I *will* tell you is that the murderer was one of Mr and Mrs Cook's triplet sons. He was born with a body like that of an oran-utang, even down to the red hair which covered most of his body. He killed Moira Findlay in mistake for his mother whom he hated. He must have thought when he saw Arlene Brown that he hadn't killed his mother and he followed her with the intent of killing her too. The family had a black and white collie dog which Leslie Cook loved but killed because of his unnatural strength. He saw both women with a similar dog and that reinforced his idea that they were both his mother. They were both quite small and dark-haired, as she was when younger."

"How did you work out who it was, Sir? I take it that you can tell us that," said Salma.

"I remembered the light in the attic and we found out that the Cooks were lying about having visitors who were going to sleep in the attic. DS Macdonald fancifully thought that it was a rewrite of 'Jane Eyre' and that Mr Cook had another mad wife in the attic."

They all laughed and Fiona Macdonald looked a bit sheepish before joining in the laughter.

"We went to visit them and demanded that we see into the attic. They sent for their daughter, Mrs Cook's stepdaughter, who was apparently the only one who could calm their son. He was tranquillised. I stupidly listened to Mrs Cook's plea to see her son for one last time alone and she stabbed him to death. Mr Knox will have a field day with that, no doubt."

"To save him from a life incarcerated in a mental institution," added Fiona Macdonald.

"What will happen to her, Sir?" asked Penny.

"I imagine that when the story comes out in court, the judge will be very lenient towards her. I hope so. The whole family and Mrs Cook in particular, have suffered enough."

"So you'll see Mr Knox, now, Sir," said Fiona.

"I will indeed then I suggest we all go for lunch. My treat."

Made in the USA
Charleston, SC
05 April 2014